Voice
of the
Stranger

Copyright © 2023 by
Published by Lethe Press | lethepressbooks.com

ISBN: 978-1-59021-744-3

Cover art: Julie Hamel
Typesetting: Ryan Vance

Voice
of the
Stranger

Eric Schaller

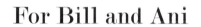

For Bill and Ani

Contents

Author's Note

The title for my collection is taken from the song "Green Pastures." The relevant lines read, "We will not heed the voice of the stranger, for he would lead us on to despair." It's a Biblical admonition to beware the call of the other. The word stranger here could be capitalized because the reference is not to "a" stranger, but to "the" stranger. We all know who that stranger is. The bloody stranger with the troublesome horns. The stranger with the phallic tail and the slithering tongue. The stranger who calls you on to despair. The Devil. Significantly, the song is also a xenophobic reminder that we never really know in what guise the Devil will tempt us. The only folks we should trust are our family and locals. Trust the mundane, those we have known all our lives. Any stranger might be *the* Stranger.

Don't look to short stories to protect you from strangers. There's a popular meme, spuriously attributed to Tolstoy and Dostoyevsky: "All great literature is one of two stories; a man goes on a journey, or a stranger comes to town." The likely originator of this meme was John Gardner who, in his book *The Art of Fiction*, included an exercise to write, "as subject, use either a trip or the arrival of a stranger (some disruption of order—the usual novel beginning)." Which is to say that sometimes, but not always, a story may feature a stranger. What's most significant from my perspective is that you as the reader, are not necessarily responding to the arrival of a stranger, sometimes you are that stranger. Also of significance is the tension between our fear of the unknown and its attraction. Moreover, this is all mixed up in the adjectives we use to signify the alien—strange, odd, weird, exotic—all suggesting the same thing but imbuing it with differing levels of dread and desire. Just remember, you as the reader are encountering every character in a short story as a stranger.

You are entering strange territory.

A note about the stories in this collection. For decades, *The Year's Best Fantasy and Horror* anthologies, edited by Ellen Datlow, Terri Windling, Kelly Link, and Gavin Grant, defined and expanded the borders of speculative fiction for readers and writers. I loved the breadth of the stories and the sense that the characters you discovered in the stories existed on a teeter-totter, balanced by a hair, between the fates of Heaven and Hell. That's a sensation I also hope you will discover within these stories. I want you to live within these stories as you might live in the world at large, never knowing what stranger awaits you around the next corner but knowing, nevertheless, that you are in for an adventure.

One last thing. Despite what I wrote earlier, I lied. A lie of omission. Despite the plot memes spuriously attributed to Tolstoy and Dostoyevsky, despite what Gardner clarified, despite your virginal embrace of a story's characters, there is always another stranger hiding in plain sight: the author. Every time you open a book, you put yourself in the hands of a stranger, maybe *the* Stranger.

But you knew that, didn't you?

I.
Past Tense

The Five Cigars of Abu Ali

"Tell Abu hello from me when he gets here. Tell him I'm sorry that I couldn't stay." Elizabeth wore her heaviest winter coat and a woolen hat, concessions to the season rather than to style, and stood beside our Volvo, its engine grumbling even though she had already allowed it to warm up for fifteen minutes. Our two kids, Mark and Mary, were strapped into the back seat from where they scratched designs into the frosted window interiors. Elizabeth's breath hung in the air, but it was such a cold January—only the masochists had gone outside for the First Night Celebration the previous week—that I half expected her words to crystallize and fall to the pavement as snow.

I nodded and chose my words carefully: "I'm sure that he'll be equally disappointed." I knew that Elizabeth had no desire to see Abu. I knew that she had in fact contrived the visit to her mother in Exeter only after we discovered the message from Abu on our answering machine giving notice, or warning as Elizabeth would have it, of his impending arrival in Boston. I shuffled my feet and rubbed my shoulders. Before going outdoors, I had grabbed the first coat that came to hand, a canvas jacket with a flannel liner, figuring that anything was good enough because I would only be outside for a few minutes. Now I knew why I only wore that jacket in the fall.

Elizabeth fumbled with her mitten for the handle of the driver's side door. "Dinner's in the oven," she said. "Don't forget to take it out."

"I'll keep an eye on it. How long has it been in?"

"It's cooked. The oven's just on warm."

"I love you," I said and leaned forward. Elizabeth kissed me goodbye but missed my mouth by an inch that was as good as a mile.

I waved as they drove off into the dwindling daylight and took some pleasure in the faces of Mark and Mary framed like twin moons in the rear window. They watched me as their mother took them away and waved their small hands in return.

Then I hurried back inside to wait for Abu.

As it happened, Abu did not arrive until after ten o'clock. By that time, I had taken the dinner—chicken sautéed in wine, roasted potatoes, and asparagus—out of the oven, the food had gotten cold on the counter, and I, having finally given up on Abu's arrival, had reheated a portion in the microwave and eaten it at the kitchen table. The food had even settled in my stomach so that the low-blood-sugar headache, which had been threatening all evening long, had retreated back into its neural lair.

The taxi that brought Abu double-parked outside the condo, and I watched him crawl out, clearly drunk, preceded by one woman and followed by another. The woman in the rear carried a small suitcase that I assumed was Abu's. I met them at the gate and helped Abu maneuver up the steps and then shuck his cashmere coat in the entryway. Even when drinking, Abu knew how to keep up appearances. Perhaps he used more cologne than I appreciated, but not one of his moussed hairs was out of place. He wore a red silk shirt and a gray Armani suit, the same suit he had worn the last time I saw him eight months ago. The difference between then and now was that previously I had worried the suit would soon be too small for him. Now it was loose on his frame.

Abu's weight loss took me by surprise. He had been thin when I first met him, lithe as a jaguar, and had played midfield on our intramural soccer team at Boston University. But he was also a man who fell easy prey to his passions. Not surprisingly, given our youth, women were one of his passions, and he had a string of love affairs all destined for heartbreak. Food was another passion. And wine. And song. I could go on. But suffice it to say, even at the most formal dinners, he licked his fingers rather than use a napkin. He gained a good thirty pounds while at college and continued to add to his girth over the years.

"Looking good," I said. "How're you doing?"

"Just fine." He made a sweeping gesture that took in both women. "This is Ann," he said, laying an arm across the shoulders of a woman with dark hair, blue eyes, and a tailored blue dress set off by a strand of ostentatiously large and obviously fake pearls. "And this lovely lady insists upon being called Sly," Abu pulled the second woman toward him with his free arm. "Short for Sylvester, I believe, but I suppose it could be for Sylvia. She won't say, although I've been buying her drinks all evening." Sly had reddish-brown hair, was skinny as a toothpick, and wore jeans and a black t-shirt with the Nike symbol.

After making Ann and Sly comfortable in the living room, I dragged Abu into the kitchen and shoved a glass of water into his hand. "What do you mean by bringing two women here with you?"

Abu giggled and raised a forefinger. "The company of women without men is a melancholy thing, but the company of men without women is enough to make one cry."

"But Elizabeth will kill me."

"I should also add that a table might as well be empty except that it be seating four. In short, you should be thanking me, for without my forethought we would simply be two lonely men weeping into our glasses of whisky." Abu emptied his water into the sink and set the glass upon the counter, the clank containing more conviction than I hoped he intended. "You do have scotch, don't you?" he asked.

"What about dinner? I have some chicken. Elizabeth prepared it before she left."

"No thanks. Although I appreciate the offer, I can think of no worse accompaniment to whisky. Besides we already ate." Abu placed a hand on his belly as if he still thought it a monument to his gluttony.

"If you supply the whisky," Abu continued, "I have everything else we need right here." He patted his suit jacket at heart level then frowned in puzzlement. He patted the other pockets of his jacket, then those of his pants. "Where in God's name... " He chomped furiously at the ends of his mustache. This was not enough to jump-start his memory and soon his whole face contorted in thought like a bar rag being wrung dry. He finally emitted a loud sigh of relief and said, "My suitcase. I have everything else we need in my suitcase."

The whisky was in the dining-room sideboard. "I was at a conference in Minneapolis last fall that had a whisky tasting in the bar." I handed Abu two sherry glasses, keeping another two for myself. "You could sample shots of three different whiskies for one price. Cardhu is what a fellow from Scotland recommended. He said that this was his favorite whisky. It's not as smoky as Laphroig, but it has a nice body to it."

"So I hear, but I have always preferred to taste with my tongue not my ears."

Back in the living room, Ann flipped through a home decorating magazine. Sly manipulated one of Mark's toys: a transformer, capable of being converted between a Porsche and a robot, but right now stuck in an intermediate stage of metamorphosis.

"Where did you find that?" I asked. Mark had been searching for his transformer up until the last minute before he left

"It was here between the cushions." Sly set the car on the end table by the couch, upside down, arms protruding upward, where it rocked back and forth like a turtle trapped on its back.

"Enough about toys," said Abu. "We are all grown-ups. My good friend George has supplied the whisky, just as I assured you that he would." He made a short bow in my direction. "I will now supply the cigars. My suitcase, if you please?" This last was directed at Sly who merely arched one red eyebrow to indicate that the suitcase in question was directly in his line of vision, leaning against the couch, and he could damn well get it himself.

Abu unzipped the suitcase while kneeling on the floor, pawed through a tangle of socks and underwear, and pulled out a Ziploc bag. The bag contained four oblong brown folders of cardboard and a tube of ivory-colored plastic. "I bought these at the Duty Free in Heathrow," Abu said. "They spray inside the bag with a mister to keep the humidity up for when you travel. Basically, it's a twenty-cent humidor." He handed us each one of the cardboard folders. "Open it up," he said, seeing Ann peer inside her folder. "That's a Cuban, a Punch corona. You can't buy those with U.S. dollars." He took his cigar out and ran it beneath his nose. "Oh, that's good."

Soon we were all sitting back, the smoke from our cigars twisting and turning on the way to Heaven like the robes of a Renaissance angel, our sherry glasses within easy reach and knuckle deep with whisky.

"Hey Abu," asked Ann, "you're a Muslim, right?"

"Mmmm." Abu smiled at her, his eyes half-lidded.

"Well then, how do you drink alcohol? Isn't that against your religion?"

"As phrased, I can only answer your question by saying: with a glass, my sweet. With a glass." Abu took a long drawn out sip and smacked his lips. "But I know what you mean. I'm sure that my parents toss and turn at night, unable to sleep, thinking about where they went wrong in raising me. They spend all day lecturing me whenever I visit them in Pakistan."

"You're not supposed to smoke either," I said.

Abu turned toward me, and I was surprised to see the wounded look on his face. "That's right. A good Muslim is supposed to avoid anything that poisons the system. But, as I said, I'm not a particularly good Muslim. I would like to blame the corrupting influence of the U.S. but I'm afraid that it is my own weakness that is at fault."

"Hey Abu," Sly asked, "what's in the bag?" She pointed to where Abu had set the Ziploc bag on top of his suitcase. It was empty now except for the capped plastic tube. "Another cigar?"

"Now that question is harder to answer than you might think. I'll tell you one thing though: I haven't drunk nearly enough to try. Ask me again in about this long." Abu held up his glass and, by jiggling his hand, made a small whirlpool of the whisky remaining in it.

Sly smiled and waited politely, but it was clear from her silence over the next half-hour that she was not a woman who appreciated delayed gratification. Meanwhile, Abu told how he got the nickname Wicky as a kid because, while playing cricket in Lahore, he had diverted a throw from mid-field into the wicket to put the runner out and he hadn't even flinched. "It was more of an accident than skill on my part," Abu said. "I didn't see the ball coming because I had my eye on a cutey, a real tomato who had just moved into the neighborhood."

When Abu drained the dregs from his glass and leaned forward to help himself to more from the bottle, Sly said, "I thought we had a deal?"

"I have not forgotten our earlier conversation and I think I am now ready." Abu spoke carefully, enunciating each syllable. "You were partially right when you guessed that there is a cigar in that tube. You may be completely right for all I know. It certainly looks like a cigar. It also feels like a cigar and smells like a cigar."

"Remember what W. C. Fields said about cigars?" I asked.

Abu paused, and the two women turned toward me.

"He said that a woman is just a woman, but a good cigar is a smoke."

Both women laughed at that, braying like donkeys.

"Believe me," said Abu, "I've done everything with that cigar except smoke it. Still, I'm not sure that's all it is. Maybe your friend Mr. Fields is only partially correct, and a cigar can sometimes be more than a smoke. But that's a long story and, if you are interested in listening to the ramblings of a poor drunken Pakistani, I suggest that we all refresh our glasses before I begin."

We did so, and he then told the following tale.

The Tale of Abu Ali

I return to Pakistan once or twice a year to buy rugs. Sometimes I travel from there to Iran—you know, Persian rugs—but I do most of my business in Pakistan. This past year, I was up in the northern mountains with Major Khan and his driver. The Major is an old family friend, now retired from military service, but in his day he fought bandits in the Karakoram and the Indians in Kashmir. He lost the tips of his ears and nose, two fingers from his left hand,

and several toes from frostbite up near the Khyber Pass. Like any old man, he remembers his youth with great fondness and he was happy to travel north and spend the afternoons drinking tea with his army buddies. Meanwhile, I searched the bazaars and went door to door, looking for families willing to part with rugs that had been in their homes for generations.

We followed a course through the mountains dictated by the Indus River. Sometimes the road was wide and paved where the Army Corps of Engineers had blasted away the mountain slopes. In other places, the road was so narrow that we couldn't take a curve without one wheel hanging over the edge, spinning in air, with nothing but that air between us and the river glinting hundreds of feet below. Once we met a bus coming down the road from the opposite direction, passengers riding on the roof as well as in the seats, and we had to back up for miles before finding a place wide enough to pass.

There were villages in each of the mountain valleys with fruit trees and green terraced fields running as far up the mountains as people could irrigate or carry water. Do you know of Hunza? From the yogurt advertisements? That's the region we were in. That's where everyone is supposed to live to be over a hundred. In Pakistan, they talk about the magical properties of Hunza water. Dannon marketed the idea that the longevity of the inhabitants was due to eating yogurt. You travel through the villages though and the first thing you notice is that everyone looks old, even the little kids who hang out, smoking cigarettes, and watch for any traveler to whom they can sell apricots and cherries if in season, or beg for money and cigarettes if not.

We would buy a large bag of apricots, stick it in the back of the Land Cruiser, and eat nothing but fruit all day as we drove from village to village. If you wanted to, you could probably trace the route we traveled by the apricot trees now growing from the pits we tossed out of the car windows.

Most of the villages lacked petrol stations so, to be on the safe side, we carried jerry cans with us that we filled whenever we had the chance. One day, we stopped at a petrol station in a town shadowed by the granite spires of the Karakoram mountains. The Major and his driver talked with the attendant while I went inside the neighboring shop. It was a ramshackle affair that could have been knocked over by a sneeze, and the owner of the shop had long ago given up trying to keep the dust off his wares. On the shelves were bags of sugar, flour, rice, and tea, various odds and ends like cigarettes, matches, and soap, and some cheap but colorful plastic toys and sunglasses. I bypassed these and made for a chest cooler in the back emblazoned with the Coca-Cola logo.

I lifted the lid on the chest, which exhaled a cool breath of air that reminded me just how hot it was outside. Inside the chest were row on row of soda bottles, green and black, Seven-Up and Coke, standing vertically like soldiers at attention.

I extracted three bottles and was about to close the cover, when there was a shudder and the clank of glass against glass. I paused. Several bottles in the rear of the chest were shivering like Pakistanis in a Boston winter.

I picked up a bottle, but in my hand it was calm. I removed another bottle from the same corner and found it also motionless in my hand. I leaned over the suspect corner, peering into the space vacated by the bottles, and saw that beneath the top layer of bottles there was another layer, as if one battalion of soldiers were standing on the heads of a second battalion.

It was one of the bottles in the lower layer that was shivering, its motion transferred to the bottles above it.

When I pulled that bottle out, it continued to pulse in my hand, alternating between a slight vibration, barely noticeable, and a vigorous shudder that caused my whole hand to torque. The bottle was covered with hoar-frost—who knows how long it had been in the cooler—and when I rubbed aside the fine white powder, I saw that the dark interior flowed more like smoke than any liquid, but a smoke thick and dark as molasses.

I bought four bottles of Coke, one for each of us to drink, and that curious fourth bottle to hide in my luggage until I had the opportunity to investigate its contents alone.

We stayed that night in a government rest house and later, after everyone was asleep, under pretext that I had to go to the bathroom, I stole outside with a flashlight, my penknife, and that bottle of Coke. Standing in the dust on a sticky carpet of mulberries, I popped the cap and turned the bottle upside down. To my surprise, nothing came out. I then set the bottle on the ground and shone my flashlight upon it, and I saw, in the light of my flashlight, a thick smoke pour upward from the bottle.

The smoke continued to flow out for several minutes, forming a mist that surrounded me and rose above me to obscure the stars. When the smoke was all out of the bottle, it reunited and began to condense. For a moment, it seemed that I stood in the shadow of a hideous giant, half-human and half-animal, for I had the impression of bristles, curling tusks, and eyes as large as saucers. But when he had finished coalescing, I saw how mistaken I had been in my first impression. The djinn—for such this creature must be, I realized—was the size of a child, one that would barely reach my waist when standing on tip-toe, and he looked entirely human.

"Free at last," the djinn cried and pumped his fists into the air. He then began to dance on his bandy legs, leaping from one foot to the other. "Free at last. Free at last." Although of child-like stature, in all other ways the djinn appeared to be a man. He had, for example, a handsome mustache and, if you will pardon the observation, prodigiously large genitals such that, as he danced, his penis slapped like a fish against his thighs.

Having given vent to his glee, the djinn twisted his head from side to side, doing so to an inhuman degree such that he faced almost backwards. He then bent his fingers back each in turn so that they touched the wrist. "Oh, that is much better. You cannot imagine what it is like to be trapped in a bottle and to never know when or if you are to be released."

He bowed deeply and extended his hand toward me. "You kind sir, are undoubtedly my benefactor, to whom I owe an enormous debt of gratitude, a debt, which you can be assured, I will be most happy to repay."

I reached down and took his small hand in mine. His palm was warm and dry and slightly dusty, his handshake seemingly firm but it gave a little to applied pressure.

"Ah, but where are my manners?" he said. "Here you are dressed like a prince, while I look like the man who played at cards and, finding that he had lost all the money in his pockets, made one final bet in which he risked the clothes off his back. You know how that bet transpired." In truth, I was only wearing a pair of light cotton pajamas, hardly the robes of royalty. Nevertheless, the djinn ran his hands lightly over his own body, sliding them down from his neck along his arms, chest, and legs. His body, where his hands touched, became blurred and then reformed so that he was no longer naked, but wearing a suit of the finest linen.

Needless to say, I was amazed at all that I had just witnessed. If questions were bees, then my head was a hive. "Who are you?" I asked. "Where did you come from? How did you get here?"

"That is a long story, a long sad story of a trusting heart and of its repeated betrayal by those that it trusted the most," said the djinn. In thinking about this troubled history, the djinn's lower lip trembled and it seemed that he might burst into tears. "But perhaps this is not the best place to tell my story."

It was only then that I remembered my own manners and invited the djinn to accompany me into the house. The djinn thanked me for my hospitality and begged my indulgence for just a moment. He picked up the Coke bottle in which he had been imprisoned and threw it with all his strength into the night. I heard the bottle shatter in the rocky field behind the house. "That takes care of that." The djinn brushed his hands against each other and a broad smile crept across his face.

Back in the house, I made a pot of tea in the kitchen and piled some books on a chair so that the djinn could sit comfortably at the table. We sat across from each other, cups in hand, and the djinn told me the following tale.

The Tale of the Djinn

Many years ago, Solomon, the great prophet, called all the djinns before him to submit to his will and to acknowledge his mastery over their domain. Those rebellious spirits that did not appear at the appointed time in his court were to be apprehended and imprisoned. Now I, having inadvertently consumed some fermented grapes the night before and then falling into a deep slumber, did not answer the call of Solomon. Awakening well past the appointed hour and realizing my error, I debated what gift would excuse me in his eyes. But Solomon had by this time already sent Asaph, the son of his chief minister, to find out the reason for my absence.

"What is that?" demanded Asaph upon entering the valley where I made my home.

I bowed deeply before him. "That," said I, "is my gift to Solomon on this special occasion, and its preparation the reason for my tardiness in appearing before him. I have built a statue of Solomon that is taller than me, and I am taller than fifteen men."

"I can see that it is a statue of Solomon", said Asaph. "But what is that smell?"

I bowed again, my nose scraping the earth before Asaph's feet. "That smell is goat dung," said I. "The reason you smell the goat dung is because the statue is newly made and has not yet had time to dry in the sun."

"And why have you made a statue of Solomon out of goat dung?" asked Asaph.

"I seek to show," said I, "that the form of Solomon can bring beauty to even the basest of materials."

But neither Asaph nor Solomon believed in the truth of my words. As a result, I was imprisoned in a copper vessel, and, to make sure that I should not escape, Solomon himself stamped his seal into the lead stopper on the vessel. He then gave the vessel to one of the djinns that had submitted to him and commanded that I be thrown into the deepest part of the sea.

I do not know how long I languished in my underwater prison. At first I kept track of my sentence in years, and then in tens of years, and then in hundreds. I counted fifteen hundred years, but sometimes I counted backwards, thinking that perhaps it would make the time pass more swiftly. For your information, should you ever find yourself in a similar situation, counting backwards does not make the time pass more swiftly. Quite the opposite, in fact.

Eventually, a fisherman, casting his nets into the sea, caught my vessel and dragged it onto the shore where he freed me from my captivity. You will not be surprised to hear that the first thing I did upon being released was to kick the vessel that had been my prison back into the sea. You can also imagine my relief and the gratitude I expressed toward my benefactor. He was a poor man, and I made him rich. He lived in a shack of driftwood, and I built him a palace grander than that of the sultan. He was alone, and I brought him the sultan's youngest daughter to be his bride.

What may surprise you is that even after I made the fisherman wealthy beyond the dreams of most men, he still went out each morning to cast his nets into the sea. He undressed, offered a prayer up to God, and waded into the sea just as he had done when a poor man. He did not even accept my assistance and said that a fisherman's luck was the provenance of God. But upon completing his work, he was happy to share the food and drink that I prepared. In the afternoons, we engaged in various sports and tests of skill. Sometimes, when bored with these activities, I carried him on travels to distant parts of the land. What he enjoyed most on these journeys was simply floating in the sky high above the domes and spires of the strange cities and watching the citizens move about their tasks like ants.

But my good nature was to prove once again my downfall. Unbeknownst to me, the fisherman's wife had become jealous of the camaraderie that existed between the fisherman and myself. Perhaps this could not be avoided for our relationship predated her entry into his life and it may have seemed that I surpassed her in his affections.

One morning, while the fisherman was casting nets upon the waves, she came to me dressed in her best silks. It is wisely said that when standing in the garden one should be doubly on one's guard for snakes but, at the time, I suspected nothing.

"My husband," said she, "has told me how he discovered you in a small vessel. He has also said that he freed you from this vessel in which you had been imprisoned for many hundreds of years."

"That is so," said I.

"Now when he told me this story I was sure that he told me a lie," said she. "But now I see that you are in collusion together, for you have just told me the same lie."

"That story is no lie," said I, "and you dishonor us all to call it such."

"It is no dishonor to speak the truth," said she. "A vessel such as you describe would not be sufficient to hold my foot, and you are much greater than me."

"If you like," said I, "I will demonstrate the proof of my assertion. Bring me a suitable vessel and all shall be made clear. Then this argument may be put behind us."

Whereupon she fetched a small pot in which she normally kept cosmetics. I then made my body take the form of smoke, as you saw previously, and entered the pot in a smooth and constant motion, continuing to do so until nothing was left without. She then covered the pot with a lid, apparently to demonstrate that I was contained completely within the pot. Having thus satisfied, to my knowledge, the point of the argument, I popped the lid loose and flowed from the pot to reform before her. "Are you now convinced?" asked I.

"Hardly," said she. I was surprised to hear the anger in her words, and, although she wore the veil, it seemed that her eyes flashed fire. "It is apparent that you can enter a vessel," said she, "but it is just as apparent that a vessel cannot contain you for you exited the vessel as easily as you entered. How then could you have been imprisoned in such a fashion as you claim?"

"That is simple," said I. "Solomon stamped the vessel in which I was imprisoned with his seal, and his seal contains the great name of God engraved on it. Even I, with all my might, cannot break such a seal."

But once again she refused to believe me and would have me prove the truth of my words. I reentered the cosmetics pot in the same manner as before. She again covered the pot with its lid. But this time she scratched the name of God upon the lid with one of her diamond rings. Try as I might, I could not open the lid from the inside, although my efforts made the pot dance about the floor.

Seeing me now trapped, rather than freeing me as we had agreed, she instead gave the vessel to a servant. She told the servant that it contained a poison that would destroy the person that opened it and instructed him to deliver it secretly to her father, that he might lock it away so as to preserve the health of his peoples.

This servant joined a caravan heading east but he never reached the sultan for, in his journey, he and his fellow travelers were set upon and killed by bandits. The bandits took his possessions, including the vessel in which I was imprisoned, and hid these inside a cave where they and many generations of bandits before them had stored their ill-won goods. I remained inside the cave for years, all the time seeing the treasures increase, with many more treasures brought in than were removed. Eventually the secret of the bandits was discovered and my vessel removed with a load of treasure. I thought that my release was now at hand, but I was to be disappointed. The new owner, finding my vessel to be made of base metal not of gold and certain symbols on the vessel that indicated a dangerous poison was contained inside, disposed of my prison by tossing it into his latrine.

I only had worms for company for the next 653 years. I know this number as a fact because I did not make any mistakes in counting this time.

My next benefactor was a laborer who, while digging the foundation for a new home, unearthed my vessel. He too I made rich so as to express my gratitude for the part he played in my release. The source of the wealth I bestowed on him was the same cave used those many centuries ago by the bandits. The men who once knew its secret had all died, taking the secret with them, and none had rediscovered the cave so well was it camouflaged, its entrance hidden behind a great boulder.

My benefactor became a well-respected businessman and the owner of many companies including a real-estate company, a sporting shoe manufacturer, and a soft-drink distributor. Having achieved great wealth and seeing his businesses continue to grow in value, he reached a point where he considered that he had more to lose than to gain. Furthermore, because his good fortune was owed to me, he considered me the most likely agent for its loss. He therefore hatched a plan to rid himself of me.

One evening he asked me to take him to his bottling factory in Lahore, where he believed that the overseer was embezzling money from him. It is wisely said that one can recognize a dishonest man because he trusts no one, not even himself. But, at the time, I suspected nothing.

Finding the books in good order, we then explored the factory to determine if all else was as it should be. My benefactor seemed distracted during this enterprise and more interested in discussing matters of philosophy or, to be more accurate, the physiology of djinns.

"I have seen you become as smoke," said he, "such that you can flow and take on different forms. Do you have all the properties of smoke or are you limited in ways that I do not appreciate?"

"I confess that I have not given the matter much thought," said I. "Indeed, owing to the extensive periods of my incarceration, I have not always had the opportunity to test the limits of my capabilities. In what property do you find interest?"

"Smoke can be divided but still retain its essence," said he, "such that even one small part of the whole is like the whole in form and substance."

"That is true," said I, "but I fail to see the relevance."

"If you have this same inherent property," said he, "you should be able to divide yourself into multiple smaller selves, each like you but capable of acting independently. For example, I have seen you enter a single vessel but, if I am correct, you should be able to divide and secrete yourself in multiple vessels." He pointed to a case of empty Coca Cola bottles, seemingly located near us by chance.

I was intrigued by the experiment that he set forward and only too happy to oblige, thinking that I might learn something to my advantage. Indeed, although my benefactor had only lived upon this earth a small percentage of my years, he proved correct, and I found myself able to do as he proposed. But no sooner had I divided myself into the two-dozen bottles than the man I had hitherto called my benefactor placed the bottles into a machine where they were immediately capped. Moreover, I soon discovered that the bottle caps were printed with the name of God so that each of my selves had no more power within the bottles than the smoke that they resembled.

Finding myself thus trapped, I knew that I had been betrayed, and my benefactor become my jailer. But God is great, and I commended myself to his mercy. I do not know if I have God to thank or simply the vagaries of machines, which are built by man, but it so transpired that, after being capped, not all the bottles were placed into the same case. Moreover, my jailer did not apparently notice the absence of the bottle you discovered until after it had been shipped to Skardu. By then it was too late.

In concluding, I must apologize for my lack of potability, but I believe that you will come to consider yourself well recompensed for your act of charity in freeing me.

"And that," said Abu, "is how I came to be drinking tea at one-o-clock in the morning with a midget djinn." Abu took a sip of whisky and ran the pink tip of his tongue across his lips.

Sly cleared her throat. "You still haven't told us about the cigar."

My own cigar, balanced on the edge of a saucer decorated with blue forget-me-nots, tenaciously clung to over an inch of ash.

"What about the reward?" asked Ann. She ran a fingernail—click, click, click—across her faux pearls. "How were you 'recompensed' for freeing the djinn?"

I said nothing. As far as I was concerned, Abu was just playing games with the ladies, the same thing he had done for as long as I had known him. It was getting late, the house smelled of smoke and cheap perfume, and I knew that I would have a lot of explaining to do when Elizabeth returned with the kids.

Abu pointed a finger at Sly and then at Ann. "Each of you has just answered the other's question."

"The djinn gave you the cigar?"

"That was your reward?"

"That's right. After telling me his story and thanking me for the hundredth time, the djinn told me that he had only one regret, that he could not immediately reward me in so grand a fashion as I deserved and he desired. The being that spoke to me, he explained, contained his essence but was greatly diminished in power. He asked leave to search for the bottles that contained the rest of himself, so that he could return to his full size and power. After that he promised to return and reward me in suitable fashion.

"I could do nothing but agree. He had asked so politely.

"The djinn then reached into his jacket and handed me a cigar. 'Accept this as token of my esteem,' he said. He explained that if I smoked the cigar it would transport me to the cave of riches. This was the same cave used by the bandits from which the djinn had rewarded his previous benefactor. He assured me that the cave of riches had been forgotten for so long that anything I brought back would be mine alone."

"So what did you find there?" asked Ann.

"I never went."

"You mean that the cigar didn't work?"

"No, I never tried. I never smoked the cigar."

"I can't believe that," said Ann. "If I had a treasure cave, you can bet I'd go there every day. You'd see me wearing so many pearls that I wouldn't need clothes."

"So many gold rings that my hands would drag on the ground." Sly giggled at the thought.

"If you don't believe me, have a look." Abu went over to his suitcase, undid the Ziploc bag, and opened up the plastic tube. A cigar slid into his hand. "Take a look at it, but please don't touch." He cupped the cigar lightly in his hands and showed it to each of us in turn. It was about the same size as the coronas we were smoking, the wrapper a little darker, and its tip twisted into a pigtail. The cigar band showed a heart wreathed in curly-cues, but without any recognizable brand name.

I don't know where the cigar came from, but Abu was telling the truth when he said that he had not smoked it.

"Don't get me wrong," said Abu. "After the djinn left me, I was ready to smoke the cigar then and there. But something held me back. At first I couldn't figure out what was bothering me. Maybe it was that the djinn seemed so polite. There was something too polished about the way he acted. If he was really such a good friend, then why was he always getting locked up? Or maybe it's because his history seemed familiar but distorted, like a story my ayah used to tell me as she tucked me into bed, but with the hero switched for the villain. Or maybe it's just because people in my homeland have learned—it may have taken centuries, but we have learned—not to trust the lure of easy money. Here, of course, it's different. Americans fall asleep dreaming of the lottery and lawsuits.

"Finally, it came down to one simple question. Even assuming that the cigar transported me to the cave, and that the cave was full of all the riches that the djinn promised, how was I to get out of the cave once inside? As far as I know the cigar may be the only way to gain entrance, in which case I would be buried alive."

"But isn't there always a magic lamp or a ring or something inside," Sly said. "No one ever stays trapped in those caves."

"Would you take the chance on that?"

"Or what if it's just a cigar?" Sly asked. "Maybe that's the whole joke. Why don't I smoke it and you watch. If I disappear, I promise to come back. I'll even give you a percentage of the treasure."

"A small percentage," said Ann.

"If you don't believe there's something special about the cigar," said Abu, "then consider this: although I have had the cigar in my possession for months, and I have never kept it inside a proper humidor, it is still in perfect condition. There are no cracks in the wrapper, no unraveling, no nothing."

"So that's the end of it?" said Sly. "You have a magic cigar but you're afraid to find out if it lives up to its reputation."

"You looking for a money-back guarantee?" said Ann.

"Well, that's not quite the end of the story. I did see the djinn one more time. If you'll freshen my glass, I'll tell you about that."

I did the honors and also topped off the ladies' glasses, draining the last few drops from the bottle. The initial giddiness brought on by the alcohol had left me and now all I felt was tired. I hoped that, with the whisky gone, the party might soon break up. "Drink up," I said.

"You should have seen the Major and me when we returned from the north," Abu said. "We had so many rugs that I had to hire a bus to follow us with them. We traveled in tandem the whole length of Pakistan, from K2 to Karachi, rugs tied to the top, stuffed in the aisle, and laid across the passenger seats of the bus. The bus still took on passengers at a reduced ticket price, fitting them into whatever room remained, and that posed its own problems. Once the Major hopped out of the Land Cruiser while it was still moving and chased down a passenger, forty years his junior, who had disembarked from the bus and tried to make off with a rug across his shoulders. When we got to Karachi, I had the rugs crated and shipped, downed one last Coke with the Major at the airport cafe, saluted him for old time's sake, and then flew to London.

"Now all the time I traveled in Pakistan, all the time I waited in London for my rug shipment to arrive, I never let the cigar out of my reach. At first, to protect the cigar, I kept it in an emptied biscuit tin cushioned with my socks. Later I bought a cheap cigar in a protective tube, and exchanged one for the other. I carried the djinn's cigar with me at all times during the day and I slept with it at night, tucked inside my pillowcase.

"In London, a month or so after I got there, I returned one evening from a pub dinner, unlocked the door to my apartment, and saw the djinn seated on the couch waiting for me. Although his features were still the same, he was larger than when last I saw him, such that he could no longer be confused with a boy.

"'Congratulations,' I said, 'I see that you have had some luck in your quest.'

"'A little,' he said, 'for my former benefactor kept one of the bottles on the dresser in his bedroom, perhaps to gloat over when alone.' The djinn wore a beautiful silver-gray suit of a quality that only movie stars could afford. He also looked more muscular than when I saw him last. Almost unbidden came the thought that he was not actually so much stronger but that, as with his clothing, he had adjusted his appearance for maximal effect.

"'But the other bottles?' I asked. 'Did you find them?'

"'Unfortunately,' said the djinn, 'my former benefactor was not in condition to answer my questions, having taken sick and become enfeebled. Thus does God punish those who seek only their own gain. But I now fear that he has buried the other bottles or cast them into the sea for I could not find them in his house or on his grounds. I still hope, however, that some of the bottles escaped him and exist beyond his control.' The djinn spoke calmly, but I saw his fists clench and a look of raw hatred sweep across his face.

"'I have faith,' I said, 'that your perseverance will be rewarded.'

"'But enough about my troubles,' the djinn said. 'How are you? I am surprised to find you in this apartment. I would have thought that, with the treasures from the cave, you could now afford something more in keeping with your deserved place in society.' The djinn fingered the couch fabric. He then rose from the couch, sidestepped the coffee table, and came to stand beside me.

"'In truth,' said I, 'I have been so busy that I have not had time to take you up on your kind offer.'

"'You should not consider this an offer based solely on kindness,' said the djinn. 'It is what you deserve.' He placed a hand on my arm in an apparent attempt at reassurance.

"'Indeed,' said I, 'it seemed presumptuous of me to take advantage of my good fortune when you were still not satisfied with your situation.'

"'It would give me the greatest pleasure,' said the djinn, 'far outweighing my personal misfortunes, to see you justly rewarded for your efforts on my behalf.'

"While speaking, the djinn gripped my bicep with increased vigor. His forcefulness, if nothing else, convinced me that I was correct in my earlier fears and that he could not be trusted. My thoughts were now focused on how I might rid myself of him. To this end, I conceived a plan that had some chance of success, but might not reflect too badly on me if it failed.

"I went to the cupboard in the kitchenette and got down a bag of potato chips, which I poured into a wooden bowl. 'Help yourself,' I said, offering the bowl to the djinn. In an apparent act of clumsiness, I sloshed chips out of the bowl, letting them fall upon the carpet where, to compound the error, I stepped on the chips, again apparently by accident, and ground them into the nap. 'Damn,' I said and went to the hall closet to get the vacuum cleaner.

"'Do you mind?' I asked politely, running the vacuum cleaner across the carpet in front of the djinn's feet. I don't think the djinn had ever seen such a machine before and, from the way his mouth twisted in distaste, he did not enjoy the noise that it made.

"In response to my request, he floated several feet up into the air. When he did, I turned the vacuum cleaner on him."

"You did what?" Ann asked.

"I sucked him up."

"Just like that?"

"I don't think the djinn realized what was happening right away. The vacuum cleaner pulled at his suit jacket. I begged his pardon. He tugged back. I apologized again. He twisted and turned, hands wrapped around the tube of the vacuum cleaner, and bobbed about in the air like some demented balloon. He then cried out, perhaps in pain, perhaps in anger. It was obvious by this point that something was very wrong.

"'Release me,' he said. 'I will make it worth your while.'

"I pretended not to hear. I also pretended not to notice the changes taking place in his features. His face turned red, his brows and mustache bristled, and his eyes enlarged until they were the size of boiled eggs.

"'Release me,' he repeated. Several of his teeth now protruded like tusks, deforming his mouth so that spittle flew with his words. He snorted like a wild beast.

"Still I pretended to be lost in confusion and unable to understand what was happening.

"He then screamed above the roar of the vacuum cleaner in a language that I didn't recognize and struggled with increased energy, flinging himself madly about the room. I was literally dragged across the floor. Then, his legs braced against a corner where the walls met the ceiling, the djinn ripped himself free and hurled the vacuum cleaner down at me. The wand hit me in the head, opening a large gash, and I fell to the floor in the coils of the hose.

"The djinn floated above me. He seemed about to speak but broke off in a fit of coughing. His chest heaved and his throat rolled and then, hacking like a cat, he expelled some small white fragments that clattered on the floor beside me. I glanced at the nearest one: it was a tooth. Seeing that, I knew what had happened to the djinn's former benefactor.

"'I will kill you,' said the djinn. 'I will grind you up and I will eat you.' He wiped some drool from his lips with the back of his hand and then stroked his tusks with a long pointed fingernail.

"Lying there on the floor, at the mercy of that evil creature, I thought that my time had come at last. But I was saved by a smell, a stink of eggs and burning tires so horrible that even shaking with fear, still I wrinkled my nose in distaste. The stench originated from the djinn, from a rip in his jacket, a rift just above his waist where a grayish smoke now leaked out to dissipate in the air. His suit wasn't so much like clothing as like a skin and, where it was ripped open, I could see inside, and inside he was all black and swirling like a swarm of flies.

"The djinn had been wounded. Knowing that, I knew that I could win our battle.

"I grabbed the vacuum cleaner up again and thrust the tube through the hole in his side. He screamed but by then it was already too late. The vacuum cleaner sucked greedily. His suit became more and more wrinkled. His face contorted and creases opened in its surface. Then his face caved in: his nose collapsed, his brow settled down over his great yellowish eyes, and the dome of his forehead disappeared altogether. As his insides got sucked into the vacuum cleaner, his skin suit deflated and flopped around like a wind sock. Then it shredded and got sucked up too.

"I ran the vacuum cleaner over the floor for several minutes and, when I was sure that every last bit of the djinn was inside, I pulled out the vacuum cleaner bag, wrapped it in duct tape, and wrote the name of God on it with a black marker. I then bought a small safe, stuffed the bag inside, spun the dial, and dumped the safe from Blackfriars Bridge into the Thames.

"But, yes, basically I sucked the djinn up... just... like... that."

Abu grinned so broadly that his teeth lit up the room.

I wish I could leave the story there at the moment of Abu's triumph. We all laughed and toasted him, not necessarily believing his words but happy to share in the illusion that such stories could be true.

"Put that djinn in the bin," said Sly, laughing like a hyena.

"Wouldn't you just love to have been there," said Ann, laughing with equal intensity.

"I'm not a hero," said Abu. "I'm just a simple rug dealer from Pakistan, more handsome than most I'll grant you and gifted in the arts of love, but just a man nevertheless. I'm sure that any one of you would have done the same if put in my position." Abu raised his glass to take a drink but, finding it now empty, looked mournfully into its bottom.

"I'm afraid that the whisky's finished," I said.

"Do you have soda? Or juice?"

"I'll take a look."

Abu followed me into the kitchen. In retrospect, I don't think Abu really had soda in mind. I think he wanted to talk to me in private, but I didn't give him a chance. Something had been building up in me all night, but I didn't recognize my anger until it boiled over.

"What a load of bullshit," I said.

Abu's mouth fell open.

"Do you think for one minute that I'm going to sit and watch you drink up everything in the house? And stink up everything in the house with your stupid cigars? All so you can get into the pants of some girls you picked up in a bar."

Abu opened and closed his mouth, gulping ineffectually like a fish on the line.

"I used to think you were a friend. I used to admire you. But I was younger then. We both were. Maybe you were different then, but I don't think so. I was just too young to recognize you for what you are."

I was surprised to see a tear start down Abu's cheek. But that didn't stop me.

"You're a user," I said. "You were a user then and you're a user now."

Abu broke down completely. He attempted to reach out for me, to place his hands on my shoulders for support. But when I stepped back to avoid him, he just stood there, arms hanging loosely at his sides, tears and snot running down his face. "I have nothing," he said. "Nothing."

I stared at him, puzzled. "What do you mean?"

"None of my shipments of rugs made it. They never arrived in London. That's why I waited there so long. I waited and waited. When they didn't show up on the ship I thought was carrying them, then I waited for the next ship in hopes they would be on there instead. And the next ship, and the next. But nothing. No records either, as if the rugs never existed."

"Is that why you came to Boston?"

"I sent a rug shipment here from Karachi, but was told it hadn't arrived either. No records for that one either. I want to go down to the docks myself and check on the shipping and receiving. That was my plan for tomorrow." Abu glanced at his wristwatch. "This morning." He wiped his nose on the sleeve of his suit.

I had never comforted a grown man before but, rightly or wrongly, my natural inclination was to do the same as I would with my kids. I held him tightly, patting his back, and murmured what I took to be comforting noises.

"It was the djinn," Abu said, whispering into my ear. "He was trying to force me to use the cigar. By taking away my wealth, he figured that I would have no choice but to use it. When I didn't, he showed up at my apartment." Abu made a valiant attempt to control himself, which brought on a fit of hiccups. "I still don't know what would happen if I smoked it."

"Oh, give it a rest," I said and pushed him away. "You and your stupid genie. For a moment I believed you but I should have known it was just another trick. Another play for my sympathy. Well save it for someone who cares."

He pleaded with me but I was out of patience and, after listening to his babble for a few minutes, I stalked out of the kitchen. He padded along behind me, his hands empty, having never received the soda that I promised him.

In our absence, Ann and Sly had been conferring in the living room, foreheads pressed together and murmuring in the cryptic tones of those that understand each other so intimately that only part of a thought need be voiced. They immediately separated upon our return and smiled. "Everything all right?" asked Ann. "I hope you boys found what you were looking for," said Sly. She ran a finger around the rim of her empty glass. "It's been a wonderful evening, but I think it time we were going. Abu, you with us?"

Abu nodded.

I followed them to the entry way and helped Abu on with his coat. Then I pawed through the closet looking for the coats belonging to Ann and Sly. I didn't remember what their coats looked like. I didn't even remember putting them in the closet. But Ann and Sly already had their coats on, having apparently grabbed them while I was helping Abu.

Abu stumbled down the steps, supported by his two lady friends.

"You sure that I can't get you a taxi?" I asked.

"The night is young," he said, "A walk in the night air will clear my head."

"We'll take care of him," Ann said.

"You can count on us," Sly added.

Then the door slammed and they were gone.

I watched them for a little while from the window of the condo. They moved slowly down the street, Abu weaving so that he was sometimes on the sidewalk and sometimes on the pavement. The streetlights are spaced at some distance apart here, small oases of light, and this makes it difficult to know what I saw as they moved away. At first, everything seemed normal enough, just Abu meandering along and the two women trying to maintain contact with him so that they could guide him. But in his drunken state Abu didn't want anyone's help. He threw off their arms and insisted upon following his own chaotic sense of direction, which led him back to the middle of the road. He was lucky there was no traffic at the time. Thankfully, Ann and Sly caught him and forced him to walk on the sidewalk. I breathed a sigh of relief and, seeing that they were almost out of sight, dropped the curtain back into place. I would clear away the glasses and ashtrays from our late night and then go to bed.

But, even as I turned, I realized that something about the final image wasn't right. Thinking back on what I had just seen, replaying the image that had burned itself into my mind, it seemed that I could still make out the shape of Abu quite clearly but that the shapes of the two women had become indistinct. It seemed that Abu walked in the company of two wraiths, hazy in outline like wisps of smoke.

I pulled the curtain open again and rubbed away the condensation that had collected on the window from my breath. By then it was already too late. The two women had escorted Abu arm in arm beyond the range of the streetlights and into the Boston night.

I thought little of it at the time, marking it down to the tales that Abu had told and an active imagination. But it has been six years now and I still haven't heard from Abu. I can't help but wonder what happened to him and what exactly I saw that night. It's not just me and my sense of guilt. Two months after Abu disappeared, Elizabeth discovered a notice in the newspaper with which she was lining the cat litter box. A body had been dragged from the Charles River, a man with no identifying documents—perhaps these were stolen from him with his wallet, perhaps he did not want to be identified. The man had a mustache but no beard, and may have been of Indian, or Pakistani, or Middle Eastern descent. Two witnesses, women, although not identified by name, reported seeing a man jump off the Longfellow Bridge that night.

But that man was not Abu Ali.

I contacted the newspapers and found out the dead man had been subsequently identified as Mohammed Aziz, a stranger to me, who had been involved with the heroin trade in Boston.

Whatever happened to Abu remains a mystery. I like to imagine that he started a new life even if I am not part of that life. Maybe he's back in London. Or Pakistan. Anywhere. Given how we parted, I can understand why he would not contact me. I hope that's why he hasn't contacted me. What still strikes me hard is just how easy it is to lose one's friends. One misplaced word or glance and they disappear, and you don't realize that they're gone until it's too late.

The cigar did not disappear with Abu. Before he left me that night, he pressed it upon me. "Take it," he said, "no matter what you think of me. Hold it. Keep it. There's not a day gone by that I haven't thought about smoking it. But when I reach for it, my heart beats faster and my palms get sweaty. I just stare at it and I don't know what to do. If I come back for it, don't let me have it, no matter how I might beg."

Now the cigar lies in the top drawer of my desk, hidden behind a pile of paperwork, in the same plastic tube in which Abu brought it into my house.

Sometimes I pull open the drawer and look at that slim torpedo. Abu was right: it doesn't need a humidor. I run my fingers lightly across the leaf wrapper and smell the faint peppery aroma that clings to my fingertips. I wonder how the cigar would smoke and, if I were to smoke it, would I find myself still in the familiar surroundings of my study or transplanted to the fabled caves of Ali Baba, my overhead light replaced by hanging strands of pearls, the rug gone and the floor knee-deep in gold coins, and, instead of my desk, a massive treasure chest spilling forth gems, gold chains, and jewel-studded crowns and swords rather than papers, pens, and pencils.

The cigar band is decorated with the tiny image of a heart and, flocked around it, the graceful curves of the Arabic language. At first I didn't think much about the writing, treating it simply as a decorative motif. But then I got to thinking about what the genie, if the genie truly existed, might inscribe upon the cigar. Through a friend, I contacted a professor in the languages department at Boston University. That professor was unable to translate the copy that I made of the cigar band, but he had contacts overseas. Distance means little in this age of the internet, and a professor at the King Faisal Center for Islamic, Arabic, and Asian Studies in Saudi Arabia came up with an approximate translation. He said it was written in Kufi, sometimes known as the character of Cleopatra, an early form of Arabic writing that dates back to the Middle Ages. The language can be translated but the true pronunciation of the words is lost in the sands of time.

In its simplest form the cigar band reads: The heart of the seed.

But it can also be interpreted as a question or a riddle, in which case it reads: How does one reach the heart of the seed?

I know the answer to that riddle.

I can't forget it no matter how hard I try.

Sometimes, when working late in my office at home, like tonight, I think about the choices I have made and how I came to be where I am. I think about my wife, my kids, my job, and my receding hairline. I think about everything I have gained and everything I have lost. I think about the night that Abu Ali stumbled into my apartment and then stumbled out, leaving nothing but this cigar behind him. Then I become aware that all the time I have been thinking these thoughts, all the time I have been handling the cigar, that I have been muttering the same words over and over again, as if two words could change everything and allow me to reclaim the possibilities that I saw when I was younger.

When that happens, like now, I push my chair back and leave my office, the cyclopean eye of the computer staring at my retreating back, to wonder through the rooms and corridors of our condo. I see where the four of us sat that night six years ago in the living room. I see where I argued with Abu in the kitchen and where I helped him on with his coat in the hallway. I see the window through which I followed the progress of Abu and the two women down the street, and I pick out the streetlight that marks the last point I saw Abu before he disappeared.

Climbing upstairs, I slip quiet as a ghost past the bedrooms and the sleepers within. I pass Mark's room. I pass Mary's room. They're not little kids anymore and sleep with their doors closed. No nightlights for them either. At the end of the hallway is another closed door: our bedroom. Elizabeth is in there, having gone to bed hours earlier.

I stand in front of the door and repeat those two words once more, this time knowing full well what I say: "Open Sesame."

The door seems to swing inward of its own accord.

Elizabeth lies in bed, curled on her side, face pressed into the pillow. Dark hair cascades in curls across the pillow and across the sheet that she has pulled up over her shoulder. She snores softly. I listen to the intake of her breath, catch the silence that lurks after each inhalation, then the barely perceptible popping noise that her lips make when they part, and finally the exhalation that leaves her lips and sounds almost like a sigh.

"Open Sesame." She stirs in bed, drawing her breaths more deeply so that the air whistles through her nose.

"Open Sesame." The third time I say those words to her, she wakes. She turns her head, rakes the hair from her eyes. She squints up at me and, seeing me, frowns.

"What the hell," she says. "What's happening?"

Hearing her speak, it's like I'm the one waking from a dream, stepping out of someone else's story and into one of my own. I just stand there and smile. "Nothing," I say, finding my own words. "The door was open. I thought you might be awake."

"Well, I am now."

I take that as an invitation.

The Watchmaker

There was once a watchmaker who lived in the town of Hinterwald, where it is said, because the town lies midway between valley and clouds on the alpine slopes of the Weisshorn, that there are but three seasons in the year. Winter lasts for six months, spring and autumn each for three, and summer, which may come but once every ten years, lasts only a single golden afternoon.

The watchmaker was known as Herr Lindhorst to most members of the town, and as Kristoff to the few who assumed intimacy with him. He lived and worked in a narrow two-story house that he had inherited from his parents, above the door of which hung an iron sign bent and forged into the shape of a watch dial. Ever since the watchmaker had been a boy known as Kris, he had drifted off to sleep each night listening to the sign creak in the mountain winds.

The family Lindhorst had repaired watches for as long as anyone could remember. If you overwound your watchspring, perhaps while distracted by the neighbor's daughter hanging her laundry, the metallic ping at your fingertips causing your heart to sink into your boots—how could any woman fall in love with such a careless man?—it was to Lindhorst's Watch Repair that you turned. If you attempted to master three tasks at once, such as reading the morning newssheet, locating your mouth with a spoonful of lumpy porridge, and checking the time on the pocket watch given to you on your sixteenth birthday, and if, as a result, your watch should tumble into your coffee cup, it was to Lindhorst's Watch Repair that you brought the family heirloom still leaking the brown droplets of your favorite roast. Invariably, your watch would be returned to you in better condition than before its accident. "Why it's just like new," you would say, examining the print your thumb left on the polished metal. You would be answered with a smile and the phrase repeated by each member of the Lindhorst family for the past three generations, "We do our best."

Kristoff Lindhorst was the first member of his family to make rather than simply repair watches. His first creation was a monstrosity cobbled together from broken springs, chipped gears, and cracked crystals that belonged in the trash bin but which had excited the crow-like curiosity of the four-year-old. The watch that Kris presented to his father for approval looked something like a mangled crab the boy had found deposited on the mountain slopes by a wayfaring seagull. But whereas the crab had clearly expired, such that even a week of warmth in the boy's pocket failed to reanimate it, the watch just as surely worked. The mechanism emitted a healthy "tick-tick-tick" and each of its eight hands spun merrily around at different speeds. At the time, the similarity of the watch to the displaced crab was seen as coincidence but later, after Kristoff's predilections became clear, it was granted that he had created his first automaton.

Kristoff joined his father in the shop at the age of six. Passersby marveled at the child who, perched on a tiny stool at a tiny watchmaker's bench, appeared to be an elf materialized out of a folk tale. "He has the eyes and the fingers," his father would say to his customers, winking a watery blue eye and waggling his own gnarled fingers. "More importantly, he has the passion."

At the age of fifteen, Kristoff made a grandfather clock. At the striking of each hour, a mechanical man dressed in traditional garb and with a permanent smile painted on his porcelain face, stepped onto a balcony decorated with carved roses. Most times the man merely bowed, sweeping feathered hat from scalp and bending so far forward that he kissed his knees, then returned to his home behind a door in a twisted oak. But when midnight struck, the man arrived with a ladder held beneath his right arm. He leaned the ladder against the clock face, climbed up five rungs, and then cleaned the clock face with a dust cloth. His motions with the cloth appeared random, but those who closely followed him discovered that he outlined the stern features of the Man in the Moon.

At the age of nineteen, Kristoff was commissioned to update the clockwork of the town hall. This was a well-loved piece that included a blacksmith with hammer and a hunter with cudgel, who glided about a circular stage to ring the bell each hour. Although once a tourist attraction, it was now old-fashioned in comparison to the more elaborate dioramas of the neighboring towns. Kristoff added a fox that wound its way through the legs of the blacksmith, snuck up on the hunter, and then, by gnawing through the strings that tethered them to the hunter's belt, released three partridges. The birds flew up with a rattle of wings and rang the bell with sharp blows from their beaks, the two men now swinging their implements at the fluttering birds rather than at the bell. The fox winked at the spectators then ran off, the money pouches of the blacksmith and hunter clenched in his teeth.

After this there was no holding Kristoff back. He traveled from town to town, taking on more and more lucrative commissions. He was served the best foods in the best restaurants and, whether the project took a day or a year, put up in the best hotels. Holidays were declared and bands played each time a piece of his was unveiled. Tourists following routes on maps that depicted the locations of his creations, returning from their travels with metal or paper reproductions to set on their mantels, the jerky movements of these poor substitutes affirming the genius of the originals.

At 31 Kristoff was without peer but, before he reached his next birthday, his career was over, and his friends and former patrons crossed the street rather than risk encountering him. Kristoff was approached in a pub, as he later said, by a man with features so nondescript that these were a better disguise than any mask. This man, who did not give his name, said that he was an agent for another who wished to remain anonymous, but who had a project truly worthy of Kristoff's skills. Needless to say, but emphasized at least a dozen times during the conversation, Kristoff would be well rewarded should he accept the commission. "You have spoken almost excessively," Kristoff said, "but I have yet to hear what you wish of me." At this the man took a square of paper from his embroidered coat pocket, wrote on it with a silver mechanical pencil, then folded the paper and passed it to Kristoff.

When Kristoff unfolded the paper, he saw that it contained a circle drawn atop a cross. "Venus," he said, understanding the significance of the symbol as soon as he said the name aloud. "You wish me to make a woman."

"Precisely. And to the specifications that I will give you."

It would have been to Kristoff's credit if he had thought long and hard before accepting the commission but, as he later admitted, he was nodding his assent before the agent had finished his sentence. It was not fame that Kristoff sought for the agent made it clear that the mechanical woman would become the sole property of his anonymous benefactor. Furthermore, given the nature of the commission, it was obviously intended for private entertainment not public exhibition. Kristoff simply desired to push his skills to the limit, and through them to create something that exceeded all expectations, his own included.

But the devil finds more entertainment in the plans of man than in any staged comedy. Two months after Kristoff had delivered himself of the commission, the mayor from his own hometown of Hinterwald was discovered by his wife in the arms of a female automaton. There is some disagreement as to what she saw, but the most persuasive rumor has it that the automaton had not one face but many, each a separate mask that could be affixed by discrete snaps to the featureless head. Among the faces could be recognized images, exact down to the slightest imperfections upon which a lover might fixate, of women well known in the community and with whom the mayor and his wife had dined on numerous occasions. The scandal that ensued had as much to do with the jealousies of those women not included in this harem as by the horror of those women who were included.

All decisions have their repercussions. The mayor suffered a brief downturn in his fortunes and won reelection by the narrowest margin of his political career. But for Kristoff Lindhorst, who was never forgiven by the mayor's wife, the change in fortune was permanent. He was obliged to carry a sign around his neck for one month on which were painted large block letters that literally translated to "Broken Bee," but in the local vernacular meant "Poor Fabricator." He was also forbidden to construct automata for the remainder of his life, although as a concession to commerce and the history of his family, he was allowed to retain the watch repair shop.

Now suppose that you were a friend to the watchmaker in your youth—perhaps it was you who foolishly drowned your pocket watch in a coffee cup—but that time and circumstance had come between you. You had heard of his fame and taken an unspoken pride in having once known this man who had risen so high. You had also heard of his fall and silently grieved that the just could be punished so harshly. On impulse, you wrote the watchmaker a letter expressing your condolences and how, although others might turn against him, your friendship remained unchanged. He wrote back a short message that ended with the words, "I am as happy now as I have ever been." You knew that this phrase could hide any manner of unstated griefs and so your heart remained troubled.

Now suppose your business took you back into the land of your youth, where the watchmaker still dwelt, and you sought him out so as to judge his state with your own eyes. The sky was jewel bright on the day you arrived, but the leaves had begun to change color and there was a chill to the gusting winds that warned of the coming winter. You found Kris, as you still called him in your mind, in the ground-level repair shop of the same narrow house that you remembered from your childhood visits. The rusty sign in the shape of a clock swung back and forth above the entrance. A small bell tinkled when you pushed the door open.

How time passes, you thought, seeing the stooped shoulders and prematurely gray hair of the man bent over the bench. It did not take much imagination to realize that his parents were now gone, buried no doubt behind the old church, and that he was alone in the world. The gray-haired man did not hurry to stand, but raised the magnifier from his eyes and set his tweezers down beside a semicircle of loose gears. He looked at you, at the supposed customer who had disturbed his work. Then, with no hesitation, as if you had not aged a day, he called you by your name.

Kris insisted that you sit down and tell him everything that had happened since you two parted. But having taken to his feet, he did not himself sit down. He bustled in and out of the back room and eventually returned with two cups of fragrant coffee, the brew flavored with cinnamon according to local custom, and a plate of sugar cookies. You blushed. Had he forgotten the incident of your watch and the coffee? But you sipped politely—there is no brew so bitter as the errors of youth remembered—and told him what you thought he wanted to know. But in spite of his interest in your affairs, you eventually turned the conversation to his life and the events that had transpired in your absence.

"I am so sorry," you said.

"Think nothing of it."

"That is not so easily accomplished. To see a man of your talents cast aside breaks my heart."

"Truly, I am a happy man."

"I find this hard to believe. In truth, I cannot imagine it. "

"My father used to tell me that everything happens for a reason and, no matter what we did in the shop during the day, finding that reason was our true calling. Understanding brings happiness."

"It is easy to philosophize. But I think you will agree that most philosophers are an unhappy lot. They are distressed by uneven cobbles, the price of tobacco, and the inequity that consigns them to poverty when they have ideas worthy of kings."

Kris laughed, an easy unaffected laugh, and you realized that the pleasure he took from your presence might have little to do with what you had to say. "Come," he said. "Perhaps this will bring understanding." He set down his empty cup, rose from his stool and opened the drawer of a neighboring bench. A dozen velvet bags were nested inside, the mouths of each drawn shut with silk cords. He withdrew a silver watch from one of these bags and laid the cool metal disk on your palm. "Here. Hold this. Look at it. Feel it."

You humored him, praising the craftsmanship.

Again he laughed. "Wind it."

You did so. "It has a very nice mechanism."

"Thank you." Kris's smile was as secretive as a cat's. He loped over to the door and, with the same delicate touch he applied to his craft, slid a bolt into place. There were two small windows on either side of the door, their panes so ancient that only distorted images could be seen through the glass. Nevertheless, he unhooked the thick felt curtains used to keep out the winter chill and let these fall across the windows. "Now," he said, his cheeks glowing in the lamp light, "Wind it backwards."

"Backwards?"

"Yes. Press the crown in and wind it backwards. Then set the watch down on the bench."

You did as told and set the watch down upon its back. For a moment the watch was still, then there was some engagement of gears so that it rocked upon the bench. Then, so quickly that you doubted your sight, thinking yourself the victim of slight-of-hand, the watch thrust forth two legs and two arms, flipped itself upright, and began to dance. As dances go it was not sublime, being more like the untutored hops and bounds of a country boy intent upon impressing a young lady than the measured twirls of the aristocracy. But as you followed the watch's movements, you felt the corners of your mouth twitch, and soon you were smiling for all the world as if you were once again a young man with no fear of the ridiculous.

"I cannot help but love them," the watchmaker said. He smiled and, although he spoke to you, he kept his eyes on the dancing watch. "They are like my children to me."

There was a beauty there, a connection that you who had now achieved a certain renown of your own, realized that you could not touch. "It must give you great pleasure to achieve something so lifelike in an object so unlike a man."

"I do not think much about such things. I just do my best."

But although you saw the beauty, you also knew your moral responsibility. It is for this reason that, after returning to your own hometown, you wrote a polite but anonymous letter to the authorities in Hinterwald. In the letter you described a narrow two-story house, on the ground-level of which was a watch shop, and certain activities, possibly of an illegal nature, that took place in that shop. Once the letter was mailed, you felt as if a great weight had been lifted from your shoulders. If summer comes but once every ten years, you said to anyone willing to listen, even if they did not understand the allusion, then it might as well not come at all.

North of Lake Winnipesaukee

"The whole continent was one dismal wilderness,
the haunt of wolves and bears and more savage men."
—John Adams

Listen. It was a beautiful winter's day when the wolf returned to Tamworth. The snow had been falling for over a week and established seemingly permanent residence on the cabin roofs and the shit-cobbled track that ran through the settlement—horse dung freezes just as assuredly as anything else in this wintery world, be it water, food, or flesh—but it was only on this day that the clouds parted to reveal the merciless blue sky, the cold fist of the sun, and the toothed peak of Coruway Mountain. The temperature was so cold... that sounds like the beginning of a joke but this settlement was well past such jokes, not when the coldest months of the year waltzed arm in arm with death. Sometimes it was so cold that brothers, sisters, any and all family members, regardless of blood, slept huddled beneath the same blanket for warmth. Sometimes sap congealed and pine trees exploded. Sometimes your eyelids froze shut. But on this winter's day, the snow thick on the branches of the pines, on this day when the wolf stalked down from the mountain and through the forest to claim its vengeance, it was only so cold the snow seemed effervescent, as if it weighed less than the air and might momentarily rise from the branches, the frozen road, and the pitched roofs, and burst like bubbles from a flute of champagne.

Champagne? A myth really, but a pleasant one, a reminder that somewhere, on another continent once called home, there are kings, queens, and lesser nobility. There are feasts and toasts, oaths and betrothals, betrayals and infidelities. Any such celebration is held all the more dear because a sparkling wine has been imported from a tiny locale in France, this also known as the devil's wine because the bottles might explode to the touch, their flowery bouquet married to a Chinese firework.

Like pines in a winter freeze.

Here, north of Lake Winnipesaukee, the settlers still remember when the snow stank of volcanic ash and fell throughout a long cold summer, how the crops shriveled and the livestock died. Here, the crows flock hundreds strong and trade morbid secrets when the cold sets in. On most days, the roosting crows shake the snow from their wings, and the branches follow suit, black replacing white as if God wrote them into existence across a virgin page. The crows watch, glint-eyed and hungry, from the safety of the trees. But on this day, when the wolf returned, the crows neglected to shiver their wings, and the snow piled on them as if they were beaked statues carved from the wintery boughs, only their eyes sliding, shifting, ever watchful.

A wolf pack is a family, united by bonds of blood. The wolf's ancestors noted the first incursions of the Pigwocket Indians and then later of the frontiersmen. The ground was fertile and well-watered, fish and game plentiful. One frontiersman returned, bringing along two Indians, sister and brother, to establish a homestead. They chopped trees, hewed the wood, and cursed the biting flies as they built the first season's log cabin. They cursed all the more when the dread winter cold set in. The Indian brother abandoned the household before the snow melted that following spring, but his sister remained. She endured the annual cycles of cold, heat, and hunger. The frontiersman was once absent for two weeks to purchase cornmeal and his now common-law wife, along with their three children, lived on watery milk alone. Once, when starving in the dead of winter, the frontiersman again absent, his wife debated whether to suffocate their children as a final mercy. More years followed, and the wolves watched as others joined the settlement, the forest ever in retreat as the settlers extended their fields for grain and pasture.

The frontiersman fathered five children in all. The youngest loved the winter and took to snowshoes as if they were extensions of his feet. Each morning, he would tear into the soft pulp of a roasted potato or, if his mother had risen early, a *bannock* of meal and water baked on a chip of maple wood. He carried a gun—children of the north learn to shoot as soon as they can walk—and was all the more valued when the autumn harvest was past and any meat, be it pigeon or squirrel, was partnered with potatoes in the stew pot. Others might curse the indignities of icy slips and falls, the disgorgements of snow-weighted branches, but he revered the unsettled beauty of the winter landscape. The pines strained Heavenward, taller than steeples, and he snowshoed beneath fragrant arches within the true house of the Lord.

The wolf family had taken every precaution to hide their den—no tracks marred the snowy hillocks outside their home—but the curious boy stuck his head into their cave and smelled the rot of old meat and bones. He heard the soft breaths of many mingled into one. The boy stole only the one pup, thinking to make it his own, supposing it superior to the dogs with which other hunters scouted for game. The boy returned to the settlement with the wolf pup coddled in his arms, his sleeves in tatters from its milk teeth.

The settlers knew only the one version of *Little Red Riding Hood*, the one in which the wolf gobbles down the foolish girl and that is the end of it. They do not tell tales of her rescue by a woodsman with his shiny silver axe. They most assuredly do not extend the tale such that Little Red Riding Hood and her grandma kill a second wolf by boiling it alive in a stew pot. Those are tales better served with champagne. The settlers bribed the boy with hard candy to lead them to the wolf den. They then butchered the wolf-bitch and her pups, the whole damned lot of them. Had not the Puritans of the Massachusetts Bay Colony placed a bounty on wolves as one of their first laws? Had not Roger Williams called wolves "a fierce, bloodsucking persecuter"? And had not the New Haven settlement once offered five pounds to anyone who killed "one great black woolfe of a more than ordinaire bigness"?

This is not the story of *Little Red Riding Hood*, whichever version you prefer. This is a story of vengeance. This is the story of the wolf that survived. That wolf had been out hunting. It was a successful hunt for he carried a broken squirrel in his jaws, its blood fresh on his tongue. In returning home, he knew to leap from root to root, to never paw the snow. He had warned his kin against the dangers of pride but he, regardless, took pride in his own acrobatics.

To no avail.

The den's entrance was crisscrossed with imprints from the rawhide lacings of snowshoes and scarred with drag marks and blood. The hunters' stench of sweat, beer, leather, and gunpowder clung to the rocks and trees, to the tufts of rent fur.

That evening, crouched belly to snow, the surviving wolf watched a jubilee in Tamworth village. The colonists built a bonfire so large the flames licked at the stars. They stripped themselves of bonnets and shirts and, cheeks ruddy, dripping sweat, dared each other to attend ever closer to the inferno. They do-si-do'ed and promenaded in the flickering shadows of the dead wolves. The larger wolves were skinned and hung from a rude scaffold. Slashed, their blood had frozen and bloomed with frost but now, in the heat, an adulteration of blood with water trickled from their flesh and burrowed into the snow. The wolf pups, some skinned and some furred, six in all, hung from nooses on the grandfather oak. They were curled, heads tucked beneath forearms, as if desirous for sleep. Forearms, not forepaws. The paws of the wolves, young and old alike, had been chopped off and strung on neck thongs, and now bounced and smeared blood on the glistening chests of the jubilating men.

What of the boy's wolf pup, the seventh and last of the litter, that which the boy would have taken as a pet and trained to track and take down game? The father told his son that the ungrateful cur had run off. That is what wild things do. They abandon you. He promised his son a real dog the next time he journeyed south. The surviving wolf, however, on returning from the jubilee, discovered ruptured snow and a shallow grave not far from the village. The snow had been stomped into place and swept with a pine bough. The blood called to him with the voice of his pup, cold and lonely and far away.

It was a beautiful winter's day when the wolf returned to Tamworth to claim his vengeance. Some say no wolf ever passed the door of the meetinghouse, but a man came out of the forest. He peeled back his cloak of wolf's fur, and revealed it still raw on the inside, bloody, a fresh kill he said, so fresh it seemed almost alive. He passed through the door of the meetinghouse on the strength of that kill. No wolf passed the door, all who attended meeting that day attested. But whatever emerged from the forest, whoever it was, he stayed in the village for a fortnight, two fortnights, accepting their honor and the stranger's privilege. He laughed with the men of each house. They hunted well he said. He skewered the meat in his bowl with a knife, spooned the gravy, and then wiped his finger along the inside rim and licked it clean with a long pink tongue. The women of the houses said little, not with their men so close, but they noticed the stranger's rich laugh, his strong hands, and his long pink tongue. The stranger stayed only a fortnight or two and then returned to the forest. He was a hunter he said and would not trespass overly long on the hospitality of the village.

No wolf passed through the meetinghouse door that day but, only two months later, all the fertile women of the village gave birth. It was a miraculous birthing, and a horrible one as well. The women's bellies swelled as if they had dined on tainted meat. They screamed and sweated and cursed their husbands. They offered prayers to the Lord and to Satan, accepting either as savior if only their pain be eased. Two months is mercifully short but can seem an eternity for a multiple pregnancy.

The babies were born helpless and had to be torn from their fetal sacs. This their mothers did by tooth and nail, as if channeling talents acquired from the animal dawn. Their newborns were endearing, none would dispute this, but they were also furred and they growled at all except their mothers and siblings. No man could have fathered those beasts, certainly not in such number—triplets were the rule, one woman even gave birth to septuplets— litters like what you find with a dog. Motherly breasts grew sore from the constant squirming attention. Wives feigned deafness when husbands demanded to know the provenance of their unholy brood.

The wolf father knew that many mothers would have no choice but to destroy the monstrous meat of their birthing. But some, because a mother cannot help but to love her children, would set their pups free. A wolf pup can run and play within weeks of its birth. These pups would stumble and roll, bat at the drifting snow, and bark at crows. They would roam and they would find their father waiting within the shadowy woods. Some mothers, also—dare anyone dispute this?—would follow their pups out through the forbidding snow and into those dark woods, there to greet the father and to join his ever-growing pack.

Listen! On a cold winter's night in northern New Hampshire, away from the babble of television and radio, away from the roar of trucks on the interstate, you might think you hear wolves howling, more than eight claws, eight generations, since the time of this tale. The last wolf bounty in New Hampshire was paid out in 1895, and wolves were thought to be eradicated. But wolves have been confirmed again in Maine, and in Canada within 20 miles of the New Hampshire border. Listen! The wolves are howling. They call not for you but for their brethren of the forest. They have forgotten that you were ever family. They are, once upon a time, your sons and daughters gone wild, gone savage into the dismal wilderness they love so well.

A Study in Abnormal Physiology

I. *"Everything about you screams the news"*

Although Darwin's most visible supporter, in truth I saw him rarely and so took an immoderate delight in our dinner engagement at the St. George's Hotel. But I was late—late!—and properly chagrinned. Even the weather was no excuse. Hadn't Darwin traveled all the way from Kent in the same downpour? I passed my sopping overcoat to the doorman and then, leaving the maître d'hôtel in my wake, shoved open the door to the private dining room his trajectory indicated. There was my good friend Darwin, feet propped before a warm crackling fire.

"Darwin," I cried.

He swung round and my heart slipped a measure. Neither his smile, for all its genuine affection, nor his unruly side-whiskers could camouflage his ashen cheeks and glistening forehead. He must be having one of his spells. Yet, for my sake, he had evaded the protective web of his sweet wife Emma to make the journey to London.

"Pardon my tardiness. I hope you were not inconvenienced."

Darwin dismissed my concerns with a wave of his hand. "My dear Huxley, think nothing of it. I have plenty to keep me occupied in here." He tapped his balding pate. He then added, smile turning mischievous, "Besides, unless I miss my guess, congratulations are in order."

I must have blanched. I thought to brazen it out but realized that every tarried second confirmed Darwin's supposition. "How did you know?" I asked. "Nettie only told me this afternoon." In truth, she was so early in her pregnancy that we had agreed to wait at least two months before sharing the information.

"My dear friend, everything about you screams the news."

"How so?" I pulled up a chair.

"Firstly, after Leonard was born, you said that you looked forward to a goodly brood, so I knew more children were in the offing."

I nodded.

"Secondly, you were late, something quite outside your character and which not even the weather could explain. So a matter of importance must have occurred today."

I nodded again.

"Furthermore, you gave no excuse as to why you were late. And so the cause was such that you wished to conceal it."

I ventured a sally. "Surely that is not enough to build a theory on?"

Darwin pressed his fingertips together. "There are also more tangible evidences."

"Tangible?"

"The pollen on your vest."

I glanced down and saw the faintest of yellow smudges on my lapel.

"Roses, naturally, for love. But also the anemone, an unusual choice but, within the language of floriography, the symbol for expectation. I recognized their co-mingled scents immediately."

"That's all?"

"That's enough."

"Really," I said, trying not to sound aggrieved, "I don't see how you do it. I admit you are right, but based on such fairy dust"—I brushed the pollen from my vest—"it seems more a matter of luck than reason."

"True, by itself each item presents a world of possibilities, but summed together, first one, and then the next, and then the next thereafter, but this single theory suggested itself. Have you an alternative?"

Darwin's eyes twinkled as if he were playing the grandest of jokes, and I wondered if there were additional clues, perhaps excruciatingly obvious, he chose not to reveal. Nevertheless, Darwin's method for reconciling mysteries was of relevance to my upcoming debate with Robert FitzRoy, and, in attempting a rebuttal, I seemed to inhabit the skin of my future antagonist. But before I could produce another viable theory, we were distracted by a commotion in the main dining hall.

The maître d'hôtel, his figure muted by the frosted glass, gesticulated and rudely latched onto the shoulder of a woman. She freed herself and cried, "But really I must see them." Then the door burst open and she stood framed before us, the maître d'hôtel wringing his hands behind her. "I am so sorry," he said. "This woman barged into the hotel and asked to see the X Club. I explained, quite properly, that your dining club did not meet today and, furthermore, even in the event it did meet, she would not be welcome. But then I let slip that you and Mr. Darwin were here for a special engagement and, after that, there was no restraining her. I will escort her off the premises if you see fit."

Judged by her clothing, the object of the maître d'hôtel's derision was a young woman of the working class. But she was wrapped in so many layers, and these were so wet and disordered, that her form was more amorphous than feminine. Nevertheless, her eyes compensated for these deficiencies of her sex. Green, overlarge, and desperate, they burned with a feverish intensity.

"Stuart Hopkinson," Darwin said, addressing the maître d'hotel by his given name. From his tone, I understood the anger he felt to see any woman, regardless of her station, so mishandled. "Water with a drop of brandy would be more suitable. And a warm blanket."

"Thank you, dear sir," the woman said. She fell to her knees at Darwin's feet. "When I heard that you and Mr. Huxley were here, I knew that God had answered my most fervent prayer."

Hopkinson, the significance of Darwin recollecting his name having not gone unnoticed, straightened his shoulders as if called to military attention. "Really, sir?"

"What are you waiting for? Drinks and a blanket for our friend."

"But she's so wet. The upholstery... " Hopkinson wrung his hands as if he wished to wring every contaminating drop from the woman's clothing.

"These should recompense you for whatever troubles you might encounter." Darwin dropped several thick coins into Hopkinson's ready hand. "Our friend has waited long enough for the most minimal of comforts."

Darwin had a grandfatherly way about him that soon set the woman at ease. Indeed, she was quite presentable once she had rearranged her cap, brushed back her wet hair, and, after taking a seat, sipped sufficient brandy that the blush returned to her cheeks. I nevertheless found her features unsettling although I could not decipher why. "Thank you again," she said, her face aglow with renewed vitality. "I am at my wit's end and you are my last and only hope."

"I'm afraid you have us at a disadvantage," I interjected. "You know our identities, but we do not know yours."

She looked to Darwin for guidance. He nodded. "Marjorie," she said, "But call me Jo."

"Surely you are blessed with both a Christian and a family name?" I said.

"You'll pardon me if I don't reveal my full name. Through it you might trace my master. He is a good man, and highly respected, but my story could do him a public disservice."

"Then Jo it is," Darwin said. He quieted me with a look. "By what means may we assist you?"

"I fear, dear sirs, that I am losing my mind."

II. *"An entertainment more marvelous than anything from* The Arabian Nights*"*

"It's my dreams," Jo said. "They've turned into a waking nightmare. I never used to think I had much imagination. I went to bed to sleep, and sleep was like the blowing out of a candle. I don't know if I dreamed but, if I did, I forgot my dreams upon waking." She heaved a sigh. "If only I could forget these dreams so easily."

Darwin laid a hand on her shoulder. "Please continue. When did the dreams begin?"

"Perhaps four or five months ago. One morning I awoke with a dream of flying that lingered in my mind. To fly! How strange, how wonderful! The airy world of my dream had no edges, no bottom and no top, and so I never feared a fall. There was just a feeling of weightlessness, of gliding about in a greenish light that darkened and paled around me. Most significantly, in recalling this dream, I realized that I had dreamed of flying before. I had in fact been having the same dream every night for weeks on end.

"At first I did not find the dream so horrible. I have little imagination, as I said, and it now seemed I was to be rewarded for those long dark years with an entertainment more marvelous than anything from *The Arabian Nights*. I looked forward to sleep as I never had before, and my dream responded. As my skills at flying improved, so did the substance of my vision. I discovered a vast palace of stone arches and circuitous hallways. Every night, I explored the palace but I never reached an end."

Darwin interrupted. "Did you tell anyone else of your reoccurring dream?"

"Only my master. He said that I should accept it as a gift, which put my mind much at ease."

"But you no longer feel at ease."

Jo lowered her distinctive eyes and nodded. "The more time I spent in this dream world, the more exhausted I became. But like an addict I longed for its nightly return. My bones, my muscles, my head ached. I could hardly drag myself out of bed in the morning. The stairs to my master's quarters rose like mountains before me, higher and higher each day, but still I climbed them and performed my duties. My master told me that I needed rest. But I would have none, for I have never lost a day to sickness in my life. There then occurred the event that convinced me I had lost my mind.

"I went to sleep as usual, knowing full well the enrapturing dream that awaited me. But I had a goal this time. I was resolved to reach the furthest end of a winding corridor, to press forward until I reached a boundary to my vision. In doing so, it seemed I flew backwards in time, sweeping past the brickwork of our age, then the stone arches erected by the Romans, and, toward the end, the somber monoliths once raised by savages on our moors. At length, I arrived at a cavern hollowed from ancient rock. This cavern narrowed into a cave, and the cave into something less, but still I had not reached its end. At last, my strength failing, I realized I must return to the waking world.

"Fear overtook me. I felt I had ventured too deep into the unknown and, like the princess in a fairy tale, must pay a price if I failed to return home before the cock crowed. The safety of my room was a distant memory, my arms were limp with exhaustion, but I flew like one possessed. A greenish light beckoned me homeward. But from behind, darkness grasped at me. Ice-cold tendrils slithered past my toes, my ankles, my knees, my waist, my very heart.

"I must have screamed, for the next thing I knew I was awake in bed and shivering. My master held me. He told me everything would be all right. He was wrong. My nightmare was far from over for, in the cold morning light, I saw that rank water had soaked through my nightclothes such that they hung like leaden rags from my limbs. Foul strands of algae tangled my arms and legs. I knew then that I had not been flying in my dream but swimming, and doing so in water that I could breathe as easily as I might air. Most horrible of all, this demonic dream had pursued me into the waking world.

"Is it any wonder that I question my sanity?" Jo's eyes brimmed with tears.

"When did this last dream occur?" asked Darwin.

"Two nights ago. I have not slept since. I am too afraid."

"You are certain that you were swimming in the dream, not flying?"

"Yes. But I have never swum before in my life. I've only waded in the Thames."

A church bell sounded in the distance and Jo started from her armchair, throwing aside her blanket. "I must return home or my master will wonder at by absence." She looked imploringly at Darwin with her overlarge green eyes and added, "But I have more to tell."

At Jo's recommendation, Darwin agreed that we should meet again the next day at a public house called The Crown and Anchor, convenient to her morning shopping route. He then pressed some coins into her palm, more than were necessary for the cab fare home. "I recommend finding alternative accommodation for the night. A change in location will do wonders for your sleep, and for your dreams."

After Jo left, Darwin asked if I had noticed the obvious. I nodded, for I had now identified what aspect of her features disturbed me so. "She is unique in my experience," I said. "I cannot place her as being Xanthochroic, Australoid, Negroid, or Mongoloid, nor some admixture of these types. Perhaps tomorrow, if she will allow it, I will apply my calipers to her skull and so resolve this mystery."

I thought for a moment that Darwin would do me the indignity of laughing, but his outburst was smothered, whether from sickness or politeness, and emerged a cough. "Good old Huxley. You are the most observant man I know, but you are also sometimes the least perceptive. Did you not notice her many layers of clothing? Did you not notice how she tidied the blanket to camouflage her belly? She, like your dearest Nettie, is with child. I estimate about six months along."

"Pregnant? She said nothing about a husband."

"You, friend Huxley, are more knowledgeable about worldly matters than I, yet even I have heard of a pregnancy occurring without the benefit of marriage."

"That could go hard on her." I felt an immediate gratitude for the good family to which I belonged. Then, remembering the strange passions that had possessed my own Nettie during her first pregnancy, I said, "The onset of these weird dreams coincides with her pregnancy. Do you think they may be a delirium brought about by her situation?"

"I hope you are right. My fears suggest otherwise. We shall know better tomorrow."

III. *"Is she dead?"*

The next morning, the previous night's downpour having dissipated into a charitable drizzle, Darwin and I met at The Crown and Anchor. I tucked into a full breakfast while Darwin drank tea and nibbled on a cold triangle of toast. He muttered a plague on the diet regime proscribed by his doctor.

Jo was late. At first we thought nothing of it. One bell rang, then two bells after the hour. Darwin shifted from tea to snuff, never a good sign. At three bells, he accosted the manager and asked if a young woman had inquired for us earlier. The manager, more intent on the racing form than on his guests, shrugged.

Darwin furrowed his brow and glared at the floor as if he hoped to decipher the hotel's history from its scuffmarks. "What a fool I am?" he suddenly cried. "Did you let a room to a young woman last night? Brown hair and about so high?" He held his hand at level with his chin.

The manager again shrugged. He had been off duty at the time, but he did have the hotel register. Six rooms had been let but there was not a Marjorie or a Jo among the signatories.

"Bother the names," I said. "A single room. One woman. Arriving late."

"A Dorothy Hopkins signed in last night at five after ten."

"Has she checked out?"

"No."

"That must be her."

We dragged the manager up two flights of stairs and pounded on the door. No answer. "I really should not be doing this," the manager protested while producing the key. He quieted when he tried the knob and found the door unlocked. The door swung open to reveal a tranquil room with a narrow bed, a nightstand, and a single chair set against the far wall. A woman occupied the bed. For all appearances she slept, wrapped in sheets and blankets, her head propped upon a pillow. "That's Jo," I said. Darwin called to her. Jo neither moved nor spoke. Her face was deathly pale. In two strides we were beside her. Darwin shook her shoulder and her head lolled to the side. I, putting my medical training to use, touched my wrist to her chill forehead and then fumbled for her pulse but found none.

"Is she dead?" the manager asked.

I did not answer but peeled the bed coverings away. A pool of blood, centered about Jo's hips, had soaked through the dress she still wore from the previous night and spread across the lower sheet.

"Her pregnancy," I said. "She has lost the baby."

"A baby?" said the manager. "But where is the baby?"

This was, in my estimation, the first intelligent remark he had made during our brief acquaintance.

"Perhaps she was assisted," said Darwin, his voice dour. "You remember how the door was left unlocked." I knew immediately to what he alluded. A woman, finding herself with an unwanted pregnancy, might resort to drastic measures for its termination. The doctors who catered to this dark practice often gained additional recompense by selling the fetuses.

The horror and pathos of the situation struck us all. The manager muttered a prayer and tugged at his neckerchief. "Fetch a doctor," Darwin said to the manager. "And the police. Huxley and I will remain with the corpse."

After the manager disappeared at a stumbling run, Darwin turned to me and said, "This is an ugly business. I do not accept the coincidence of this poor woman's death so soon after her meeting with us."

"You do not think she died in childbirth?"

"I think the process was orchestrated. Are there not methods that can be employed to induce labor?"

I kept up with the medical literature although I had not recently practiced. "There are physical means, such as the rupture of the membranes, a method commonly employed by midwives. An article in *The Lancet* also reports promising results when women are injected with a pituitary extract from female dogs."

Darwin returned to the dead woman and, with a whispered apology, hiked her dress up past the waist to expose her abdomen. He pointed at a small puncture on her left side crowned with a glistening ruby droplet. "I believe the second method may have been employed here, perhaps in conjunction with the first. Note also the consistency of the blood." He flicked the skin adjoining the puncture. The bead broke and trickled down her side. "In Herefordshire, two summers ago, a dozen cows hemorrhaged and died. The causal agent was traced to mildewed hay. A grain of the compound produced by that fungus is enough to prevent clotting so that even the smallest nick is life-threatening."

"Then it is murder. Of both a mother and her child." A rush of anger blinded me. I could not help but imagine my dearest Nettie in a similar position.

"I fear it is something even more horrible. I suspect the child was delivered prematurely and stolen from Jo at the intentional cost of her life."

"Why?"

"Undoubtedly for some evil end. But if the child still lives—and I think it might—there may yet be a chance to save it." A haunted look came over Darwin's face and he wiped a frail hand across his forehead. "We must save the child."

I bowed my head, awash with the memory so recent and so painful of my own son Noel's death. I remembered his funeral, his cold body lowered into a hole from which he would never rise. I, like Darwin, do not hope for reunion beyond the grave. Darwin, however, had suffered three times over in this respect. I still do not know how he stood the sorrow. "For Annie," I said, naming his favorite daughter.

"And for Charlie and Mary, and for your sweet Noel."

"Cannot the police arrest this fiend?"

"The culprit, even if we knew his identity, has covered his tracks so well that there is no evidence of foul play beyond our own conjectures. An unwed mother. A botched abortion. The situation is far too common."

"What can we do?"

"Do you have your calipers?"

Caught off guard, I nevertheless patted my coat pocket.

"You said that Jo's physiognomy disturbed you, and I think there is still time, before the police arrive, for you to make your measurements. In analyzing the data, you may disregard the time you spent aboard the HMS *Rattlesnake* as Surgeon's Mate studying oceanic invertebrates. Your more recent studies on the lobed-finned fish are most pertinent."

"And then?"

"I believe you have an impending debate with FitzRoy. Or have you forgotten?"

IV. *"Show me a gemmule"*

My opponent in the debate at the Workingman's College was the same FitzRoy who had once captained the *Beagle* but who now implored adherence to Biblical creation. In truth, although I attempted to uphold my popular sobriquet as *Darwin's bulldog*, my mind was not on topic. I kept recalling the decrepit bedroom scene from that morning and the story, disturbing and most mysterious, that my calipers told. I wondered if Jo had been once employed as a fishmonger. Might she have acquired her Piscean features through a Lamarckian process, akin to how dog owners take on the characteristics of their pets? I wondered what further researches into the matter Darwin pursued, alone, while I entertained the restless crowd.

Perhaps I was more distracted than I imagined. How else to explain the ease with which the mundane FitzRoy ambushed me? I was attempting to explain how Darwin's theory of gemmules enabled traits to be passed from one generation to the next when FitzRoy, a malevolent glint to his eye, extended his hand. "Show me a gemmule," he said.

I was flummoxed. To say that a gemmule was too small to be seen by the naked eye, or even by aid of a microscope, seemed a prevarication. I hemmed. I hawed. Then, as if sensing my discomfort, a member of the audience stood, raising himself with the aid of an ebony cane, and asked if he could relate a relevant example. The man was large, of about my age, and with an unsmiling mouth that lent his utterances a weight commensurate with his frame. "Within man himself, during his growth from fetus to adult," he said, "do we not see dramatic changes take place that span but a single generation? We do not know how this happens, but just as assuredly it does. Similarly, rather than argue the existence of a mechanism for transmutation, should we not instead seek it out by all means at our disposal?" With that final question ringing to the rafters, he settled back into his chair, forcing a squeal from its strained supports.

The stranger's example raised my dander back to a fighting pitch, and I concluded the debate strongly. "To be a man one must think, truly think, otherwise one is much less than an ape"—I speared FitzRoy with a glance—"one is nothing but a noisome fly that buzzes about laying the maggot of an idea hoping, merely hoping, that it might someday take wing." Then I was down among the audience, shaking hands, pounding shoulders, and accepting congratulations on my performance.

The weighty stranger did not step forward into the crush but stood to one side, casting a cold eye on the proceedings. In truth I found the stranger's attitude more disturbing than FitzRoy's ignorant bravado, for it seemed that buried within his corpulent frame lurked an alien intelligence that looked upon mankind and found us all wanting in some fundamental respect.

V. *"Do not turn around"*

I did not rejoin Darwin until that evening, responding to a message to meet him at an address on Park Lane and which ended with the admonishment to, "bring your stick." The walking stick in question was of stout oak, its handle a snarling bulldog cast from bronze. Darwin's request suggested imminent trouble.

The Darwin I discovered was so coifed and pomaded that I hardly recognized him. Darwin swung us out of the current of pedestrians and we took position in the shadow of an awning. He reached into his jacket pocket, extracted a packet of calling cards, and passed these to me. I looked at the top card. The first line read, *Lawrence C. Wilderman.* Beneath that was the suggestion of a business, *Goshen and Wilderman, Proprietors.* And then, beneath that, the brief description, *Purveyors of the Finest Clamps, Forceps, and Specula*.

"Who is this Wilderman?" I asked.

"That, my friend, is you. I am your business partner, Frederick Goshen. I had the cards printed this afternoon."

"For what purpose?"

"To effect an entrance. Legally," he said, eyeing my cane. "Keep your eyes on number 12." I squinted in the direction he indicated and was met with a sharp elbow to the ribs. "Try to be less conspicuous."

I rubbed my side. "Who lives there?"

"That is the residence and practice of Dr. Paul Monroe, the employer of our late friend Marjorie Constable."

The doctor's name was vaguely familiar. "Monroe? Are you certain?"

"Ninety-nine parts out of a hundred. I learned his identity within the hour of our separation this morning although, as I said, most of my time was spent on the tedious task of establishing our pseudonyms." He located my ribs again with his elbow. "I insist you refrain from displaying an obvious interest in our quarry."

I shifted position so I would be less sorely tempted. "How did you learn his identity?"

"Do you remember why Jo came to the St. George's Hotel?"

I thought back to the events of the previous night. "To find us?"

"In a way. But how many servants would know to look for us at the St. George's Hotel? More curiously, according to the maître d', she had in fact come in search of the X Club. The existence of your dining club is hardly a matter of public renown."

I nodded. "I have done my best to keep our circle a secret known only to initiates. If I follow your reasoning, Jo must have learned of the X Club from her master. Moreover, given the nature of our club, he has a scientific bent and has acquired some stature in society. But surely there is more?"

Darwin smiled. "Even though she did not intend to reveal it, I knew within seconds of our meeting that Jo's master was a physician, most likely with surgical leanings. Did you notice her perfume?"

"Perfume?"

"Women are well acquainted with the use of aromatics for attraction but there are few, perhaps none, that consciously choose ether. That is a scent peculiar to the medical profession, and one only acquired by a woman when she is in close contact with such a man."

"Contact? Do you mean... ?"

"I do not use the word *contact* lightly. Yes, I suspect her pregnancy derived from the relationship she intimated with her master."

"Then the physician who presided over her death, the man who stole her child... " The bloody scene recalled itself to me in all its horrid detail.

"That was her master. The unborn child—his child—was more dear to him than her life. I shudder to consider why."

I shook my head, stunned that such a beast roamed our city. "This man, this creature, how can you be certain it is Dr. Monroe?" The name burned like bile in my throat. "Surely there are hundreds of physicians in London?"

"True. But before she died, Jo revealed her master's address."

"She told you?"

"Nothing so exact. But she chose our meeting place at The Crown and Anchor, and indicated it was along her shopping route. Significantly, the manager gave no indication of knowing her. Based on this I concluded that The Crown and Anchor was close enough to her home to be familiar but was not a business she frequented. A range of five blocks, with the public house as its epicenter, seemed a good starting point for my search. There were also a few minor clues that further narrowed the possibilities." Darwin seemed about to expound on these when, without changing tone or tempo, he said, "Keep talking as if we are just two friends out for a pleasant stroll. Most of all do not turn around. A messenger has arrived at number 12."

It took all my self-control to resist the temptation to peek. "A messenger?"

"Although I am all but convinced that Dr. Paul Monroe is our man, there is still that one chance in a hundred that I am wrong. This is the final test. There! The door has opened. The messenger has been admitted. We will soon know. You may turn around."

The door to number 12 was closed and I might have thought the messenger a figment of my friend's imagination but for the flickering of shadows in the transom window. After five minutes, the door opened. I held my breath. "It is only the messenger," said Darwin. "His work is done." The messenger's departure was followed by another five arduous minutes. Then a hansom cab pulled up to the opposite curb, blocking our view. Darwin grabbed my arm, and we perambulated a dozen steps until we once again held an unobstructed vantage point.

The door to number 12 swung open. A heavy gentleman shuffled into view, backlit, in his one hand a leather bag weighted with the implements of his trade, in his other hand an ebony cane.

"Dr. Paul Monroe," hissed Darwin. "Our quarry has taken the bait."

I gasped. I recognized the doctor from my debate with FitzRoy. He was the audience member who came to my aid when I stumbled over the concept of gemmules. What's more, I now also remembered when I had previously heard of Paul Monroe. George Busk had recommended him for inclusion in the X Club but, unable to command a majority, had dropped his petition. "I know that man," I said and—while the footman assisted the doctor into the cab and then, with two flicks of the driver's whip, the cab rattled down the street—entertained Darwin with my short tale. I concluded with the question, "What message could possibly incite the doctor's convenient exit?"

"Would it help if I told you the messenger is named Erasmus?"

"Your brother?"

"The same."

"Then, unless I miss my guess, you wrote the missive and can enlighten me as to its contents."

"It was merely the report of a birth, one I thought our doctor might find of interest, of a child born with a vestigial tail. In Fobbing."

"Fobbing? Then the doctor will be gone for hours."

"That is my hope."

VI. *"One scent is missing"*

The door opened at Darwin's knock and the footman, reminiscent of a fox with his sly eyes, pointed nose, and wisps of coppery hair, leaned out. Darwin presented his card and I did likewise. "Goshen and Wilderman, purveyors of the finest clamps, forceps, and specula," Darwin said. "We have an appointment with the esteemed Dr. Monroe." Darwin withdrew a velvet roll from his jacket pocket and, patting it, elicited a muffled jangle. "Our instruments are imported from the four compass points, even from so distant as the Orient."

The doorman looked stricken. "I am sorry, but Dr. Monroe was called away on an emergency. I do not know when he will return."

"We would be happy to wait if you would show us to the sitting room." Darwin passed him a shilling and, not for the first or last time, I marveled at how the seemingly inexhaustible fortune of his family greased the wheels of protocol.

Two more shillings and we were established on a stiff-backed bench in a claustrophobic room at the far end of the hallway, our only comfort two glasses of a mediocre sherry. The room held an empty coat rack, a desolate shelf, and a table that under better circumstances would have supported a copy of the evening newspaper. It was not a room reserved for esteemed guests and my mind turned, as it would, to the missing comforts of home. I wondered how my wife could ever forgive me for abandoning her so soon after her confidence of the previous afternoon.

"I have a question," I said.

"Are you still troubled by the manner in which I uncovered your wife's pregnancy?"

This was indeed the question that preyed on my mind. In spite of Darwin's noted acumen, the clues he had paraded before me seemed too meager to warrant their conclusion. But I refused to grant Darwin the satisfaction of having so closely followed the current of my thoughts. "What is in your pocket roll?" I asked, hoping to resolve this mystery at least.

"Some tableware from the hotel. I don't know what would have happened if our man had demanded a closer look. Kindly crack the door ajar so we may keep an eye on him."

The footman returned twice to check on our comfort, or lack thereof, before disappearing downstairs to the kitchen. This gave us the opportunity to sneak upstairs. I followed close behind Darwin, taking two tense steps to his one, my cane at the ready. The first two doors were locked but the third opened into the doctor's consulting room. This was dominated by a massive desk and towering bookshelves bowed beneath the weight of musty volumes. A coal fire smoldered in the grate.

"This is more to my taste," I said, eyeing the comfort of an upholstered chair.

Darwin shook his head. "There has to be more. What do you smell?"

"Books. Tobacco. Coal smoke."

"Exactly. One scent is missing: ether. Where does our doctor perform his surgeries?" Darwin paced the room, muttering to himself. "There has to be an entrance in here somewhere. He would want to be proximate to his library." He now stood before the bookshelf, nose inches from an embossed spine. He pulled out the volume, passed a finger across the top to test for the dust that was noticeably absent. "Aristotle's *History of Animals*. And over here... "—he pulled out another volume—"Saint-Vincent's *Dictionnaire Classique d'Histoire Naturelle*. A most interesting choice of reading materials for a physician."

"Not just his reading materials." I pointed to a skull that served as a bookend. "An orang-gutang, otherwise known as the wild man of Borneo."

"He has souvenirs from all over the world." Darwin rapped on the carapace of an armadillo and, although I am sure he would disavow such a random act as initiating his next train of thought, I cannot but think that the hollow echo was the impetus for his immediate response as well as much that came thereafter. "What a fool I am," Darwin cried. "There must be a door, a hidden door!" He proceeded to rap his knuckles against the walls. Of greatest interest to him was a space at one corner of the room, a yard in width and adjacent to the bookshelf. This space was empty save for the ceramic sculpture of a snake twined around a Negro. "The sculpture has been recently moved," Darwin said, pointing toward a circular indentation in the rug. I had no trouble lifting the sculpture and, in accordance with Darwin's observation, found that the base precisely fit the impression in the rug.

But there we were stymied. Although Darwin continued with his rappings and tappings, the expression on his face shifted from hope, to irritation, to, at last, simple befuddlement.

Giving up his pet hypothesis, Darwin wandered the room. He pressed and pulled on knotholes, lamp fixtures, any protrusion he found. I followed suit but met with an equal lack of success. He then turned his attention to his own forehead, drumming his fingertips as if to jog his brain into activity. This may have done the trick for Darwin, with a small cry, returned to the empty corner and, dropping to his knees, ran a finger along the join where the baseboard met the floor. "Yes! There is a gap of at least a quarter inch. Note also the abrasion to the wood." He then rose to his feet, grasped the edge of the bookshelf, and pulled. A large section, a yard in width and extending from floor to ceiling, dislodged and slid along the wall.

"By Jove," I said. A doorway was revealed and a winding stair leading down.

VII. *"It moves"*

A grayish light suffused the circular stairwell, sufficient to discern each step and thereby avoid mishap. I took the lead in our descent, brandishing my cane. The light originated from concealed crevices that opened into the house proper. Most interesting were a series of lenses set into the walls by which we could spy on what transpired in the neighboring rooms. We passed from the first to the ground floor, and from there to the kitchen level, where we discovered the red-headed footman, like a fox in the henhouse, romancing the kitchen maid in his master's absence. The steps then passed below the basement level, the light dimming and the air becoming still, and came to an abrupt halt before a windowless door.

Darwin almost bumped into me. "We're here," he whispered.

I cracked the door open and peered in. I was met with the blackness of the tomb. Only my nose proved up to its sensory task, alerting me to the caustic odors of the chemist. "Should I fetch a lamp?" I asked.

"I am sure the doctor's laboratory is provided for."

I fumbled along the wall and, coming upon a knob, turned it clockwise. Light flared from a dozen lamps and illuminated two long tables sheathed in metal, a glistening palace of interconnected glassware, and shelves congested with flasks of all shapes and sizes. Darwin and I explored Monroe's secret laboratory. I was not sure what I hoped to find, but it was all morbidly fascinating. The body of an executed criminal, or so I surmised from the mark of the rope around his neck, was spread-eagled on the nearest table. His chest cavity had been cut open and his organs, some still attached, exhumed and placed in trays containing a yellowish liquid. Two bloody stumps on his right hand revealed the positions of amputated fingers. I lifted the disfigured hand, stiff with death, and was met with an unexpected shriek alongside my ear. I whirled, cane raised. Ghostly fingernails skittered along my spine. I pulled a velvet drape aside to reveal an ornate cage and a pet budgerigar. I wondered what purpose it served but then, on closer inspection, saw the bird's legs had each been removed and replaced with a human finger. Monroe's avian experiment gripped its perch with the white-knuckled ardor bequeathed by the dead criminal.

I transferred my attentions to the shelves and discovered canisters containing a zoological menagerie, some desiccated, others preserved in spirits. A cabinet door opened to reveal glass baubles that entombed a succession of human embryos. These demonstrated more clearly than any display I had ever seen how an embryo passes through developmental stages approximating its own evolutionary history. A pinkish embryo no longer than my finger joint mimicked a bug-eyed minnow with gills. Another appeared amphibious with its webbed hands and feet. From there, they took on more generalized mammalian forms: a nude mouse, a curled piglet, and, finally, hunched and naked primates that aspired to humanity. To my consternation, however, I perceived greater variability among the embryos than I would have suspected possible.

I called to Darwin. "Would you look at this?"

"What do you have?"

"A fetus. Human, I believe, but unlike any I have seen."

"How so?"

I paused so that I might describe the creature more exactly. By my estimation, based on its size and development, it was six months old. However, it still preserved characteristics of an immature form. Pinkish membranes spanned the digits of its hands and feet. Gill slits parted behind its ears, revealing downy frills crimson with oxygenated blood. It lacked obvious genitalia, suggesting a female, but I could not be certain given its erratic development.

"I would describe it thusly," I began. But there I halted, my senses taking flight like game birds at the huntsman's blast. What I saw was clearly impossible. The left hand of the fetus shifted. I hypothesized it a swimming motion, perhaps attributable to a current within its aquatic prison, only the movement was so perfectly executed that it brought the fetus face to face with me. Then, and for this I conceived no possible explanation, the lids of its eyes sprang open to reveal irises of the deepest, most captivating blue. "It moves," I croaked.

Darwin was beside me in an instant. He clapped my back. "Our efforts are not in vain. The water baby lives."

"Water baby?"

"Yes. Jo's child. The result of Monroe's experiments. Through injections and drugs he halted the development of her fetus, maintaining its aquatic physiology. These treatments also had the side effect of inducing the changes you observed in Jo's physiognomy, affecting not only her bone structure but her mind. We must rescue the poor innocent before Monroe returns." Darwin hoisted the crystalline globe from its shelf and thrust it into my arms. The child within turned a back flip—I noted that fins decorated its arms and legs—and beamed, positively beamed at me. Bubbles trickled from the corners of its lips.

We were already too late.

Even as we turned for the exit, I heard a sarcastic harrumph. Dr. Monroe stood in the doorway, his ponderous bulk more impenetrable than the door itself. The red-headed footman leered over his shoulder.

"To what do I owe the pleasure of this visit?" Monroe said, his voice thick with evil. "You have taken the names of Goshen and Wilderman, but I wager those names never passed the lips of your mothers. Why do Darwin and Huxley, two esteemed members of the Royal Society, prowl my laboratory uninvited?"

Before Darwin or I could make rejoinder, Monroe seized the footman's lamp and hurled it in our direction.

*

VIII. *"I have a confession to make"*

"Look out!" I cried, but I mistook the missile's trajectory. It burst among the glassware, destroying several flasks and spattering flaming oil. Unbalanced, the towering ensemble of beakers, flasks, and tubing swayed, then crashed among the flames. Acid fumes fogged the air and fresh spirits fed the blaze.

"The door," I gasped, thinking only of escape. My eyes and throat burned. I pulled my neck cloth over my mouth and nose, following Darwin's example.

"Closed and locked," said Darwin. Our captor had fled, leaving us to die. The inferno was already beyond hope of control. Cabinets erupted. Jars exploded. The budgerigar emitted a horrendous shriek, flapped its smoking wings, then tumbled from its perch still aflame but silenced forever.

"We are not finished," cried Darwin, "Help me with the carpets." He tugged ineffectually at the corner of the one nearest him. His weakness had returned.

"The carpets?" Their oriental patterns danced with flame.

"Yes. There must be access to the sewers from somewhere in this room."

I moved to his aid, but our efforts revealed only stonework. Another carpet met with the same result. "What makes you so sure?"

"Jo awoke from her dream soaked with water. She certainly did not wander through the streets in her nightclothes. Also, Monroe had a means to dispose of his dissections. Indeed, the proximity of his laboratory to the lost rivers beneath London was key to my locating... " His voice broke in a hacking cough.

I peeled back another burning carpet to no avail. Sweat trickled down my temples and spattered on the floor. I sucked at my singed fingers.

Darwin wished to communicate one last item of importance. "I have a confession to make," he said. Those terrifying words, if nothing else, convinced me that the hour of our demise had arrived at last.

"Yes."

"I must tell you how I deduced the secret of your wife's pregnancy."

"A final clue?"

"I am ashamed to admit it... " He paused, glanced about the laboratory as if a spy might lurk within its fiery embrace, then blurted: "I was told the secret."

No man, most especially Darwin, would fabricate a lie under our dire circumstances, but I found his revelation more impossible to credit than his earlier deduction. I had only learned of my wife's situation the previous afternoon and, such is her sanctity, that she would have informed no other. "You were told?"

"Yes."

"By whom?"

"My brother Erasmus."

This only compounded the mystery. Was all London privy to matters of my bedchamber and my heart? "How would he know?"

Another fit of coughing, but nothing can dissuade Darwin once the arrow of his mind has been loosed. "Just as the lost rivers permeate the subterranean levels of London, unseen and oft forgotten"—he pulled at a carpet and in doing so reminded me once again of the urgency of our situation—"so too does information race along those avenues least noticed."

Fire skipped along a shelf. Glass vessels exploded into blue flame. Half blinded by smoke and acid fumes, I kicked aside the rug with which Darwin wrestled. Nothing. I wanted to remind Darwin how Nero fiddled while Rome burned, but forced my impatience into a semblance of temperance. "This is no time for riddles."

"The servants. Your housekeeper noticed the signs of morning sickness in Nettie—how could she not given her proximity? Once a servant learns of a situation, so too do her friends, and the friends of her friends, and so on... but there, I have made my confession and now we must return to our task." Darwin spoke in a hoarse rasp as if the fire had taken root in his throat. He fell to his knees and crawled about the floor, head tilted as if gripped by dementia.

It has been too much for him, I thought. What little faith I still possessed, like my anger at being duped, turned to ash. Nevertheless, I continued my efforts with the rugs if only because it had been Darwin's last wish. Monroe's laboratory enclosed us in its Hellish mouth, licked at me with tongues of flame, choked me with its smoky breath. I pulled feebly at a rug, no longer remembering why.

A whisper, barely discernable above the roar of the fire, stopped me. "Over here," Darwin croaked. His head was pressed against a flagstone, his knuckles raised in a cat-like stance. Then I understood his strategy. He was rapping on the floor as he had recently done on the walls of the consulting room. "It was not under a carpet, after all," he said. A broad stone shifted in its setting and slid aside.

"Nor is our adversary so imaginative as I had credited him," I said. But my hopes were immediately dashed. Under the flagstone was an iron grating. And the iron grating was locked. "Can you pick it?" I pointed at the hasp lock, large as my fist and with a keyhole into which I might have poked my little finger.

"No time."

Can you imagine how I felt? Freedom, life itself, was only inches away. I saw the metal rungs of a ladder that descended to the sewers. I felt the cool up-rush of air, heard the delightful trickle of water. But none of this was for me. I would roast in the horrific oven of Dr. Monroe's laboratory.

Then, like Venus appearing to shame the darkest night, I heard these words: "Your cane."

Of course! My cane swung from a loop at my waist. I set aside the globe that contained the water baby. Its glass was warm to the touch. Its charge implored haste with innocent eyes. I inserted the oaken shaft of my cane into the grate and leaned my weight upon it. Metal creaked but did not give.

"Not the hinges. The lock."

I shifted position. Pressed down. Metal squealed, then popped. A stud flew free. Another. The lock tumbled into the shaft and, from deep below, I heard the ecstatic plunk of its entering water. I swung the grating back. The abyss was a stairway to Paradise. "After you." I gestured for Darwin to precede me.

He did not budge. "You did the lion's share of the work."

"This is no time for chivalry." The fire roared.

"But you have charge of the water baby. "

There was no arguing with Darwin. I did as he bid. Ten feet down, the metal rungs came to an abrupt end. I kicked at air but found no support. Unbalanced, I fell not knowing how far below the lost river ran.

IX. *"Follow my voice"*

I landed on my back, the water baby's globe cradled safely in my arms. The depth of the water was a mere three feet but I could not avoid dunking my head into that stench-filled slime. I righted myself and wiped the muck from my face. "Take care," I called to Darwin, his form silhouetted by flames. A portion of the inferno detached itself and, descending toward me, revealed itself to be carried in the hand of Darwin: a chair's leg, one end populated by flame.

Although popularly known as the lost rivers, this name is a pleasant-sounding holdover from history, a suggestion that what was once a river shall always remain so. Nowadays, rife with the daily waste of three million Londoners, these underground tributaries yield a dank trickle, thick as molasses, that only aspires to join the majestic Thames. Nevertheless, I detected a faint current in that ooze. "This way. Follow my voice." I waded through foulness. Darwin slopped along behind, his torch casting a dispassionate light that revealed all too clearly his haggard, limping form. Darwin seemed a ghost of himself.

"Are you all right?"

"Yes. Make haste. The danger is not past." Darwin's voice was a faint croak.

I do not know how long we traveled. A wearisome hour, most assuredly, but it may have been many more. Nor do I know the distance we covered. Our steps seemed to demark the intestinal tract of a gigantic serpent that wound its way beneath London, an Ouroboros who, should it ever awake, could suffocate the city in its mighty coils. Moreover, sometimes this serpent split into a many-headed Hydra intent on deception. But no matter the temptation of a larger corridor, always we followed the current, however miserable it might seem, knowing that it must flow to the Thames and our eventual freedom.

Darwin's torch gave out. At first I thought we moved in utter darkness, but that was only the after-effects of the flame. As my eyes adjusted, I detected phosphorescence from the fungi that encrusted the ancient stonework. Revealed were the strange greenish arches and hallways, the labyrinthine magnificence that Jo had referenced from her dreams. Still we journeyed and, eventually, I beheld a sharp point of light that was no bedazzlement of the senses. It persisted no matter how I blinked or rubbed my eyes. A star! Yes, a single lonely star spangled the night sky at the far end of our prison tunnel. "Almost there," I cried. I hoped my beleaguered friend would take heart. I hoped even the water baby, whose globe I encircled with my arms, might recognize in that spark an end to our trials. But then, just when our safety seemed at hand, from behind came a roar like a steam engine pulling into the station. The earlier warning from Darwin came back to me in force: "The danger is not past."

I turned and saw a sight to blind even the Pope's jaded eyes. A seething wall of water bore down on us, flooding the sewer from floor to ceiling. The bowed form of Darwin was but a miserable insect cowering before it. The rage contained in our approaching doom seemed the very spit and venom of our adversary made manifest. Indeed, I have no doubt the flood was the work of Dr. Monroe: he had opened a sluice gate upon finding us escaped.

I had only seconds to react but, in that elastic time, I saw to my right an iron ring set in the wall. I flung myself at it. A skeletal hand barred my way. Death come to lead me from this mortal coil? No, only the remnants of a prisoner once chained and left to drown in the rising tide. I knocked the bones loose and slipped my arm through the ring, gripping it fast in the crook of my elbow. Safe. Or safe as anyone could be when trapped like a rat in a world intent on his drowning.

Darwin was not so lucky. Like me, he turned to the wall for succor but, unlike me, he found no protrusion to offer relief. He scrabbled in vain. His eyes widened in fear. At the last moment, he gulped a lungful of air and dove, seemingly into air, but the water reached out and grabbed him in its fist. Then, as if disappointed, it batted him aside. His body somersaulted toward me in the foam, and I swung myself out and toward the oncoming wave. One arm tethered me to the iron ring, the other reached for my friend. The water slammed into me so hard that I wore its bruises for a week but, wonder of wonders, within its crushing embrace my fingers made contact with the twisting, churning fabric of Darwin's coat. I was not so much pulling Darwin to safety as holding him against the vengeful flood.

I saved Darwin. But at what cost? In so doing, the globe containing the water baby slipped from my hands. There had been no decision involved, no weighing in the balance the life of a friend, a fêted scientist who had experienced all the good and the ill that can span fifty summers, compared to the life of a child, an innocent who had respired upon the earth less than fifty hours and this only as the captive to a madman. I simply reached out in blind hope to aid my friend. But, although the world might condemn my actions, although I lost the living, breathing object of our adventure, I would do the same again if given Hell and all eternity to decide.

Darwin safe in my arms, I watched the lost globe as it sailed away upon the receding wave, a crystal bubble aimed at the stars. For a few haunting seconds it seemed it might survive intact. Then, as if compelled by a demon's hand, it spun toward a protruding buttress and shattered. The water baby—a flash of pink against the gray—slipped into the murky stream, and left not a ripple to mark its memory. I do not know how long I watched in vain for it to reappear, but my attention was only diverted when the cold weight of Darwin proved too much for my arm. "Careful," he cried, finding his footing on the newly scrubbed sewer floor. "I believe the Doctor's tricks exhausted, but it is foolish to tarry."

X. *"Welcome"*

We stepped forth from the sewer into a night like any other, I suppose, but never have the stars in the sky and the lights of our city seemed so beautiful, for they announced our escape from the underworld and the renewed possibility of hearth and home. Yet we were cold, wet, and tired beyond all endurance. We stumbled along a stone path bordering the Thames and, a little ways down, on the lee side of a ramshackle structure that leaned dangerously far over the river,

I saw the friendly glow of oil lamps and heard the voices of my own countrymen raised in joyous fraternity. There, I resolved to take our chances and our rest.

No grand enterprise will set foundation near the noxious fumes of an open sewer, and our destination proved no exception to this rule. Indeed, in all my travels, never have I discovered so strange a domicile. From a distance I assumed it a cottage. On approaching I thought it a shack. Up close I was hard pressed to call it anything but flotsam cast up by the Thames. Pressed against the moldering apartment building was a derelict pile of wave-polished timbers and barrel staves, tattered sails, pottery shards, an upended basket, and even, I am convinced, the skeletons of a dog and a gigantic rat. Nevertheless, the edifice assumed a vaguely domestic shape. Most strange of all was the name affixed to the splintered board that overhung the canvas door: *THE ST. GEORGE'S HOTEL*. Yes, it had the same name as the public house where we had first met Jo. In height, the door was a little below that of an average man and we stooped to enter. I blinked my eyes against the unaccustomed glare.

"Welcome."

I recognized but could not place the voice.

"What may I offer you to drink?"

The man's angular silhouette was also familiar.

"Be warned, the only choice is beer, unless you have brought something to share."

An expectant scrape of chairs as the other occupants of the low room, a half-dozen in all, leaned in to listen to our conversation.

I shook my head. "We have nothing." I pulled the soaked pockets of my jacket and pants inside-out. "Nothing." And now, to my dismay, I recognized our host. He was the same man, or else his very twin, that served as the officious maître d'hôtel at the uptown St. George's Hotel. Any hope I had for charity disappeared.

But this man was as like, and unlike, the other maître d' as it is possible for two brothers to be. His eyes sparkled. His voice was animated. His hands fluttered like a dove's wings. Then, as if to both confirm and deny his identity, he said, "You paid handsomely for your friend's comfort. Whatever I have here is yours."

"Thank you." These words could not express the emotions of my heart. I extended a hand. "Thomas Huxley, forever at your service."

He returned the favor. "Stuart Hopkinson, as ever, at yours."

The other occupants were all scavengers from the flats—mud larks, I've heard them called—their clothes caked with the pungent muck of the

Thames, and these rearranged themselves so that we might be seated in closer proximity to the coal fire. I wrapped Darwin in the towels Hopkinson fetched and applied myself to rubbing life back into his inhospitable frame. Hopkinson entertained me with his observations about the world, circumstance, and the collision of the two. I have not space to repeat all that he said, and will content myself with the following, which, I believe, unriddles the mystery as to why two establishments named the St. George's Hotel exist in London, so different in all respects save the commonality of Stuart Hopkinson. "There," said Hopkinson in reference to the uptown St. George's Hotel, "no matter the quality of my suit, I will always be in service to another. Here, although the circumstances be not so fine, I am and will always be my own man."

In these convivial surroundings, augmented by a medicinal draught of beer, Darwin made a rapid recovery. The morbid gray of his cheeks was replaced by a pinkish hue, like roses blooming by a factory wall, and the furnaces that stoked his eyes were lit once more. He pushed the towel shrouding his head back to his shoulders. "I hope to never repeat such a water cure," he said. "Yet, against all odds, we have survived."

I, now that the danger was past, felt only a burgeoning sense of failure. The death of Jo. The loss of the water baby. Doctor Monroe's escape. Each was a dagger to my heart. "We accomplished nothing." I pounded my fist on the table.

"Nothing? Imagine what would have happened if we had not been here."

"He murdered the woman who loved him." In saying this I knew it to be true, and thought of how love had doomed many a good woman.

"Monroe's laboratory is destroyed, his work discovered, and now he must flee."

I rose from the table, almost bumping my head on the low ceiling. Perhaps something could still be accomplished. "Let us call the police before he escapes the country."

Darwin motioned for me to resume my seat. "What are we to do, tell the police that we broke into Monroe's house, rifled through his belongings, and stole from him? Would you trade these warm lodgings for a prison cell?"

"Stole?"

"Monroe would count the water baby as among his possessions. Even if the police followed our lead, all evidence has been destroyed in the fire. No, we must take our satisfaction in knowing we have put a stop to his predations."

I took a bitter drought from my mug. "Do you really think the threat of Monroe is over?"

"For now," Darwin said. "But in a world absent of God and the devil, I am afraid his kind cannot resist the temptation to assume the form of the deity and, in doing so, take on the aspect of a demon. He will reappear, although perhaps under another name." Darwin's voice trailed off as he tried out various permutations of our adversary's name, "Martin, Marlowe, Montrose, Moreau... "

"But what of the water baby?" The pain this question engendered in my breast took me by surprise, and I wondered if Darwin noticed the tears that flooded my vision. I, like Darwin, am not a religious man. I grant neither the existence of God nor of an afterlife. To have failed the water baby was to have failed utterly in our task, and to have failed also the memories of our departed children.

"Monroe is an evil man, but did he not create something of beauty, of wonder, in spite of his evil?"

I nodded. In my mind's eye I saw once again the sweet child with her pale blue eyes, sensitive mouth, and gills that flushed crimson. I saw the delicacy with which her tiny hands and fins fluttered against the water in her crystal globe. And I saw, and could not shake, that final image of her lithe form slipping from its shattered prison to disappear into the wave that almost drowned us. "Do you think she might yet survive?" I am not given to prayer, but this question was nothing else.

"I believe the water baby will seek the sea and there find others of its kind."

Darwin's vision astounded me with its audacity. Not one infant, but many, a tribe of naked children prospering in the same waters that held sharks, squid, and any number of carnivores, not least of which were blood-thirsty fishermen with their hooks, nets, and harpoons. "What makes you think that others of its kind exist?"

"To go from none to one is infinite in conception. But now, having seen an example of one, it is but a small step to conceive of two. And if two, why not three? If three, why not more?"

"I follow your logic, but do you really find this plausible?" I wanted to understand Darwin, to have him brush aside the cobwebs of my stubborn disbelief. His response, for the first time in memory, disappointed me.

"With some things," Darwin said, "it is not a simple matter of reason." He picked up a charred stick and stirred the fire. He seemed afraid to meet my eyes.

I stared at the tiny flames raised from the guttering chunks of coal. In those fire-sprites I saw Annie, Charlie, Mary, and Noel, robbed from us when they had burned so brightly and been extinguished after so short a time. But, although I might dwell on loss, in my heart I knew that Noel would not wish it so. Had I not two other children among the living, and another on the way, all of which deserved my love?

I could not suppress a smile in remembering Nettie's belly warm beneath my tentative palm—had this really occurred only a day ago?—as I sought to decipher a heartbeat, too early I knew but I optimistically persevered and demanded in vain for Nettie to hush her laughter and joyful tears. In thinking of this tiny life growing within Nettie, soon to take its place in my arms, it seemed that I better understood the water baby. She too, for now I could think of the water baby as nothing but a she, had embraced the waves, reaching out to them as to her natural environment. She entering the water without a backward glance for the world she abandoned. Rather than witnessing a death, I had witnessed a birth, a beautiful, miraculous birth such had never been witnessed in all the eons of man.

As if reading my thoughts, Darwin said, "Consider what you and I survived this night. Fire, water, and a monster intent on our destruction. No matter the dangers, I will never take odds against life."

II.
Present Tense

Smoke, Ash,
and Whatever Comes After

There's nothing special about the bureau. It's waist-high, has four drawers with round knobs for handles, and is painted a cheery yellow. Peter painted the bureau three years ago, smothering the earlier blue coat with a color of his daughter Tracy's choosing. Ursula used stencils to add flowers, each composed of blade-like leaves and a stem that supports a many-petalled bloom.

"It bit me," Tracy says. She extends her hand as a reminder, palm exposed to display the ragged wound. A protruding staple had snagged her flesh and drawn blood. Further discussion revealed a history of antagonism. Pinched fingers. Corners that cracked her temple. A bare toe stubbed, purple and painful to the touch for weeks afterward. A brutal litany that extended back further and further the more Peter probed.

"Don't worry, I'll take care of it," Peter says. He hefts the sledgehammer he dragged up from the basement.

"My things," Tracy cries.

And so, before the demolition can begin, there's the removal of drawers from the bureau, the upending of the drawers on the bed, the returning of the empty drawers to the bureau, and the taking stock of the items disgorged from the drawers. Tracy performs this duty while seated cross-legged on her bedspread, brow furrowed in concentration, lower lip protruding. She focuses on several purses taken from one of the upper drawers, popping these open and inventorying their contents.

Peter pokes half-heartedly at the piles of clothing. These are wadded and wrinkled, and exude the musty smell of old pinewood and dryer sheets. Peter pulls at a small shirt that seems familiar—the PRIN of PRINCESS and a sparkly crown perched on the letter P—there's a photo on the refrigerator of Tracy wearing it at a birthday party. The shirt is tangled with its neighbors and, when he pulls on it, drags other clothing along.

Peter slaps the whole mess against the bed but it refuses to come apart. He feels a wave of revulsion as if he has performed this action on Tracy herself. It isn't just that it's her shirt and that he has abused it—an overzealous tug on Tracy's arm comes to mind, his stomach lurching at the memory—it's because the tangle of clothing approximates the shape of a child. He holds one arm, but there's another arm composed of purple tights, and a central trunk and two additional limbs. These are distorted, bulging in some places as if sick with cancerous tumors, slack elsewhere as if missing joints.

Most disturbing is the thing's head. This is what convinces Peter that the bodily shape is no accident. The head is abnormally small, a knotted sock, ripped and teased apart at the top so that it forms a tangle of whitish hair. There's real hair also, of the sort you find in corners furred with dust. The head possesses no obvious facial features but, when glimpsed out of the corner of his eye, the wrinkled fabric appears disconcertingly human in its expressiveness.

"Where did this come from?" Peter shakes the floppy thing in front of Tracy. It is almost as big as Tracy herself.

Tracy sets her pink purse down. "I made her."

"You made it?"

"A long time ago." She frowns. "I was a lot younger then."

"Three years ago?" Peter is sure of this number. That is as long as they have owned the house, have owned the bureau.

Tracy shrugs.

The thing in his hand is malformed, abandoned, and it inspires a sorrow in Peter that borders on guilt. He picks at one of its knots. Threads stretch and break. It's as if the fabric has grown together, the connecting threads as thin, taut, and alien as spider silk. "You made her?"

"I wanted a baby sister."

Tracy's words penetrate Peter's brain like needles, memories stitched in pain. Ursula had gotten pregnant the year after Tracy was born but they had opted for an abortion. The timing hadn't been right. Peter remembers the arguments, the reminders of his unemployment, and of his fatalistic acceptance of a logic so absolute it seemed demonic, as if he were a wooden puppet forced to dance in flames. Tracy is too young to know about the abortion, of that Peter is almost sure.

"Are you okay?" Tracy asks. This is currently her favorite phrase and she uses it with a frequency that divorces it of meaning.

"Do you still want your doll?" he says. He wants her to say yes.

She shakes her head. "It's stupid."

Peter sets the doll down. It disappears chameleon-like into the piles of colored fabric.

Tracy returns to her investigation of the purses. "Did we get everything from the drawers?"

"I think so."

"I can't find my earrings."

They recheck each of the drawers for the pair of pink plastic clip-on earrings that Tracy describes. The earrings are flower-like with five petals each. The longer they search for the earrings, the more often Tracy describes them. In some ways Tracy is very much like her mother.

"I'm sure they're not here," Peter says. He removes a drawer and holds it at the level of Tracy's waist so that she can see how empty it is.

"Maybe I left them at Marcie's."

"Marcie's?" The name doesn't ring a bell.

"From when we had the sleepover."

"We can get you some new ones."

"They were my favorites."

"Do you still want to destroy the bureau?" Speaking these words, Peter realizes that it is he most of all who wants to destroy the bureau, as if its destruction can wipe out the past. Ursula has gone shopping and Peter knows, if she were here, she would propose an alternative to its destruction.

Tracy's brow furrows once again. Her hatred is pure and unashamed, Peter's merely a corollary to hers. Watching her emotions take visible form, wriggling like worms beneath her skin, Peter realizes that only children can feel such emotion, and only children can inspire such emotional extremes in adults. "Let's kill it," she says.

"We have to burn it," Tracy says. She is dwarfed by the shattered remains of the bureau. In the end it was easy, dishearteningly so. The bureau threw itself on their mercy but they had no mercy, Tracy least of all. She pulverized its wooden bones with her hammer. She pried joints loose, yanked screws, and danced on the products of her demolition, drunk with joy.

"Burn it?" Theirs is an old house and there are fireplaces on the first and second floors. Three years earlier, on a cold and blustery autumn evening, Peter and Ursula had poured glasses of Pinot Noir and lighted an inaugural fire in the living room. The romance lasted all of fifteen minutes, just long enough for them to smell the smoke that trickled down the stairwell, courtesy of the second floor fireplace. By the time they had the fire drenched, the second floor had become chokingly, teary-eyed full of smoke, the sheets and curtains ruined. They hadn't had a fire since.

"Burn it, please."

Peter and Tracy pile the broken wood onto a blanket and drag it down the hallway and into the master bedroom. The second floor fireplace vents directly to the outdoors and so, unlike the living room fireplace, shouldn't pose a problem. Peter had tried this logic on Ursula but she would have none of it. A recent expert on fire-codes, courtesy of the Internet, Ursula said that just because it was acceptable a century ago didn't mean that it was ever safe.

Peter arranges fragments of the bureau into a teepee on the fireplace bricks. A piece slides and his structure collapses. He tries again and fails, and again. Rubbing alcohol and newspaper do the trick and the sodden mass erupts into flame. The smoke, sweet and stinging, hovers as if unsure of which direction to pursue and then, following Peter's urging, slides up the chimney. He turns to gather more kindling and almost knocks Tracy over. "We learned about these in Sunday school," she says. She traces an image among the leafy curlicues on the fireplace surround, a creature winged but so stylized that Peter cannot tell if it represents a bird, an angel, or a demon.

"That's nice," he says.

The fire takes hold and Peter feeds it additional remnants from the bureau. The cheery coat of paint on a board blackens and blisters and the flames eat away at the wood. The fireplace exhales warmth. "How do you like your fire?" he asks Tracy.

She raises her palms to the heat. "I'll be right back," she says. She scampers from the master bedroom and Peter hears her feet patter down the hallway. He adds more wood and pokes at the fire with one of the bureau's legs, sending sparks up the chimney. Tracy returns dragging the wretched bundle of clothing, her doll. "You forgot this," she says. She thrusts the thing's limp arm toward him.

He freezes, heart hammering, unsure why he feels so taken off guard. The bureau leg quivers in his hand. He returns his attention to the fire and pushes wood near the front toward the hotter interior. He carefully flips a broken section of drawer up to lean into the flames. Tracy has still not

ERIC SCHALLER

retracted her doll. He taps the bureau leg against the brick flooring. "What do you want to do with that?"

"Burn it."

"But you made it. As a sister." His voice catches in his throat.

"It's nothing." She shakes the thing and its knotted limbs flop about, vagrant of purpose. "I don't want it anymore."

"You may sometime, when you get older and want to remember what you were like as a girl."

She glowers. "It's stupid," she says, the same argument she used before and to which there is no rebuttal. She gathers the clothing together and, before Peter comprehends her intent, tosses it into the fire.

For a moment all he can do is stare at her, not believing how readily she has consigned this part of herself to the flames. "No," he cries, his heart rent.

"I told you I don't want it."

His vision blurs. Tracy says, "Are you okay?" He doesn't answer. He turns from his half-crouch, fearful of what he will find among the flames. The doll writhes, its loose limbs afire, cloth fluttering like wings. Peter catches a glimpse of the thing's wrinkled face, its features now all too human. Its hair flares in an eruption of hungry oxidation and he gags at the stench. The thing's hopeless eyes stare at him, holes in a burning face.

The fabric gives up its shape among the flames. Bones poke through the combustion, ghostly and small, like baby's bones. But they aren't baby's bones. Some are the size of bird bones, as if from a chicken or a crow, others thin and fragile as those of a mouse. There are also teeth and these disturb Peter more than the bones. Some of the teeth are canine-sharp, others blunt as molars, perhaps from a raccoon. He throws the bureau leg into the fire, sending the teeth and bones skittering into the ash.

"Tracy," he says. His voice carries a suitable Gregory Peck-like intonation, a father who understands the innocence of childhood but who still demands answers.

No answer.

"Tracy?"

He rises, rubs knots from his calves. When and where has she disappeared? He has a vague recollection, while he was distracted with the fire, of her saying she is going downstairs to make a sandwich. Maybe that was from another time. He limps to the doorway of the master bedroom, his left leg numb and now tingling from holding position so long. He calls again, "Tracy."

He shuffles down the hallway, checks Tracy's bedroom. The bed is jumbled with her clothes and he has the impression that she is lying there, as invisible among the clothing as her doll had been before. "Tracy, are you here?" he says. He upends the piles of clothing. He drops to his knees and peers into the darkness under her bed. This was Tracy's favorite hiding spot a year ago, one she retreated to whenever punished, scooting as far back as possible, out of reach in the dark, silent and pouting. "Tracy?" He waves his arm underneath, bats something soft. He sneezes. It takes a moment for his eyes to adjust to the dim-lit space. There is nothing but a few balled-up socks and board games. The dust is undisturbed except where he has raked his sleeve, something he should have noticed right away.

He stands, calls again, "Tracy." His voice echoes. Her bedroom seems larger, almost foreign now that the bureau is gone. He can see its silhouette on the wallpaper, the colors brighter where the bureau has stood than the surrounding area which, sun-bleached, retreats ghostlike from its imprint.

Peter checks the bathroom, although its open door already announces Tracy's absence, and the spare bedroom, then hurries downstairs. The kitchen is empty. There is none of the mess Tracy would have left if making a sandwich. No plastic bag, bread slices disgorged, crumbs and a twist-tie on the counter, no jars of peanut butter, of jelly, no stickily gobbed knife. "Are you hiding? If so, it isn't funny. Please." Peter's voice sounds too angry. "I'm sorry. You're scaring me. You don't like to be scared and neither do I." He pauses, breath held, alert for any sign of her presence. Little creaks, a passing car, the smell of smoke, a spiciness to its scent, his fingers pressed against the counter. It's funny how seldom you notice the feel of things, like fingers, normally only doing so when touch turns to pain. "Tracy?"

Up until this point, Peter has imagined Tracy's absence but not truly believed in it, feeling that they have embarked on an elaborate game of Hide-and-Seek. Now he's scared. Ursula bought him a wristwatch for his birthday. It's heavy and awkward, but he wears it because it was a gift and because she made the effort. How much longer until Ursula returns home? He has to find Tracy before she returns.

Tracy is not in the house. The front door is ajar, but he can't remember if that's how he left it earlier. "Tracy," he calls. He scans their front yard, the neighboring yards, a momentary eye contact and he waves in response to their neighbor Charlie as if it's an ordinary day. "Tracy." He can't bring himself to bellow her name, afraid that will broadcast his inadequacy to the neighborhood. "Tracy." He bellows her name anyway. His neighbor Charlie stares but says nothing.

He jogs along the flagstones from the front door to the driveway, and from the driveway to the street. He wipes sweat from his brow, his temples. He turns in a circle, shielding his eyes against sun glare. "Tracy." There's a maple at the end of their driveway, the leaves red but clinging to the branches. Autumn arrives later each year. The air is sickly warm. "Tracy." He jogs along the sidewalk. "Tracy." There's no reason to run, no destination, but he has to keep moving.

Two blocks away is an undeveloped strip of land that runs perpendicular to the sidewalk. Bordered by young trees, it has something to do with the sewer lines, a touch of wildness that extends fingerlike into their neighborhood. The leaves have turned yellow and the uncut grass has also turned yellow and loosed its seed. People walk dogs here and a path has been beaten by their passage. This is one of Tracy's favorite places and maybe he subconsciously chose this route because of that. She could be hidden among the trees or sprawled among the weeds. He cups his hands and calls into the emptiness. "Tracy."

Peter remembers how, soon after Ursula and he bought their house, Tracy found a dead cat in the grass and, pulling at his hand, brought him over to see it. The corpse was desiccated, jaws locked into the snarl it had bared at the car that killed it. Peter wrapped his hand in a plastic bag and pulled the corpse loose from the grip of secretion-bound grass. The body with its cardboard-stiff fur released a stench so strong it stung his eyes. They held a funeral, mostly for Tracy's benefit, burying the cat in the strip of flower garden that bordered their yard. Peter thinks of Tracy's doll and of the sequestered bones and teeth, a child's magic visited on her mimicry of a sister. He wonders, were he to return to that garden grave with a spade, would he unearth the cat's remains or find nothing no matter how deeply he dug.

"Tracy."

A honk.

Peter whirls. A Toyota in the far lane, Ursula's Toyota, has slowed. She has returned from her shopping trip. Ursula rolls her window down. "Hey sailor," she says. Unlike most of their women friends, Ursula has not cut her hair and it froths about her shoulders, a coppery red more fiery than the strawberry shade Tracy inherited. Discovered, trapped, Peter almost gags. He jams his trembling hands into his jean pockets. He wants to run, to disappear along that grassy path, maybe to find Tracy, but most of all to just keep running, to run so far, so fast, that he might outrun his failures.

"You're back," Peter calls, his tongue ash-dry. He makes no move to cross the traffic lane that separates him from his wife. "How was shopping?"

"I've got groceries." The implication is that Peter will help her unload these back at their home.

Peter glances left and right and beyond the car to take in the familiar span of their neighborhood. It is possible, just possible, that Tracy will choose this moment to reveal herself, to peer around a maple's trunk, to emerge from behind a fence or a hedge, so near that he should have guessed her hiding place. Nothing, just the advancing roar of a lawn mower that devours and mulches the autumn leaf-fall. The man restraining the mower wears oversize sunglasses. He turns at the edge of the far sidewalk and retreats along its length.

"... stopped at Kohl's on the way home to buy her something new to wear."

Peter nods, not sure what part of Ursula's story he has missed but agreement is good family policy. His queasy stomach informs him the conversation has already turned to their daughter. He has to tell Ursula, to employ her help before it's too late. "Ursula," he says. He pauses not knowing what to say next. There is a shadowy movement in the passenger seat. A forearm flashes beneath the sun-spattered windshield. A ripple of hair, straw-colored and timid as a fresh-kindled flame, appears and is gone.

Tracy?

Peter starts across the traffic lane. He knows that distorted silhouette in the passenger seat, has known it since he cradled his newborn daughter slick with blood at Saint Mary's Hospital. He marked its transformation from chubby-cheeked baby to inquisitive toddler to puckish girl. "Tracy," he calls. "Tracy." A hand stretches past Ursula's blouse and waves. That gesture disperses his ghostly fears and gives his lungs license to breathe.

Another car approaches, slows, and comes to an unwelcome stop behind Ursula's Toyota. She shrugs. "Meet you back at the house." Her car lurches forward and the smell of exhaust envelopes Peter. He casts one last look at the strip of undeveloped land, then jogs homeward after her. He understands now what must have happened. Tracy ran away on a lark, bored with the demolished bureau, the fire, his company. She was probably only a few blocks away when Ursula, returning home from shopping, intercepted her. Now here she is chauffeured home in style.

Peter turns up the driveway, his legs already rubbery, a stitch in his side. Leaves crunch underfoot. Ursula is out of the car, beckoning him over. When he reaches her, he bows, panting. "How was shopping?" Has he already asked her that? He lays a hand on Ursula's arm and breaks into a fit of coughing.

"Allergies?" Ursula asks.

He nods, tastes salty phlegm and autumn smoke.

"Sorry for being so late," Ursula says. She wears open-toed sandals even though it is late in the year. Her toenails are enameled a red darker and bloodier than the color of her hair.

"No problem." He waves her concerns away. "Where's Tracy?"

"Over there." She gestures at the car and Peter's heart blooms. Vindication. The passenger door hiccups then opens, propelled by a spangled sneaker. A child, a girl, *his* girl, slides off the seat and out of the car.

"Tracy!"

Ursula is in his way, blocking his view. "Don't just stand there," she says. "Grab a bag." Grocery bags are arrayed orderly as teeth across the rear seat. Ursula presses a button on her car key and the trunk yawns open. Tracy, his Tracy, circles the far side of the car.

"Daddy." Tracy appears around the trunk, bypasses Ursula's hip.

"Tracy," he says, his voice shrill. Déjà vu all over again, her name having been repeated so often it seemed a spell to turn back time. He squats and she runs to him, arms outstretched as if they have been parted for days, even years. She throws her arms around his neck and he hugs her. "You scared me so much," he says. The pang he feels is a mixture of grief and love. He luxuriates in her physicality. "Tracy," he says. He hoists her into the air, something she's outgrown but he can't help himself. She throws her legs around his waist. "My little monkey."

"We would have arrived home earlier except for *your* daughter," Ursula says. Her emphasis on Peter's role as progenitor encompasses exasperation and amusement.

"Did you do something to upset your mom?" Peter asks Tracy. He receives a solemn headshake in response.

"We were all finished," Ursula says. "We had already checked out and gone to the car, but then Tracy insisted we go back."

Checked out?

"She wanted to buy new detergent for the washing machine. She said ours made her clothes itch."

"Really?"

"But that wasn't the end of it. She said the dress she had on gave her a rash because of the detergent."

What was all the talk about shopping and clothing?

"We stopped at Kohl's on the way home and I bought her something new to wear so that she would give me some peace."

Peter twists his head, his five o'clock shadow scraping Tracy's warm flesh. She wears a lemon-yellow blouse. He tries to remember what she had on earlier but all he recalls is the raggedy doll and its pink shirt with the sparkly PRINCESS logo. He can smell Tracy's clothing, the astringent chemicals that department stores used to combat mildew.

"You bought a new dress?" He can think of nothing else to say.

Tracy tilts her head and something small bats his cheek, near his eye. He flinches. It's an earring, a child's earring. It's pink, plastic, and shaped like a flower. Tracy points behind him. "Daddy, look."

He turns and follows her finger's trajectory back toward their home. He glances at the house long enough to confirm its existence and then returns his attention to Tracy. Her face is white behind her freckles. Her earrings are pink. She's wearing a new dress.

"What is it," he asks. He whispers because she's so close and because he's suddenly afraid.

Tracy does not immediately respond. Her arms encircle his neck. She pulls him in more tightly. Her eyes are wide, her face pale, and she wears the earrings his daughter has lost. His heart hammers in his chest and sweat trickles icily down his temples. "Look," she says again, insistently.

Peter raises his eyes. Tracy presses her forehead against his, the spot of contact warmer than the unnaturally warm autumn air. He breathes in her scent. Her hair smells like smoke. "Are you okay?" she whispers. He stares over her shoulder at the house that Ursula and he bought only three years ago. At first there is nothing. Then, as if Tracy has known what is going to happen all along, flames erupt from the chimney and their tongues, yellow, lithe, and pointed, lap at the sky. Blue turns to gray and ash begins to fall, silently and more softly than any rain.

Three Urban Folk Tales

I. The Postman

There was a postman whose father was a postman and his father a postman before him. Like them, the postman wore a blue-gray uniform with a stripe down the pants leg and, like them, he delivered mail on six days out of the week, resting on Sunday as was the tradition. Times change and traditions change, and many of the postman's brethren took to wearing running shoes. Some even wore spikes so as not to slip on the icy winter sidewalks. But the postman still wore black leather shoes and polished these to a high gloss before he went on his rounds each morning.

The postman walked most of the time, but at a pace that made the pedestrians seem statues frozen in mid-stride, he a breeze sliding amongst them. Over the years, he came to know his postal route so well that he could predict under which awnings the birds would build their nests and the number of icicles that would descend from any given rain gutter. He could have walked his route blindfolded. He even did this once at night, when the entire city was dreaming, just to prove to himself the possibility, and did not stub a toe.

When your feet know the path then your mind is free, and so the postman was never bored, whistling a tune as he walked that put the birds to shame.

One day the postman found that roadwork had begun on the street adjoining an apartment building to which he delivered the mail, along the route that he normally followed. Large machines now tore the street apart and other machines layered asphalt and tar, all under the supervision of men in uniforms. Furthermore, a tape of orange plastic with the words "NO TRESPASSING" blocked his path.

He approached the tape and touched it with his right hand.

A man dressed in blue and wearing a yellow hard hat called out to him. "Can't you read?" the man said. The question did not invite an answer.

The postman was bound by his code of employment to deliver the mail and so he decided to follow another route to the building, one of which he had heard but previously had no reason to use.

The route he chose was down a dark and narrow alleyway and was shorter than his normal delivery route. But, as luck would have it, he was set upon by a pack of dogs just when he thought he had reached the door to the building. These bit him and ripped his clothes, then raced off taking the bag of mail with them. The postman did not know whether to follow the dogs or to run off in the opposite direction. He sank to his knees and wept, for he was a proud man, and resolved to try yet another route.

The next day he followed the alleyway where the garbage from the apartment building was stored. Officially, the garbage was removed once a week but, at the time of this tale, the garbage collectors had been on strike for over a month and garbage overflowed the trash bins and accumulated in great mountains along the alleyway. The day was hot and the smell of garbage intense. The postman covered his nose with a handkerchief, but to no avail. He passed out from the odor and, while he lay oblivious, rats came from the garbage and took his mail to line their nests.

On the third day, the postman returned to his former route, even though roadwork was still in progress. He ducked beneath the orange plastic tape that read "NO TRESPASSING," passed between the machines that tore the road apart, and avoided the other machines that layered asphalt and tar. The men who supervised the machines called to him using profane names, but he blocked his ears and continued on. In this manner he successfully reached the apartment building and delivered the mail.

Nevertheless, his shoes had become so encrusted with tar that he was never able to scrub them clean.

II. True Love

"You will find your true love in the city." This is what the young girls of the country tell one another in hushed voices so that their parents do not hear. The girls make secret pacts, sealed with blood and kisses, to leave home together when they come of age. These promises, like most, are soon forgotten by all but a few. It is these few who leave the country for the city. They find jobs and apartments, cats to name after their favorite drinks, short cuts to sushi bars, and parking places that no one else even knew existed. But they never forget why they came to the city in the first place.

There was a young woman who came to the city and, to make ends meet, took a job at a copy shop. A man came into her copy shop every day. He wore a gray suit and carried a black briefcase from which he would take the papers he had her copy. He barely spoke and it was several weeks before she noticed him, and several weeks more before she began to expect him. One day she saw that the papers he gave her to copy were blank, and then she knew that he was in love with her.

Never let it be said that love is all in vain. The man found his voice, and soon they both were calling each other by pet names in public. A year flew by with walks in the park when the sun was out and movies when it rained. In the evenings, they would eat at the woman's favorite sushi bar and try to guess the occupations of strangers that walked by. On weekends, they would buy discounted day-of-show tickets, park at a convenient spot the woman knew was always miraculously empty, and go to the theatre.

If love were simple, then this tale would be over. But one day, the man missed a date with the woman and, when she tried to call, she found that his phone was no longer in service. When she inquired around the city as to his whereabouts, she was only able to learn that he had quit his job and left with no forwarding address. She waited for a call or a letter from him. She invented reasons for why he might have gone. Sometimes she cried and at other times she bellowed in anger.

Still, he did not return.

The woman decided that perhaps a man's heart is an open book but, if so, then it is written in an alien language. This is what she told her friends over drinks, and they laughed and said that the city was making her bitter. She said no, just men.

Not long after that, while she was in the lobby of her apartment building, she noticed the postman sliding envelopes into the rows of postboxes that serviced the apartments. She admired the calm efficiency with which he performed his task. Looking at his face, she realized that he was a young man, not much different from her in age. Glancing downward, she saw that his shoes were encrusted with tar. Because she had a kind heart, even if outwardly bitter, she invited him up to her apartment for a snack while she tried to clean the tar off his shoes. On the way up in the elevator, they began to talk and they were still talking the next morning when the rising sun reminded them that they had to go back to work.

So the woman found her true love in the city and, if the two are not divorced, then they are married still.

III. As Above, So Below

The city is not one city but many. Beneath the city of men and women lies the city of the rats. The mayor of this city had a daughter who was considered entrancingly beautiful. She had dark eyes, long whiskers, a glossy brown coat of fur, and a pink tail that could circle her body twice around. Her father desired that she should marry a lawyer, a banker, or a businessman, professions that in the city of the rats refer to those who steal, store, and exchange the food and trinkets that they value so highly.

The daughter said that her husband could be as poor as a church mouse. She had but one requirement, that he not be boring.

Many suitors came to win her hand in marriage. They performed acrobatics, acts of ventriloquism, sang songs, and danced. They did complex calculations in their heads based on any mathematical question she might ask. They guessed the identities of playing cards hidden inside a cereal box. Some, it is true, even had help from the mayor, who hired acting coaches so that his business partners might appear in a better light. But nothing worked. The daughter would eventually raise a small well-formed paw to stifle a yawn, and the suitor would be dismissed.

One day a young rat came forward to beg audience with the mayor's daughter. He was not handsome, nor was he rich. But his eyes were bright and his paws were clean, as rats will say when they wish to say something nice about a poor relative. Moreover, the suitor said that he would not entertain before the mayor's whole entourage, but insisted upon entertaining the mayor's daughter in private. You can guess that tongues began wagging at that.

But the daughter, intrigued, reminded her father that she could more than take care of herself. The mayor did not answer. Instead, he scowled at the suitor for a full minute. He then laughed, for truly the suitor was of such nature that he would have difficulty inspiring fear in a mouse and, that being the case, how could he ever inspire love in his daughter's heart.

Once alone with the mayor's daughter, the suitor undid a large letter, still in its envelope, that he had been carrying.

"What is that?" asked the mayor's daughter.

"This," said the suitor, his whiskers twitching, "is a story from the city of men and women."

The letter that the suitor read told of how a young man from the country fell in love with a beautiful country girl, but could only admire her from a distance. Whenever he tried to approach her, his legs would turn to lead and hold him fast to the ground. Anytime she came near him, his tongue clove to the roof of his mouth such that he could not speak. Nevertheless, when she came of age and left home for the city, he followed her. There in the city, she, thinking that he was from the city, fell in love with him. He, playing the role of a man that she might love, found that he could finally talk to her. But, although he did not initially realize it, he was trapped. He could tell her nothing of himself, only of this person that he pretended to be. So he had spun more and more lies as to who he was and what he did. Finally, sick of the lies, he had fled the city to go back to his home in the country. Now that he had finally told the truth in this letter, if she still loved him, she could find him there in the country. If not, he would never bother her again.

The rat suitor folded the letter back along its original creases and returned it to its envelope.

"What happened next?" asked the mayor's daughter.

"That," said the suitor, "is another story. In the city of men and women there are more stories than there are stars in the night sky or hairs on a healthy rat. Some stories are meant for a large audience. Some like this one were written for a single person. The woman for whom this story was intended never received it, and so you and I are the only ones who know it. But if you will invite me back for tomorrow, I will tell you another such story."

"Yes," said the mayor's daughter. "Tomorrow. And tomorrow's tomorrow. And all the tomorrows thereafter."

If rats can marry, then they are married still.

Wildflowers

Who's to say why a man does what he does? Hunter Wilson was seven when his parents emigrated from New Zealand to the U.S., but he still remembered with nostalgia the wooly clouds of sheep that drifted across the emerald hillsides, hard work to care for, but what life doesn't involve hard work? Hard work or not, their farm failed, and Hunter's father convinced his mother they should seek the glittering haven of New York City. A world away, a new world, a new life.

Hunter's parents had all the enthusiasm of young love even after a decade of marriage, but failure embraced them more tightly than love. Hunter was eleven when his parents traversed North America in a lumbering Buick Roadmaster, a hacking dinosaur ticketed twice by police for not maintaining minimum speed on the interstate. Once in Los Angeles, even failure took a back seat. His parents opened a copy shop, expanded the business to several more shops, and banked enough funds to entertain a college education for Hunter at UC Davis.

Which is where Hunter met and fell in love with Sharon Milne, her eyes so pale and blue she wept at the dawn. She dipped her head when she said hello, and her emotions sometimes so overwhelmed her that she shivered as a substitute for language. But she could also balance a spreadsheet, make it roll over like a puppy ecstatic to have its belly scratched, and that was a skill beyond Hunter's mastery. Sharon studied agriculture but had never farmed or raised livestock. Hunter had. And so, after graduation, marriage and migration to the foothills of the San Juan Mountains in Colorado.

What goes round comes round.

A sheep ranch, although barely a ranch by local standards, more like a toy if you credited diner gossip. "We'll aim for the high-end organic market," Sharon assured Hunter. Their parcel was small but abutted Bureau of Land Management acreage, the grazing permits a handful of pennies per month. During the daylight hours of their first summer, Hunter and Sharon constructed fences and sheds, interrupted only by Hunter chasing Sharon around their homestead with carpentry nails protruding as fangs from his mouth. *Wolf and sheep* was the name of that game, and you can guess how it ended. Come evening, Sharon crafted stained-glass suncatchers to decorate their mobile home, and Hunter tried to interest their dogs in leftovers from black-bean burgers and tofu omelets. That September, they purchased Corriedale sheep at cost from a Kiwi transplant who Hunter's dad knew through the friend of a friend.

The birth of their first lamb the following April should have been a cause for celebration, a generational signpost driven into the land as a claim. Not so. The mother ewe, blood dribbling from her rear, nuzzled the stillborn lamb. She licked bloody goo from the lamb's nose and forehead, seemed to entreat it to breathe, to stumble to its tiny hooves, to suckle at her painfully engorged udder. Sharon shivered then screamed, screamed almost too late because she had never witnessed a birth and didn't know what to expect, "Its head, the lamb, in the middle of its head, it only has one eye!"

Who's to say why a man does what he does? Hunter, at age nine, on a rare weekend excursion with his parents to Coney Island. Late August, the weather unseasonably cold, Hunter's windbreaker a joke even though zipped to his chin. The billowy lines of the Cyclone roller coaster rose tsunami high over the other rides but were empty of cars, the entry gate locked. "You promised," Hunter said. Dad scanned the vicinity for lights and swirling, rattling motion. "What about the Wild Tea Party?"

Hunter glowered. Sailing around in oversized teacups? That was for babies. "I'm cold," Hunter said.

One of those looks parents love to exchange, each blaming the other for their current predicament.

"What about... ?" Hunter pointed to a long, low building decorated with canvas banners that flapped like leaden wings in the wind. Strange men, weird women. Lightning bolts, mermaids, and swords. Red lettering bright as the ketchup on the lukewarm hot-dog he had tossed half-eaten into the trash.

"That's a sideshow." Mom's lip curled.

"So?" Dad said.

"A freakshow.

"At least it's indoors," Dad said. Cold fingers of rain explored their collars and cuffs.

Indoors and warm. That should have been sufficient, but Hunter's wooden seat was hard against his bony butt. Worse yet, a hefty man in a sodden winter coat settled directly in front of Hunter and so, although the emcee's patter revealed the premise for each performance, Hunter enjoyed few of the visual details. A woman supposedly coiled like a snake inside a box to avoid sword thrusts. Another allowed herself to be strapped to a chair and her hair stood on end when an electrical switch was thrown. The emcee, not to be outdone, swallowed fire, nails, and items proffered by the audience. Hunter cringed when his dad laughed too loudly at the complaint, "How in the holy Hell am I supposed to get my watch back?"

The uncomfortable dream of the live show was allayed in part by the displays on the way out, these available at the minimal cost of one dollar per adult, children at half-price. "We'll only be a minute," Hunter's dad said to his mom in response to Hunter's insistent tug. The taxidermied mermaid and gryphon, their chimeric stitches still showing, were so obviously fake as to be laughable.

The thing in the jar was something else.

The wide-mouth jar was much like one that had held pickles at Hunter's neighborhood deli. The thing submerged in the yellow liquid was deformed but clearly once alive, its skin hairless, rubbery, and loose around its bones, if it had once had bones. Four doughy clots formed its legs, ending in soft, translucent hooves. Its head was too large for its body, too large really for the jar, and was smushed against the glass, its ears folded and crumpled like water-logged cardboard. A bulbous white tongue protruded from the lipless mouth. Most horrible of all, the thing had only one eye, a single immense eye of a glazed blue that stared back at Hunter and invited him to blink. Each time Hunter blinked and returned the stare, that thing still stared out at him.

Hunter read the fly-specked label on the jar. "What's a cyclops?" he asked.

The chest freezer was large enough to accommodate a horse. The veterinarian, ten years Hunter's senior and with the tiresomely long name of Constantine Hurley, filled in a tag and tied it to the bag containing Hunter's dead lamb. There were two other packages in the freezer, a cat and a small dog Hunter guessed based on the shape and size of the bundles. The vet slammed the freezer lid closed on what was mostly cold air.

"Let's take a look where you've been grazing your sheep." Constantine's lip was creased by a scar, a white line that extended into his dented cheek and which distorted his every proclamation into a lisp. Stigmata, Hunter wondered, perhaps due to a mishap with an unruly charge.

"You want to drive up there? Now?"

"If that's where you grazed your sheep."

"I have a permit."

"That's not my point."

It was a good half-hour drive in the vet's Ford pickup, one that still smelled of the showroom, and then, after the gravel road ended in scrub, another twenty-minute hike through brush. The peaks of the San Juan's were crowned in blinding white, the ground they hiked frozen in the shadows, and trickling runoff and boot-sucking muck where warmed by the sun.

"I like it up here," Hunter said. An understatement. He inhaled the chill mountain air, tasted it like stars on a clear winter's night.

"I can see why." Constantine pulled on a pair of disposable vinyl gloves.

"What are you looking for?"

"Hold your horses. We'll see soon enough."

Not five minutes later, Constantine paused in his tracks. A smile crinkled his scarred lip. "Here we are. *Veratrum californicum.*" He poked with his hiking staff at a torpedo of nestled green leaves, these protruding from the warmed soil as if folded in prayer. "Also known as false hellebore, or the corn lily."

"This?"

"What did you expect, a black-eyed Susan? That's a joke. A flower with eyes, one eye, get it?"

Hunter didn't laugh.

"It's too early in the season for false hellebore to send up an inflorescence. Those can reach almost six feet in height." The vet raised his arm to above eye level. He then jabbed with his staff and lacerated a leaf near the tip of his Lucchese boot. "There's your culprit." He held the impaled leaf fragment up for Hunter's examination.

Hunter backed away.

Constantine grinned wickedly and returned the point of his staff to the soil. He removed the leaf with his boot toe. "False hellebore is poisonous. The poison, not surprisingly, is called *cyclopamine.* You catch the allusion?"

"Like in the fairy tale."

"Yes, but the cyclops is real. Consume false hellebore and, instead of giving birth to *liddle lamzy diveys*, pregnant ewes birth *liddle lamzy cyclopseys.*"

Constantine tapped his forehead for emphasis. "Luckily, the lambs are usually stillborn. Like yours."

"What am I supposed to do?"

"The obvious. Don't let your pregnant ewes graze here. Should you have the time and inclination, you could spray the weeds with *Roundup*. Kill them off." The vet then added, seemingly as an afterthought, "I'll hang onto your one-eyed lamb, if you don't mind. There are people who have an interest in such things."

Hunter remembered the pickled pig in the jar at Coney Island. The one cyclopean blue eye and how it stared at him, never blinking, a window into his future as it turned out. He smiled. For the first time that afternoon, the vet was speaking a language Hunter understood. "A fifty-fifty split on whatever you make?"

"Shake on it."

Love is two hearts burning as one. Sharon had said this to Hunter back when they were both undergrads at UC Davis and lying on their backs, fingers entwined, naked under a scimitar moon. At the time, Hunter had thought it the most romantic thing he had ever heard. But young love, despite movies to the contrary, is not eternal.

Sharon had a temper. There were arguments, some exorcised by feverish lovemaking, others not. Sharon had initially helped with the sheep herding, had claimed to love the slow moving and silent days, vaporous clouds in the sky and wooly clouds on the hillside. But after the stillbirth, the birth of that *thing*, that wet and twisted creature with the one horrible eye...

"It was staring at me."

"It was dead."

"Dead or not, it saw me. I still see it in my dreams."

"I can't do everything alone."

"I threw up. I was physically sick."

There were fights. Sharon threw a dinner knife at Hunter. It missed him by a good foot, perhaps on purpose. The wall preserved a dent from the knife handle like a memory that could not be forgotten or forgiven. Hunter shoved Sharon and she fell to the floor, heavily. She clutched at her stomach. That was when, Sharon still on the floor and snarling in pain from her bruised hip, Hunter weaving above her like a punch-drunk prize-fighter unsure whether he should return to his corner, that she announced her pregnancy.

*

Who's to say why a man does what he does? Neurobiologists propose that 98% of our brain's activity occurs unconsciously. Most decisions are made by the evolutionarily ancient reptile brain in concert with the limbic brain where our emotions reside. The more recently evolved neocortex, the pride of *Homo sapiens*, operates at a much slower rate and, if it accomplishes anything to our benefit, rationalizes decisions after the fact. After the fact. In other words, all that millions of years of evolution, all that this insanely complicated neural wiring of our neocortex has granted us is an ability to congratulate ourselves over what a dinosaur did instinctively.

Or to put it another way, after an exhausting day of herding sheep on the slopes of the San Juan mountains, not a week after their knock-down, drag-out fight, a fight in which Sharon revealed she was pregnant, Hunter returned home and served her a salad of hand-picked wildflowers.

"What's this," she said.

"An apology," he said.

Assuming some level of intent on the part of Hunter, whether conscious or unconscious, and not eliminating an all-too-likely mistake in plant taxonomy, the most parsimonious rationale for the contents of the salad was a desire to abort Sharon's pregnancy as a prelude to separation or divorce. The truly cynical might remember the enthusiasm with which Hunter greeted the possibility of making a few extra dollars from selling that first stillborn, one-eyed lamb. How much more might a similarly featured and stillborn human fetus fetch if brought to the attention of certain connoisseurs of the monstrous?

Regardless, after learning of Sharon's pregnancy, Hunter demonstrated an almost obsessive level of concern for the health and status of their fetus, this increasing in proportion to the ballooning of Sharon's belly. Such an attitude is not unusual for first-time fathers, and is readily excused as the only manner by which they may participate in the miraculous transformation that occurs within the body of their pregnant wife.

There was a heartbeat.

The ultrasound, although of typical poor quality, was sufficient to reveal the tiny, bent penis. These milestones settled Hunter's edgy emotions. He looked forward to the birth of the child he could now refer to as his son.

"We'll call him William, after my grandfather," Hunter said.

"I never met your grandfather, but I like the name." Sharon said.

Whatever Hunter's thoughts, conscious or unconscious, he could not have anticipated a poisoned fetus coming to term. He could not have envisioned Sharon grunting in the delivery room, her hair sweat-plastered to her skull, her fist white-knuckled and knotted with his.

The baby was born blue-tinged and bloody but alive. The midwife cursed and left the room. Hunter and the doctor exchanged whispers. Her voice ragged, Sharon demanded to hold her newborn son, her baby Billy. A nurse administered a sedative, and waited ten minutes for the sedative to take effect before allowing Sharon to clutch her Billy to her chest. Sharon had been forewarned that the faces of the newborn are ugly, that they are wrinkled and ruddy as discarded apples, but she was not prepared for the blank skin where a nose should protrude. She was not prepared for the single, mercifully lidded, eye centered in Billy's forehead.

Sharon gasped. Her body spasmed. Billy rolled sideways and found the nipple of her left breast and began to softly suckle. Sharon pushed the creature away. Milky saliva dribbled down her engorged breast. Her newborn's mushy lips puckered with embryonic lust, dank as rotten fruit. It was then that Billy opened his eye and stared back into hers, an ocean of misery to drown in, the pupil of his singular eye the same pale blue as that of her own two eyes.

Who can blame Sharon for finding a lover? She was married, but Hunter hardly looked at her and, when he did, he bit back his words and disappeared for a week to herd sheep in the mountains. The doctor had assured them that this thing they had brought into the world could not survive, that they should not become attached to it. But a month passed, and then another, and another, and the nightmare did not end.

Two long horrible years passed and the creature, that thing, their son, Billy, sequestered in his bedroom and administered to by humming, gurgling machines, clung to life as tenaciously as a twisted, stunted mountain pine. Sometimes he called out in a language of grunts and howls. Sometimes he clenched the muscles of his arms and legs and curled up like a spider. And then there was his eye, always that eye, a saucer pale and blue, the rarity of his blinks, a gaze that could not be met without tears and recriminations. By this point, Hunter and Sharon had established a cover story to address any malignant rumors: they had lost their first child but were recently blessed with another. It wasn't a compelling story but it was the best they had.

It was just bad luck that the lover Sharon took was the veterinarian. Although perhaps not surprising. After all, Constantine Hurley's job as a vet required he pay regular visits to the ranch. Still, bad luck just the same.

Constantine was tracing the areola of Sharon's left breast with a wetted forefinger, his attention rapt while her nipple hardened to his touch, when he foolishly mentioned how her husband had sold him three stillborn lambs afflicted with cyclopia. "Not that I'm complaining," he said. "It's good money for the both of us. For all of us."

Constantine then proceeded to give Sharon a detailed account of the effects of false hellebore and its toxin, cyclopamine.

Sharon focused on the ceiling for two long minutes, the veterinarian's attention to her breasts, formerly to the left and now to the right, a distraction at best. The baby monitor emitted the glottal rhythm of Billy's mouth-breathing. He was awake. He might have but a single eye but sometimes it felt as if he could see further with it than she ever could with her own two eyes, that he watched and judged her, always, even through walls. Sharon's cheeks, drained of blood, were cool and gray as week-old snow. She shivered. She threw aside the sheets, stumbled from her bed, and, behind the locked bathroom door, puked an acidic sludge into the sink.

The murder weapon was a Henckels knife, from a ten-piece block set Hunter and Sharon had received as a wedding present. The target was Hunter's brain, the three-pound blob of electrical jelly that contained all his memories and desires: his courting of Sharon, their mobile home scarred by her hurled dinner knife, the sheep drifting like somnolent clouds across the New Zealand hillsides, later ranging across the San Juan's and nuzzling at a broad-leafed weed, *Veratrum californicum*. A weed, a lamb, a child. The last, the vital link that joined Sharon and he together, separable only by death.

The murder occurred in June, the month that heralded the arrival of mountain spring with floral fireworks. Often as not Hunter camped out with his flock, sometimes for weeks at a time. Not so this night. He called an acquaintance on his cell phone, a Peruvian herdsman named Angel Alverez who was employed at a nearby ranch and who relished the isolation of the slopes. Angel reports the deceased seemed happy on the night of his murder, that he cantered home in mountain shadow, and called out in parting, "Don't let the bedbugs bite."

Dinner that night was linguini, a favorite of the deceased. The sauce was commercial, but the deceased's wife, Sharon, augmented it with hot pepper flakes, canned artichokes, and homemade meatballs. The deceased drank two glasses of wine with his meal, and a third thereafter. An emptied bottle of Barn Owl Red was recovered from the recycle bin, the liquid residue consistent with a recent discard.

The deceased fell asleep on his couch, in front of the television, the combination of carbohydrates and alcohol taking a predictable toll on his faculties. The deceased's wife Sharon retired to and slept in their bedroom. The door to the bedroom was closed, and she claims to have heard nothing, to have been unaware of the murder until she arose the following morning to make coffee.

Sharon remembers hearing a morning talk show on the television. She doesn't remember which network, or who hosted the show, just the background mutter while she puttered around the kitchen. She tip-toed so as not to wake her husband. She pulled the kettle from the burner before it whistled and chose instant coffee rather than risk the cacophony of fresh ground. All this is in the police report. She claims not to remember a thing after that, not dropping the cup of coffee on the living room carpet, not dialing 911, not hearing the shrill siren of the cruiser, not clutching and hanging onto, of hyperventilating, of blubbering onto the decorated chest of the policeman she admitted into her murder home.

That was when Sharon exhibited "suspicious behavior," according to the police report.

Sharon attempted to block the door to her son Billy's room, crying out, "My son's in there. You mustn't disturb him. He's sick. Sick." At the time, there had been no call for the police to investigate that particular room, they being needed to document the bloody and horrific murder of Hunter Wilson on the living room couch. Subsequent investigation revealed that Sharon's son suffered from a congenital deformity—cyclopia—and she may have been embarrassed to have this revealed. Or, based on the police needing to forcibly remove her and the murder weapon then being discovered in Billy's crib, perhaps she wanted to protect her son from a murder charge.

The blood on the blade of the Henckels knife was confirmed to be that of Hunter Wilson, as were the bloody stains on Billy's blanket. Fingerprint analysis confirmed Billy's prints on the knife handle, and no others. There was some conjecture the handle had been wiped clean prior to the appearance of Billy's fingerprints.

What was the motive for the murder? This question was not resolved.

The marriage of Sharon and Hunter had been a loving one, according to Sharon's deposition, the birth of Billy bringing them even closer together in the face of adversity. Could Billy, given his infirmities, have escaped his crib, obtained the knife, and then had the wherewithal to commit such a horrendous act? Billy's physical abilities were revealed, at least in part, by a movie retrieved from Sharon's iPhone. It's not much, and some might find it painful to watch. Billy curls and uncurls his limbs, and then performs some sort of parody of a crawl on the vinyl pad of his crib, one in which his chest and cheek never leave the pad. "You can do it," Sharon says. "He's crawling, he's really crawling," Hunter says.

Even granted the potential culpability of Billy, could it have been an accident? Cheese and crackers were found on a side table proximate to the deceased, a late-night snack, but missing the knife employed to slice the cheese. Billy, having escaped his crib, may have been searching for his long-absent Daddy. Two eyes are needed to establish depth of field. Two eyes are needed to establish a three-dimensional world. Could the murder have been a mistake, horseplay come to a bad end?

There are discrepancies if you compare the police and the coroner's report. The police report notes a likelihood of instantaneous death, no resistance by Hunter Wilson to the fatal blow, consistent with the subject being asleep at the time or, if awake, knowing the identity of the assailant. The coroner's report notes a slice across the interior of the fingers as if the victim might have come to a sudden realization of his impending mortality even as the blow was struck. The police report suggests that death might have been painless. A charitable interpretation of the coroner's report suggests otherwise.

In the end, what does it matter? A man does what he does. The man was stabbed through the eye. The man is dead. Instead of flowers, a donation is requested by the surviving family to support the efforts of a local veterinary clinic.

All We Inherit

Sunlight glanced off snow, whiter than white, sharp as memory. David blinked back sun-addled tears and stepped onto the deck, clutched the railing. "Careful now," he said to his son Brad. The wood, gray and bowed with age, was glazed with ice. Two steps down and he stood within the humped channel of snow he had shoveled the previous day. His rental car, a blue Ford glittering with frost, was parked in the driveway.

A scratching sound and David realized, too late, that Brad had clambered up the snow bank behind him. Brad thought he had seen something last night. Or heard something. The icy crust broke and Brad fell through. His eyes mooned. "It's cold," he cried. "It's in my *boots*."

"You're alright. Follow me. Put your feet in my footsteps." David circled Brad and forged ahead. David wore an old pair of his dad's Red Wing boots, the leather abraded, the heels broken. He found it disturbing that he and his dad shared a shoe size. Brad followed as instructed, his steps oversized to match David's. Thankfully, there were no more complaints about the snow or the cold.

Shrubs had been planted around the house perimeter. David could not identify these in their winter decrepitude nor recall them to memory. This saddened him. Time alienates us from our own past, he thought, but he just as quickly rejected the notion. He had far too much evidence to the contrary.

Animal tracks were punched into the snow outside Brad's bedroom window. It was the same bedroom David had slept in as a boy. "A deer." David traced the twin points of the hoof print with his finger. "That's all it was."

"It knocked." Brad smiled. David hated that smile, like a submissive dog exposing its belly.

"Deer don't knock."

"What's that?" Brad pointed to where the windowpane was smeared with something frozen. Maybe saliva. Maybe snot.

"That could be anything." But the frame was scratched, the clapboards burnished. "The deer was polishing its antlers. That's all. Not knocking."

A swatch of hair had fallen across Brad's left eye and David made to brush it aside. Brad flinched, but his face brightened in the next instant. "Can we follow them?"

"Follow what?"

"The tracks."

"Which ones do you want to follow?" There were two sets of tracks. One came from the tumbled stonewall near the road, the other headed toward the barn.

David was pleased to see Brad study the tracks before answering. "That way. That's where it went." He pointed at the barn.

"That's right."

It was a short hard slog to the barn. The deer's hooves had dragged arrow-like grooves in the snow. "There was an apple tree here when I was kid," David said. "It gave good apples but its trunk was rotted out. It slanted and I used to pee into it like a trough."

"You didn't have a toilet?"

"My dad didn't like us to waste water."

("You think we got a goddamned ocean in the holding tank?")

Brad giggled. "What happened to the tree?"

"I guess it died." It was strange how all conversations turned to death.

The barn was twice the size of the house. It loomed gray, tall and torn, almost black against the snow. David peered through the slit between the door and jamb. Dim shapes emerged from the darkness. There was a John Deere riding lawn mower. Nearby was an aluminum truck cap hanging from chains, and behind that a Ford Escort station wagon, its tires decayed into gluey tar—David remembered riding in it, his dad steering, his mom in the suicide seat, and he sharing a blanket in the backseat with his brother Jamie. Rakes, tools, and engine parts were piled against the walls. Deer skulls leered from the beams.

The barn's shadow was thick and cold and crept inside his coat collar. He shivered. He should burn the damned thing down. The barn, the house, everything. Let these and his memories burn to ash and be swept away by the wind.

Brad, grasping David's coat, tried to see around him.

"You okay?" David asked.

"Yes."

"We can stop if you want to."

"I want to see the deer."

"The tracks go behind the barn."

Brad nodded. His teeth chattered.

"A little further. Then we'll go home and I'll build a fire." The fireplace was one of the farmhouse's few consolations.

They skirted the barn and walked within its bulging shadow. The drag-mark behind one of the deer's hooves was longer than the other. "I think the deer is injured," David said. Nevertheless the prints appeared almost dainty where it stepped across a barbed-wire fence and disappeared into the woods. David held out his hand. "No point going in there," he said. The forest looked beaten and ugly, nothing like what he remembered. Many trees were down and their dead branches protruded like spikes through the snow.

"What do you want for lunch?"

"Pizza!"

David had anticipated that request. They had flown from Chicago to the Burlington airport the previous afternoon and then, while driving across the state to his childhood home in Hillgate, they stopped at a Cumberland Farms to stock up on frozen pizzas along with some snack food.

("Eat it. It's the same as Jell-O."

"It doesn't taste like Jell-O." Jamie snuffled back tears, glanced at his brother David, a prayer for help. David had finished his bowl, swallowing so fast the spoon clanked against his teeth. David hadn't tasted it going down but he did now. He was trying not to retch.

"It's better than Jell-O. It's called aspic. *I read about it in a book."*

"But Daddy," Jamie whimpered.

"No backtalk. There's more to a deer then venison steaks."

"But it's got hair and bones in it.")

David had eaten two slices of pizza, Brad one, when his cell phone buzzed. It was Annie, not the call from Stephen he had anticipated. "It's your aunt Annie," he said to Brad. Annie was Brad's birth mother, a college friend of David's who, after he and Stephen got married, had volunteered to carry their child.

David accepted the call. "This is a nice surprise," he said.

"I tried calling earlier but didn't get a response." Annie's voice was distorted by static.

"We were outside, exploring."

"You're with Stephen and Brad?"

"Just Brad. Stephen's in LA, with some advertising client."

"But you and Brad?"

"We're in Vermont. At my dad's old house. There was a break-in and the police called and asked me to check it out."

"Oh no!"

"No big deal. It was a couple of weeks ago. Meth-heads, probably. Looking to score something they can sell for a fix." He took a deep breath. The break-in had affected him more than he admitted. The kitchen door had been kicked in and there were stab marks in the walls. The cord to a landline phone had been chopped into pieces and tossed, along with glassware, down the basement stairs. "There's so much crap in the house, it's hard to tell if anything is missing."

"You said the break-in happened two weeks ago?"

"Yeah. I didn't have time to take off from work until now." David was employed at an accounting firm in Chicago, one that specialized in corporate tax preparation.

"That's not it then. I had a dream last night." Annie was always having dreams. She claimed she could pick up vibrations from the future when asleep.

"What'd you dream?"

Annie evaded the question. "You say Brad's with you in Vermont? Can I talk to him?"

Brad had chewed his second slice of pizza back to the crust. "Wipe your hands," David said, "Your auntie wants to talk to you." Brad wiped and then folded the paper towel like a napkin, fastidious as Stephen in his habits, before setting it on the table. David could only hear Brad's side of the phone conversation. There was talk about the Bulls, about the airplane flight, and then, finally, about the events of last night.

"It was a big deer," Brad said to Annie. "A buck. It came to my window and knocked." A wavering buzzing noise while Annie spoke, then, "I don't know. Maybe he just wanted to talk to me... He told me how beautiful the forest is at night. He said it's like a palace... We tried to follow him but he went into the woods. Daddy said we had to stop... Daddy cooked me pizza... I won't go into the woods... I promise." Brad handed the phone back to David.

Annie had changed in those few minutes of conversation. Gone was her Buddhist complacency. "You need to get away," she said.

"Away?"

"You need to leave that house."

"Why?"

"A horned creature visited Brad last night. It invited him to follow it into the woods. He may call it a deer, a buck, but you and I know it was no deer."

"Is that what you dreamed?"

"Not exactly."

"What did you dream?"

"I dreamed about spring peepers."

"Frogs?"

"Yes. The peepers were calling. It was the middle of winter and they were calling from beneath the ice. They were so loud, they drowned out the wind, the traffic, everything. It was a warning."

"Let me guess," David said, "Then you woke up and found your alarm ringing."

Annie didn't immediately respond. When she did, her voice was subdued. "Yes," she said. "But that doesn't mean I'm wrong."

"Don't worry," David said. He knew enough not to contradict her. "We're just staying here long enough to take care of this break-in business."

The last time David had seen his dad alive was on his birthday, four years ago come July. His dad had called beforehand and, after castigating him once again for his chosen profession—"There's no provision for an income tax in the Constitution"—said he needed to discuss something that could not be discussed over the phone because, you know, the government is always listening. At the end of the conversation, he said he'd turn 64 in two months, sufficient advance warning that David could not beg off on the birthday visit.

David had parked his rental in the driveway but his dad would not allow him into their old house. David could only imagine how decrepit the place must look inside. Instead, he drove his dad to an ice-cream stand in Wells River. An elderly couple waved to his dad, and his dad waved back. That surprised David. He had assumed his dad was a pariah wherever he traveled.

The girl behind the counter was young, her smile so optimistic it hurt. David ordered a strawberry ice-cream cone, his dad vanilla. "Give me a full medium cone," his dad said, "not the small mediums you usually dish out."

David cringed. "Don't worry, I'm paying," he said to his dad. "It's your birthday."

"You've got to remind them. Otherwise they'll screw you every time."

"She can hear you."

"I want her to hear me."

The girl gave his dad the largest medium ice-cream cone known to man, along with a paper cup in case he had to rescue the top-heavy creation, and then didn't charge them for it. "It's your birthday," she said.

"Thank you," David said.

"What did I tell you?" his dad said, as they headed back to the car. "You've got to let them know what you want or you'll never get it." His dad limped on the way to the car, worse than David remembered. His dad was always going on about alternative medicines—homeopathy, bioelectromagnetic healing, chelation therapy—but he couldn't resist a sugar-loaded ice-cream cone.

The item that could not be discussed over the phone, which his dad refused to reveal until they had driven into town, embarrassed the ice-cream girl, and then returned home, mushy cone in hand, was a folded sheet of paper. He'd been carrying it in his jeans pocket the whole time. He still refused David entrance but was willing to let him stand in the driveway and unfold the dirty sheet in his presence. The paper contained an inventory, a list of the hidey-holes his dad had constructed in the house. Not what was inside these, just their location.

"There's one thing I want you to know," his dad said.

"Yes?"

"I'll kill you, if you reveal any of this to anyone. This is my house, my property."

David had forgotten to bring that mothy sheet of paper with him when he flew out for his dad's funeral, but he had remembered it this time. He prowled the house, boards creaking underfoot, curious to uncover whatever legacy his father considered worth hiding. Maybe rumors of a hidden fortune had inspired the break-in. The best discovery so far, and that wasn't saying much, was a leather bag of pennies secreted in the deer skull mounted above the fireplace.

"This is so cool," Brad said. He dug among the pennies. "Why'd he keep these?"

"They're real copper pennies from before the feds switched to cheaper metal."

"Are these worth a lot?" Brad gazed in awe at the penny in his hand.

"Each is worth a little more than a penny. But not much more. Maybe you can buy yourself an ice cream cone." The talk about copper made David edgy. Among the first things he'd checked in the house after the break-in were the copper pipes in the basement, in case the meth-heads had sold these for scrap.

The next spot was in the kitchen. "Stand back," David said, thinking about booby traps. He wiggled a cabinet drawer out and shone the light from his cell-phone into the cavity. A screw protruded from the wood. David gripped the screw with a pair of pliers and, his arm at full extension, pulled the false panel loose. He wrinkled his nose at the smell. There was a mouse nest rank with piss and crap behind the panel. Its shredded paper was tinged newspaper gray, not the green of legal tender.

No great loss there.

Next up was the attic. David's light played across a chimney, old furniture, and cardboard boxes. Some of the boxes were ripped and tumbled over, their contents disgorged. He pointed at the boot prints scuffed into the dust. "They were up here," he said. He circled the scuffed area. "But they didn't find this." David cleared electrical cords off two hooks in the far wall and, using the hooks for leverage, pulled out the planks that formed a hidden panel.

"Cool," Brad said.

Inside was a Marlin rifle with lever action, his father's favorite when deer hunting. "I wondered what became of this," David said. He ran his fingers along the walnut stock. He picked up a box of Remington cartridges. "He taught me to shoot when I was just about your age."

("You're not a man until you can hold a rifle steady and hit where you aim, and you sure as Hell better aim to kill or you've no right to hold a gun.")

"Really?"

"Wipe that look from your face. I'm not going to teach you to shoot. It's dangerous and, besides, Stephen would kill me."

"Shall we call Stephen?" David asked. David and Stephen had decided, before they embarked on the adventure of raising a kid, on using their first names so as to avoid the confusion of Dad and Dad.

Brad was seated next to David on the living-room couch, gnawing on a slice of cold leftover pizza for dinner. There was a fire in the fireplace and the room was toasty. "What time is it there?"

"California is three hours behind the East Coast."

"Is Stephen still at work?"

"We'll see." David got out his phone. "I want you to do something for me. Please don't tell him about your deer, okay? You saw how that upset Annie even though it's just a silly deer."

Brad nodded, smiled. He always gave in just a little too easily.

Stephen answered after the third ring, but his voice was drowned in static. "Too much static," David yelled into the phone, not knowing if Stephen could hear him. He ended the call and redialed, but was met with the same storm of static. He shook his head and shrugged for Brad's benefit. He held the phone next to Brad's mouth. "Tell Stephen goodnight."

"Goodnight."

"Tell him you love him."

"I love you."

He returned the phone to his ear. "I love you," he said to Stephen. "We'll try again tomorrow."

Static answered.

David woke with a start, not sure why.

Brad and he had fallen asleep in the living room, each on their own couch. He wanted Brad nearby where he could keep an eye on him. He'd adjusted Brad's blanket, and layered on a second blanket for later when the room grew chill. He'd then stretched out on his couch and pulled a blanket around his shoulders. The last thing he remembered from before falling asleep were the flickering shadows on the deer skull above the fireplace.

He'd dreamed. The dream was so uncomfortable it might as well have been a nightmare, even though nothing really bad happened. Like that deer skull above the fireplace. It was there in his dream but its teeth were unnaturally large, not something you'd find in an herbivore, more like what a buck might dream for itself when it heard coyotes wailing. Mom and Jamie were there in the dream also. They were young and beautiful. They looked like they did back when David was a kid and both were still alive. They sat on the far couch together, laughing and talking. David wanted to join in, but he couldn't understand a thing they said. Only static came out when they spoke. The static was visible, like flecks of metal.

David knuckled his eyes, wondered how long he had slept. The room was dark, the coals in the fireplace pink beneath a layer of ash. He could make out humped blankets on the far couch from where he had put Brad to bed. That was the couch his mother and Jamie had been sitting on in the dream. They were sitting on Brad's couch but he was absent from the dream.

Where was Brad?

Suddenly suffocated by fear, David fumbled for his phone and flicked on its light. He trained the beam on the far couch.

The blankets were jumbled, shoved aside.

Empty.

"Brad!" The name was sand in his throat. He flashed his light around the room. Brad was truly gone. Under any other circumstance it would have been to pee. But not here, not after last night. David flung his blanket aside. He stumbled against a low table—"Shit!"—and hobbled to the kitchen. He passed the bathroom, empty as he had thought, and made for his old bedroom. Its door was ajar. The window? Please God, he thought, don't let Brad have crawled outside. Not after Jamie. Not after that.

There was a pathetic lump on the bed, hunched against the pillow. Brad. He was curled on top of the blankets wearing nothing but his pajamas. He shivered in his sleep. David sat down beside him. "Brad," he whispered. He placed a hand on his shoulder. He rocked him gently, rubbed the tense muscle. "Brad," he said.

Brad twisted beneath David's touch, his eyes clenched shut against the light. "Daddy?" he said.

"Yes?"

Brad uncurled and looked around, puzzled by his surroundings.

"You're in my old bedroom," David said. "Why'd you come here?"

"I thought I heard the deer."

"I didn't hear anything."

"He was calling. But he didn't knock."

"So you came back here?"

"I tried to open the window but I couldn't." Brad looked apologetic. "I guess I fell asleep."

David hugged Brad then crossed over to the window and tested the latch. Outside, the barn loomed above the moonlit snow, the darkness of its silhouette deeper than that of the forest or the sky. As he watched, a piece of that darkness separated itself from the barn and made its way haltingly across the snow. It was a large buck, crowned with antlers. It stepped awkwardly, letting its weight drive each hoof through the icy crust. It favored its right rear leg.

"I think he's hurt and wants help," Brad said. "He said he loves me. He wants to show me his new home."

"Who said this?" The buck rippled in the moonlight, hard to distinguish from its shadow, from puffs of swirling snow. It stepped across the downed fence and disappeared into the woods.

"Grandpa."

*

Four granite posts sunk into the ground and almost buried beneath the snow marked the Elkin family burial lot. Eroded headstones of slate and limestone dating back to the 1830's protruded from the icy crust. The headstone of David's father was of polished granite but, like his ancestors, it included the phrase *Memento Mori*. "That's Latin," David said, "No matter who you are, rich or poor, we are all going to die."

David had decided, after cleaning up around the house and hauling trash to the dump, that Brad and he should visit the Hillgate cemetery. "The important thing is that this is your grandpa's grave. He's no longer with us. He passed away. That deer you saw, that's just a deer. Maybe it's sick or something. That's why it behaved funny."

"Is that Latin, too?" Brad pointed out an 1868 headstone:
Mh lovely babe and haft
Thou fled
To the cold manfion of
The dead

"That's a poem for somebody's baby who died a long time ago. It says here that her name was Susanna. They wrote English different then, using *f* instead of *s*." He took Brad's mitten in his hand. "Now I want to show you another grave. Jamie's. He was my brother. He would have been your uncle if he had lived."

Pain welled in David's chest.

If he had lived.

Dad had shoved David and Jamie barefoot out the door and into the snow one January evening. He'd locked the door behind them, maybe as a joke, more likely as a lesson in toughness, in resilience. David had danced in place, the cold like needles in his feet. He pounded on the door, and continued to pound until Dad relented and let them back in. Jamie had broken down into tears. Dad mocked him as a crybaby, grew angry when he continued to cry, and banished him upstairs without dinner. Mom, who snuck up later to bring Jamie food, had been the one to discover he'd crawled out the window and onto the frigid roof.

Jamie had sat outside for hours wearing nothing but underwear and a t-shirt.

David brushed the crust of snow off Jamie's headstone. He couldn't speak, not without his voice breaking.

David's mom wasn't buried with the rest of the family. She became unhinged after Jamie's death. She wandered the house in her nightgown, eyes red and sore from crying. "God has abandoned us," she said. Finally, admitting defeat,

David's dad called her sister in Connecticut, who drove up the next day. The sister didn't return Dad's calls or respond to the letters he sent, and it was only much later they learned Mom had passed away.

(*"I visited your brother today. Nobody there but Jamie, me, and the Lord. You're off at college learning to rob people, while I'm here alone. My leg hurts but that doesn't stop me from visiting Jamie and keeping his grave clean. I took a weed whacker to it. Wonderful thing. You should have gone into engineering and done something to help people. Jamie misses you. He misses his big brother who's run off to college and is now too important to pay him attention. Jamie misses his mother too. I'm all he's got left."*)

David grabbed Brad's arm, not roughly he hoped, and half-walked, half-dragged him back to the car. David was helping Brad on with his seatbelt when his cell phone buzzed. He pulled it from his pocket, surprised.

"Stephen," he said.

"I've been trying to call you."

"Sorry, the reception here sucks."

"Where are you?"

"Out running errands with Brad." David wasn't sure if it was a good idea to mention the cemetery. Stephen would accuse him of being morbid and push therapy once again for his *unresolved issues*.

"Can I talk to Brad?"

"He's already reaching for the phone."

Brad, of course, told right away about visiting the graves of Grandpa and somebody else, he forgot. He mentioned the gravestone for the baby girl, and said her name was Susanna like in the song. "You know," he said, "Oh Susanna, don't you cry for me, I've come from Alabama with my banjo on my knee." There was a long pause, and then Brad said, "I know. Grandpa's been visiting me. I think he misses us."

The rush of adrenaline hit David like an electric shock. He snatched the phone away. "What did you say to him?" he asked Stephen.

Stephen went on the defensive. "I just told Brad how no one is ever truly gone. Gravestones mark the body, but the souls of our loved ones live on. They watch over us."

"Oh Jesus. You would say that."

"I find that a comforting thought."

"Now you've got Brad convinced he's really been talking with ghosts. That's the last thing I need." He glanced over at Brad who was fiddling with the zipper on his coat.

"Sorry." Stephen's voice trailed off, the hurt evident. "Maybe it's not as bad as you think. A guardian angel."

"You don't know my family."

"The fact is, we know who probably did it," the cop said. He was a little younger than David and his posture suggested pride in the sagging weight of his duty belt. David had scheduled the meeting with him while back in Chicago, after he got word about the break-in.

"Who?" David stood in the driveway next to the police cruiser. The wind stung his ears.

"The Threshers, most likely."

David remembered a few of the Thresher kids from high school. They were small, wiry, and had spidery hands that were always fiddling at something— clicking a lighter, tugging on a baseball cap, rolling and unrolling a shirtsleeve— always fiddling as if nothing could ever be made quite right. "If you know who did it, why don't you arrest them?"

"That's the way the law is here. Maybe it's different where you live. Here, if you don't catch someone in the act it's just a slap on the wrist."

"Why do you think it's the Threshers?"

"The two suspects, a young man and his sister, were caught on video selling copper guttering for scrap in Hardwick. The guttering was imported, with a manufacturer's mark. It was stolen from a Victorian house about a mile from here."

"You still couldn't arrest them?"

The cop grimaced. "Trafficking in stolen merchandise isn't the same as stealing. They can claim they found the stuff dumped by the roadside. On the positive side, the suspects haven't been seen around here since your break-in. They may have gone to Florida."

"I hope they rot down there." David was surprised by his anger. He wanted to sound professional.

"Did you inventory the house?"

"I took photos with my phone before I cleaned it. It doesn't look like they took much of value." In truth, David didn't know what, if anything, had been removed. "What do you think about selling some of the stuff left here? Maybe at auction?"

The cop shrugged. "That's not really my line of business."

"You must know someone who could handle an auction. Maybe sell some of the furniture." He remembered his visit to the barn. "What about the riding mower? That's almost new."

The cop raised an eyebrow. "You're not serious."

"Why wouldn't I be?"

"You don't know what happened?"

"What are you talking about?"

"Your dad." The cop couldn't meet his eyes.

"Yes?"

"Did you see the plastic tarp over by the mower?"

David thought back to when he had peered into the barn the day before: the truck cap, the old station wagon, the shadowy corners, the deer skulls lashed to the beams. "I don't remember any tarp."

"Maybe someone removed it. I wouldn't want it around."

"Why not?" David was annoyed. He wanted the cop to get to the point.

"That's how he did it. He got up on his mower—he loved that thing—and pulled the tarp over himself."

"He was running the engine?"

The cop nodded.

The cold day felt suddenly colder. "The death certificate said heart attack."

"The doctor did you a favor. Death by carbon monoxide poisoning is just like labeling it a suicide."

"Why in God's name would he do that? He seemed okay when I last saw him." David remembered the old bastard limping out of the ice cream shop with his super-sized cone. Four years was a lifetime ago.

The cop drew a slashing line across his thigh with a forefinger. "Diabetes. The doctor said he was going to lose that gamey leg of his. I might do myself in, if I got news like that."

David was confident the deer would return and he just had to be ready. He took position in a chair by the bedroom window, Brad tucked into the bed nearby. He had a thermos of coffee and his dad's deer rifle in his lap. A bullet was one of the simplest solutions in the world. Kill that damned deer and there'd be no more talk about Grandpa and guardian angels.

It was another moonlit night and the deer would be obvious when it crossed the snow. He surveyed the field, the barn, and the woods. He sipped his coffee. He checked the time on his phone. He watched the slow traverse of moon shadow.

A crash and he awoke. *Where am I?* Then he remembered and the horrible realization sank in that he had dozed off. He'd dreamed he was awake, dreamed about watching the field, the barn, and the woods. He felt in his lap. The gun had slipped to the floor. Its crash had awakened him.

God, let me have dozed for just a minute. David almost dived for the bed, for Brad, to confirm his presence.

Rumpled blankets. Brad was gone.

He looked out the window. Nothing but the moonlit snow, the old barn, and the jagged line of forest. What had Brad said last night? He'd been called outside, by his grandpa. Now he was gone. David stumbled to the door. It was unlocked. Brad's jacket still hung on its hook, but his boots were missing. He was outside without a coat.

"Brad," David called from the doorway into the invading cold. His voice was small, the universe painfully empty.

His only answer was a distorted echo from the hills.

He wanted to rush outside but knew that would be stupid. He had to be logical. Logic meant returning to the bedroom and grabbing the gun and the box of cartridges. Logic meant putting on his coat and his boots. Logic meant racing back to the bedroom because he had almost forgotten his phone.

"Brad," he called again when he got outside. "Brad." He searched the driveway for fresh sign but found nothing. Then, on the trail Brad and he had broken earlier up to the barn, he saw the distinct impressions of small boots. The barn door was dislodged, exposing a slit that pulsed, that darkened and paled, as if the barn were breathing.

Sick with fear, he ran. He almost fell. He did fall. His fists punched holes through the icy crust, and he shrieked in surprise and pain—he had forgotten his gloves—but he hung onto the rifle. He scrambled to his feet, wiped the blood from his knuckles. His legs were wobbly. An icy mist spilled from the barn entrance. It engulfed him when he slid the door open. He switched on his phone light. The glittering mist rose from the plank flooring, dissipating as it extended up toward the hayloft. Moonlight through the windows cut pale shafts into the mist. He shuffled forward, blinking against the stinging crystals. Cold raked his throat and chilled his lungs.

Brad was a ghostly lump seated on the riding mower. His hunched shoulders strained against his pajama top. He faced away, head sunk beneath his shoulders. "Brad," David called. He spoke in almost a whisper, not sure what he feared to disturb. Brad did not respond but something else stirred in the shadows behind the mower.

David disengaged the safety on his rifle. He slipped sideways, ducking to avoid the truck cap hanging from its chains. A few more steps and the buck came into view. It was larger than any deer he had ever seen, but lumpy, misshapen. The buck had been kneeling on its rear legs but, speared by David's phone light, it now rose. Its lips were only inches from Brad's and something fleshy, thicker than a tongue was forcing its way down his throat. Brad's eyes were white with agony. Tears glistened on his cheeks.

David raised the rifle and shot without thinking. Blood spattered the mist but the bullet had only grazed the buck's back as it sprang aside, as it hauled something thick and wormlike from Brad's mouth. This coiled and thrashed as the buck retreated behind the station wagon.

David ran to Brad. The boy had fallen forward, head lodged against the steering wheel, arms loose at his sides. David raised his limp body back to a seated position. Brad was cold, his forehead clammy. He did not blink when David shone a light into his eyes, but his breath was warm. "I'm going to get you out of here," David said. He wrapped his coat around Brad's shoulders. He started to lift him, was relieved to hear him cough but, at that moment, encumbered with Brad in his arms, phone in one hand, rifle in the other, he was hit from behind.

David stumbled into the mower, cracked a knee against metal, and dropped Brad. He tried to grab the mower for support and something sharp raked his arm. He fell. His knuckles smacked the floor and the phone skittered away, its light a funnel of swirling mist. A hoof slashed David's face and he covered up. A blow to the crotch and he cried out, knees buckling into fetal position.

The buck reared above him, silhouetted by moonlight. David still had his dad's rifle. He struggled with the rifle's lever to chamber a new round. Too slow, for the buck dropped on him before he could raise the barrel. One hoof struck his chest, narrowly missing his throat. The other hoof knocked the rifle from his hands and sent it clattering across the floor.

The buck backed into the mist.

Weaponless, David tried to rise. He had just gained his feet when the buck charged. A prong punctured his shoulder and he gasped in pain. The other antler ripped along his forearm and snagged his sleeve. He grabbed hold of the antlers and hung on, his face pressed into the musky fur of the buck's forehead. The buck shook him, grunted in annoyance. David was a dead weight, his legs dragging across the floor. The buck paused, not sure how to recover the advantage, and its panting breaths seemed to echo David's own wracked breathing. The buck's breath smelled like rotten meat.

The buck jerked sideways, dragging David along, and then stepped back across his body to straddle him. Once again David was at the mercy of its hoofs. The buck tried to kick him, but almost crumpled from misplaced weight on its lame leg. Something warm spattered David—salty piss—and he, shocked, lost his grip. The buck pulled its head free, reared, and drove its front hoofs into him. He rolled away. He threw a handful of straw. A hoof slashed his forehead, and blood spilled into his eyes.

He rolled into the barn wall. Tools crashed around him. He found a trowel and threw it, heard it bounce across the floor. The deer was on him again, striking with its hoofs, its antlers out of reach. He was numb, bruised. Every breath hurt. Off by the riding mower, he caught a hint of movement. "Help," he cried.

His world reduced itself to the hoofs strobing between shadows and moonlight, the repeated blows on his torso, his arms, his head, the awareness that he was being beaten to death. A small shadow rose behind the buck. He heard a blow. The buck turned. Another blow, glancing, and a shovel flew free to bang against the wall. Too distant for him to retrieve. But the interruption allowed him to search the floor again. His fingers closed on metal tines. A pitchfork. He turned the fork away from his body and stabbed upward at the descending shadow. Contact twisted his wrists, pain like razor wire. The buck screamed. The pitchfork was torn from his hands. He heard it scrape the floorboards, along with the beat of hoofs as the buck ran out into the night.

"It's not over yet." David had wrapped himself for warmth in an oil-stained blanket he found in the barn.

Brad nodded. He wore David's coat and moved as if in a dream. Blood crusted the corners of his mouth and David wondered if his throat was permanently damaged.

They followed the trail of deer blood past the strands of barbed wire and into the woods. The night sky paled toward dawn in the east. David limped. He carried his dad's rifle in his left hand. His shirt was sticky with blood and his right arm was useless. He broke trail and Brad followed in his footsteps.

They passed the frozen body of a young man protruding from the snow. He had been gored in the chest. His face had been chewed off, and pink frost bloomed in the hollows of his eyes. Nearby was a bulging knapsack. A little later they passed the contorted body of a young woman. Her seated corpse was braced against a tree, a pool of frozen blood in her lap. Her face, too, had been chewed off. The two vandals who robbed the house had never made it down to Florida. David took a dark satisfaction in this.

A little later and they found the pitchfork beside the trail in a steaming spillage of blood.

They caught up to the wounded buck where it sheltered beneath an overhanging ledge of rock. It crouched on decayed leaves out of reach of the wind and snow. Fingers of mist reached up from the mulch but could not hide its presence.

David squatted in front of the buck, steadying himself with his rifle hand. The buck's belly was bloodied where punctured by the pitchfork tines. The blood had spread and stained the leafy bed. "Have a seat," he said to Brad.

Brad took a seat on a boulder.

"I should put a bullet through its skull. But I won't do that. Do you know why?" David poked the rifle barrel at the buck's head, tapping it near the eye. The buck twitched its head aside and kicked. Its rear leg was clearly lame.

"Stop that!"

The buck froze in place. Gooseflesh rose on David's arms. The thing was a monster, but it understood him. *Possession.* That was the word for it, something he had not been willing to admit until now, although he should have guessed the evil inside his dad would find some way to live on. Those bulges growing thick and misshapen beneath the buck's skin, were those tumors? Maybe the deer's body was at war with itself.

"I'll tell you why I won't kill it right away," David said. His words were directed as much to the buck as to Brad. He rose from his squat and pounded his boot heel into the deer's lame leg. He felt the bones splinter before he heard them. The buck screamed. Foam dribbled from its mouth.

Please.

At first David wasn't sure if he had heard correctly. The voice was that of his dad's, buzzing in his head like a demonic wasp. The voice repeated itself.

Please. I hurt.

The buck's brown eyes were glassy with tears, with agony.

Give him to me.

David shivered. The horror of that request. The pain and self-pity in the voice could not hide its lust, its jealousy of the living and of their warm healthy bodies. David raised his dad's rifle awkwardly to his left shoulder, his good shoulder. He wasn't used to shooting this way but the target was so close he couldn't miss. He aimed for the spot he had ripped open with the pitchfork. He squeezed the trigger.

Blood gouted from the buck's stomach. The buck screamed again. Its scream was filled with pain and horror, and an almost human sense of betrayal.

David lowered himself to a seat next to Brad on the boulder. His left ear rang from the shot. He ignored the buck and its tortured cries. "Normally, if you were hunting you wouldn't shoot like that. You shoot to kill when you're hunting, what's called a *clean* shot. That way the animal doesn't suffer. If you hit the animal and don't kill it, then you track it down, to finish it off, humanely. Do you know why I didn't deliver a clean shot?"

"Because you were angry?" Brad's words emerged in a rasping whisper.

"Damn straight. That thing tried to kill us. It's been trying to kill me all my life. It killed my mother and my brother." David choked up. "It doesn't deserve a clean death."

"What are we going to do?"

"We're going to make it suffer. We're going to watch it die. Then we'll know it's over." He brought his heel down on the creature's broken leg and ground at the shattered bone. More screams. He smiled with sweet satisfaction.

Words burned themselves white-hot into his mind: *I brought you into this world. I gave you life. You owe me.* There was anger, there were demands, there was pleading. *He's such a little thing. Such a weak thing. He means nothing to you.* David hugged Brad, not knowing how much he heard. After a while the words stopped and the beast simply glared at them.

David became aware that the tumorous bulges had shifted position, like pieces of a puzzle rearranging themselves. Even as he watched, he could see slowly, almost imperceptibly, a sliding forward, a humping accompanied by a soft tearing noise as skin separated from the subcutaneous tissue. The tumors congregated on the near side of the deer's body, closer to Brad than to David.

"You're not getting him," David said. "Maybe you think he's weak but he isn't. He'll fight you and you'll fail." David turned to Brad. "You see that thing." He pointed at the largest of the lumps with the rifle barrel. "I want you to shoot it." He pressed the gun into Brad's hands.

"I don't know how."

"I'm going to show you."

Emotions warred across Brad's face. "Okay," he said at last. His voice sounded older, tired but determined, as if he recognized that some day he would have no one to count on but himself.

"The first thing you need to do is to expel the old cartridge and seat a fresh one in its place. You do that by pushing on this lever by the trigger."

Brad pushed the lever and the spent cartridge popped out.

The tumorous lump inched forward, the skin rippling over it.

"Now you pull the lever back. That chambers a fresh round."

Brad pulled the lever back.

The tumor strained against the buck's skin. The skin stretched, seeming to groan as it tore.

David released the safety and helped Brad position the rifle against his shoulder. He adjusted the rifle's muzzle so it was aimed at the target. The buck's hair parted and a portion of the tumor emerged from the rent skin, raw and glistening.

David wrapped a hand around Brad's right ear to protect his hearing. "Go ahead. Shoot."

Brad squeezed the trigger. He tumbled backward, unprepared for the recoil, but did not drop the rifle. The bullet ripped into the tumorous lump, passed through it, and ejected a spray of hair, blood, and pus from the far side.

David helped Brad back onto the boulder.

The lump was still.

"Good shot."

Brad smiled.

"Let's try another. There's a box of ammo in my coat pocket." David tapped the pocket on the coat Brad now wore. The shells jingled. "We're going to blow that old bastard apart bit by bit, piece by piece, until there's nothing left alive."

Hell and a Day

Cobwebs might be the better metaphor, after all. Derrick still didn't understand how the movie had gotten recommended to him by the **Amazon Prime** algorithms. He'd lost track of the plot early on. The acting was amateurish or maybe the director employed stilted dialogue for artistic reasons. That level of artificiality used to be all the rage. The choice of camera angles to frame the scenes was also limited. All Derrick saw of the house was its front porch and the lower half of a bay window on its second floor.

That little was enough to rip aside those cobwebs of memory. He knew that porch. The creaking steps, the topmost one with the protruding nail. The waterlogged pink couch he sat in the one time, never to repeat that mistake. The screen door with holes large enough for mosquitoes the size of elephants to fly through. Not that these attributes were all so obvious from the cinematography. There was a white plastic chair on the porch, not a couch, for example. But he knew that porch, of that he was certain.

Almost certain. Even should he be proved wrong, Derrick still needed to sort out his feelings about that time. Not from nostalgia, at least he didn't think so, but from a peculiar form of curiosity as if he were a detective investigating his own past.

Derrick remembered the house as an old Victorian monstrosity remodeled from time to time to keep up with the times, but it hadn't been remodeled in a long time, and much of the later remodeling had been accomplished with a sledgehammer. Doorways had been opened through the horsehair plaster and were still fringed with powdery threads and crumbled lime. Many of the original doors had been removed—maybe they had been burned for warmth during one of those dread Michigan winters—and blankets nailed up to give some sense of privacy. Still, you could hear everything that went on around you. Hear but not always understand. There were many sounds in that old house, a subliminal cacophony, some human and some otherwise.

Derrick's bedroom had once been a corridor, narrow with no windows and moth-ravaged blankets tacked to the ceiling at both ends. He shivered on a thin futon pressed tight against the wall. That futon had been left behind by a former resident and it served as his bed when he slept and as his couch when he was awake. The futon was better than the floor, but not by much. Other residents passed through his room at all hours. He would wake in the dark, disturbed by a cold draft and see a shadowed form, almost, as a blanket flopped to rest.

He had a lamp, somebody's art project. Autumn leaves were pasted onto its shade but these had flaked off in the bulb's heat. Still, it was immensely satisfying to switch on the lamp and stare into its cracked and ruddy glow. To switch the lamp on and off and on again as if he, a modern Prometheus, could bring fire into the darkest of caverns.

The other thing he remembered of his room was the peeling wallpaper, layers and layers of it. Some of the designs were so incongruous they made him laugh. A maid swinging in a tree, another carrying a crook and driving a frolicking lamb before her. The tattered skin of the wallpaper taunted Derrick. Maybe he was drunk, maybe stoned. He tore at the wallpaper and uncovered another layer that swirled with a tantalizing and granular darkness. He thought this part of a hidden design. He eviscerated the maids and shepherds. Then, his fingernails caked with something more than wallpaper paste, he recognized the design for what it was, an explosion of fungal spores and hyphae that had proliferated in their hidden splendor for decades.

That movie. The one on Amazon Prime, it had something to do with a group of people, unrelated by blood but perhaps friends, that lived together in the same house. In that respect it wasn't too far removed from Derrick's Lansing experience. The reason the house didn't appear often enough on screen from his perspective, the reason the movie plot held so little relevance, was because each of the protagonists had a job. A job! The movie expended the bulk of its time following each resident through a mundane day on the job, and then reunited everybody over a communal meal and explored how they transmuted the drab events of the day into something more toothsome, although largely fabricated.

Boredom piled upon boredom.

Kill me now.

The house in the movie had got him to thinking about his old house in Lansing. But it was more than just the house and its porch, more than memories of his bedroom buried in the umbilical interior. Derrick barely knew his roommates. By sight, sure, but the personal histories that a true friend will share, these were more than anyone in that house was willing to reveal. Derrick operated on chance associations, cartoon versions of his housemates: Jacob with the ass-length hair; Lewis who loved to imitate Horshack's laugh from reruns of *Welcome Back, Kotter*; Henry who made joints appear out of his sleeve with a magical flourish; Mary with the frizzy hair... Mary was alright... she cooked the best chili and made sure he ate now and then.

Not her. Not Mary.

There was this one woman.

Miraculously, when Derrick was at the absolute nadir of his life, drowning in mud as some might say, a failure to his friends and cast adrift to the slums of Lansing, there was a woman who joined him in his room at night and cuddled and rubbed herself against him. She clutched him tight to her bony chest, and they would make love and she would cry afterwards, her tears wet and tickling against his skin. Not out of sadness, he believed, for it seemed her sobs were from the relief she found in warding off whatever demons drove her to him.

She never stayed through to the morning, and Derrick would secretly acknowledge her exit as a cool draft from their shared blanket being lifted and then another draft as she tugged aside the blanket door and passed out of his bedroom. He didn't know whether she was a housemate or not for he never saw her during the day. She didn't wear perfume, at least if she did it wasn't anything flowery. There was an unwashed funk about her, from sweat and the sour smells a body makes if not washed daily. Nothing bad, a bodily smell. The smell of life. Together, that smell and their lovemaking reminded him that they both, if no one else in the house, maybe in the whole goddamned world, were still alive and stealing a little warmth back from the night.

Derrick had fallen asleep while watching the movie on Amazon Prime, but it preyed on his mind. It would be no exaggeration to say it colored his dreams. The house. That woman. It wasn't a nostalgia thing, more like he felt compelled to fill in the chinks in his memory. It disturbed him how he remembered so little about that time. He'd put the house and that woman behind him, invented a new life through no special skill of his own. He was comfortable in his new skin. But still, he wondered.

He'd quit Michigan State, been *separated* in the vernacular of the university, and migrated from East Lansing to Lansing proper. He stayed in Lansing for less than a year, although perhaps longer, who knew for sure? There had been an intervention. He had truer friends than he might have guessed. He still owed them, his life perhaps, although they knew better than to expect equitable recompense. Someone pulled strings with someone they knew at Wayne State University, and he got a job in their library system. Derrick found comfort in the quiet, in the claustrophobic walls of books, and in the smell of paper, whether the mustiness of old parchment or the caustic odor of fresh ink. In the ability to lose himself.

A decade flew by like the riffling of a book's pages. And almost another in the same manner. He'd had the same job all this time and he was now good at it. *Indispensable* as one superior referred to him. Then he saw that movie on **Amazon Prime** and those intervening years slipped away.

He drove up to Lansing on a cloudy Saturday morning in early May. It was raining but it was a soft rain and the weather forecast promised a let up by the afternoon. He didn't remember the address of the house where he had once lived. He tried Cherry Street. He tried Walnut Street. Those names sounded familiar. In the end he drove all the way into East Lansing and then drove back again to emulate the bike route he had once traveled. He rediscovered the house on Hillsdale Street, a few blocks southeast of the capitol, in an historic district grown so small that you missed it if you blinked.

The district had been on life support even when he lived there and now it was heaving its last breath, gobbled up by cheap prefab businesses and dirty acres of asphalt. The old Victorian was smaller than he remembered and more faded, a ghost of itself. The oaks looked autumnal in spite of their spring-time efforts. Part of Derrick was afraid. Maybe those chinks in his memory were chasms, big enough and dangerous enough that he could fall in and never clamber back out.

Derrick climbed the spongy porch steps. He avoided the protruding nail by reflex. There was a white plastic chair where once the sodden pink couch had been situated, just like in the movie. But the plastic chair was slumped, one leg molten, the seat blackened and sagging as if it had been in proximity to fire. The remnants of the screen door were crumpled in one corner of the porch. Snagged in the door's frayed wires was something flesh-colored. Closer inspection revealed it to be a human nose, a rubber prosthetic. Its presence, like that of the chair, seemed to confirm that the house had been used as a movie set. Derrick knocked on the front door and felt that peculiar sensation of déjà vu, like when he had first knocked on that same door so many years ago, back then with the chill evening drawing close and he knowing he had no other place to crash should he be turned away.

This time his knocks rang hollow and there was no answer. Confirmation the house was deserted. The front door was locked but, around back, the kitchen door still responded to a well-placed kick. A yowl, seemingly out of time, like a rusty nail yanked from a board. Sitting in front of him on the yellowed linoleum and speared by a ray of sunlight was an orange tabby. It was *the cat*. How could he have forgotten it?

Sometimes memories are like that. Not something cloaked in cobwebs ready to be swept away to reveal the features of the hinted form. Sometimes a memory is lost, leaving you with no evidence of its existence, but then you open a door and it's crouched there in broad daylight and ready to pounce.

An orange tabby. The cat had been there that first evening when Derrick entered the house so long ago and the cat was here waiting for him again almost two decades later. Orange fur grew out of a lumpy abomination of a face. No eyes, no nose, just a moist toothed hole on one side of its skull, the bordering fur caked with dried spittle and food remnants.

The cat, then and now, was repulsive.

The shadows that once slid through Derrick's room at night? Sometimes they weren't his human housemates. Sometimes it was the cat. And sometimes the cat was more than just a shadow. Sometimes Derrick woke to hot breath on his cheek and the smell of rotting death, and that horrible cat would be so close it was a wonder it hadn't crawled onto Derrick's face and suffocated him in his sleep.

How could the cat have survived all these years? The tabby's crushed and distorted skull had suggested a miraculous recovery following a vehicular mishap, although no one in the house claimed knowledge of such an event. Maybe it was all genetics, the original cat having died but bred and passed on its defects to a future generation. Nevertheless, here Derrick was in the house again, and the tabby was yawning and stretching and arching its back, and it was like that old joke about how a cat will always seek out the one person at a party who has allergies, because that damned monster was mewling and sidling up to him and begging to be scratched.

Derrick could imagine the house as it might be advertised in a real-estate listing: Solid bones with many original features: hardwood floors, a stone fireplace, wood trim, an oak staircase with hand-carved bannister, an antique claw-foot tub. What wouldn't be mentioned were the holes in the walls and windows, now stuffed with newspaper, and the water-damaged ceilings, the stained plaster bellying loose of its pins. And the stench, that claustrophobic miasma of mildew and cat piss. Derrick pulled the collar of his tee-shirt up and over his nose, I'll just take one quick look at my old room, he told himself.

The tabby had followed him into the living room and now hopped onto a dirty couch and scratched at the greasy cushion. Dust and orange fur clouded the air. The couch was the same pink one that had once graced the porch but was now layered with grit and fur like sedimented time.

Derrick's room had been on the second floor. He slid his hand along the bannister, hand-carved and curving upward alongside the stairway. He slid his hand along the smooth, wooden bannister and took each step carefully one at a time. He focused on the creaks and give of the treads beneath his sneakers. His hand on the bannister and, before he understood exactly why, he jerked away, the bannister suddenly becoming something warm and other beneath his palm, a memory bestirred.

That woman, the one that used to slip into his bed. He had always known it was her by her smell, by her thin and sweaty muscles, by the way she melded into him. But there was this one time when she slipped beneath his blanket and she pressed her pelvis against him and an erection quivered against his hip. Her erection. Nothing like his own, not by its feel or by its shape. Long and thin and curved, smooth, like it had been fashioned from polished wood or bone. But warm, so warm that he could not mistake it for anything but her flesh.

Just that flash of memory, communicated from the banister to his brain, Derrick aware in that singular instant from his past that it was still her but that she was different, male it seemed, but not in any way that he would call human. Not as judged by his understanding of anatomy. Just a flash, and not connected to any particular time either. Was it the first time she crawled into his bed, or later, or even maybe the last time? He didn't know. All he remembered was that it was unique to their lovemaking. A mistake, perhaps, on her part. Or an invitation.

*

Ana. That was her name.

The cat never had a name, not that he remembered. It was just the cat.

Derrick worried at that memory of Ana like a tooth cavity all the long drive home. Home to Sterling Heights. To his safe home and to his safe job at Wayne State University. His memory of Ana seemed like it should be significant. Like it could reveal what was real and what was a sham. Like Ana had to be one of the two. Male or female. Like she had revealed her intrinsic nature to him, but he still had to choose.

Ana had once clung to Derrick in his windowless room and said things like, "I feel you." Empty phrases that seemed profound in the moment, clichéd in daytime memory, but welcomed with her nocturnal return. "I feel you." Empty phrases that demanded an answer.

"I feel you too."

"I feel you with me all the time, even when you're not here." Ana dug her nails into Derrick's back.

Derrick moaned. It was dark, and his nose was buried in Ana's hair.

"You are always with me." Ana's nails were razor sharp, and it wasn't until the next morning that Derrick discovered the bloody furrows in his skin.

"Even if I were a thousand miles away?"

Ana's chin slid up and down against Derrick's chest.

"Ten-thousand miles away?"

"No matter how far away or how dark the night, I would feel you with me. Even should I be blinded, I would feel you with me as you are now in my arms."

"And what then?"

"If I called to you, would you come to me?" Ana's tears trickled wet and warm against his skin.

Derrick knew what to say in response. "Yes. No matter how far away or how dark the night, if you called, I would come to you."

*

118

That movie, the one Amazon Prime had recommended to Derrick, he called it up and replayed it on his iPad as soon as he returned to his apartment. *Hell and a Day* was its title. Its advertising poster depicted residents screaming black-mawed, teeth glistening bony white, in front of the flaming silhouette of a Victorian mansion. The mansion looked nothing like the one featured in the movie, nothing like the one Derrick had visited in Lansing. Derrick had left the house at a run and, exiting through the kitchen, he had been accosted once again by that damned tabby. It mewed to high Heaven as if to reprimand him for not coughing up a tin of Fancy Feast. The cat feigned starvation but it certainly didn't look starved.

The general plot to the movie was just as soporific as Derrick remembered, all the more so because he didn't grant himself the respite of alcohol or sleep. Boring, but at least the majority of the movie made some sort of sense. It was the final scene that threw him for a loop. It was as if the film had given up on its plotline altogether. A quick cut, right in the middle of the dinner-time conversation, and Derrick was suddenly aware the cast members had assembled in the front yard. Maybe for a wrap party although, as far as Derrick could tell, no director or support staff were present, only the cast.

The cinematographic quality of that final scene was not as high as what had come before, the colors yellowed like in an old home movie. Folding tables were set up on the lawn, these then layered with paper tablecloths, stacks of paper plates, and plastic cutlery. Two grills smoked. Derrick could almost smell the char of burgers and hotdogs. It was late afternoon. Citronella candles had been lit. The cast congregated, laughed, and told their stories. You couldn't really understand anything they said. The camera glided among them and caught close-ups, but it didn't linger long enough to capture the gist of conversation. That camera, its movements were something that could only have been accomplished by the action of a remote-controlled drone.

Hell and a Day. Cinema aficionados still love to debate that final scene. Not for the same reasons, necessarily, that co-opted Derrick's attention. It was one of those arty cinema verité scenes so beloved in the late sixties and early seventies, and which directors recreated decades later as an homage to the gutsy film-making of that era. In that final scene, the actors removed parts of themselves as they exited the house or wandered into the camera frame. They abandoned prosthetics and excess clothing, seemed to strip themselves naked although they were fully clothed beneath.

A late arrival circled a lilac tree and tripped over a pile of rubbery cast-offs. These bounced across the grass, buoyant as Styrofoam ghosts. The late arrival, vaguely familiar, joined a group of actors who talked and laughed. Gooey adhesive dangled from faces and arms. There weren't a lot of actors, maybe a dozen, two dozen at most, but these were enough to fulfill the requirements for a party scene. This was just the sort of thing that seemed avant-garde back in its day. The showcasing of the actors, a reminder to the audience that whatever had come before was artificial, that there was another layer of reality if you stripped away the gauze of Hollywood dreamland.

And there was Ana. Ana was always Ana.

Derrick had never seen Ana in the light of day. He knew her from the way the shadows clung to her, from how he remembered her sculpted in the illumination of a 60-watt bulb, from the sensual familiarity in how she rubbed up against the other actors. Derrick could almost smell her, smell Ana as she clutched him in the windowless night of his claustrophobic room. Smell her as she murmured about how she would always find him no matter where he was, and how he had replied, promised really, that he too would always return to her, should she ever call for him.

Not only Ana. Derrick also recognized the other members of the household, now freed of their prosthetics: Jacob with his ass-length hair; Lewis with his hyena-laugh adopted from a popular sit-com; Henry with more joints up his sleeve than fingers on his hand; Mary who... they were all there at the party, sycophants rather than actors. They were all engaged in a complex dance, a dance in which no step was repeated but which always orbited around Ana. Ana was then, as always, their gravitational center.

Derrick halted the film and tapped the arrow for rewind. The actors reupholstered themselves in their earlier prosthetics. Not Ana. The front door gobbled her up. Derrick paused and advanced again. Ana was Ana. No prosthetics. Always Ana. That meant, unlike the others, the daily drudgery of her work away from the house had never been documented in the film. Her work only involved the house, as if she were its resident curator. An invisible guardian angel.

The afternoon party repeated itself and Ana wandered around to each cast member, draping an arm, seeming to confide secrets so personal that they couldn't be communicated in the bits and drabs of conversation captured by the drone camera. At a certain point, Derrick realized the party must be breaking up because there were so many fewer guests. Just Ana and a handful of the actors. The light was fading. Late afternoon had become evening. Derrick tried to follow Ana's movements, even though the camera did not always share his fascination with her. Off to the left, only a portion of her body on camera, Ana encircled one of the few members who remained at the party with her loving arm, a woman with frizzy hair. Then the woman friend was gone.

Derrick halted the film again. Again, he hit the rewind arrow. Yes, Ana had kissed the woman with the frizzy hair. Mary? Now forwarding in slow motion, the woman with the frizzy hair turned and returned the kiss. There was an understanding, love perhaps, but even as their lips joined, the woman with the frizzy hair was already fading from sight, not ghost-like or some obvious cinema trickery, but like she was nothing more than atoms and energy, and now those atoms no longer had the coherence, the foolish desire, to fashion themselves into a human form. The woman's features, even her clothing, faded into something generic, and then even these failed to cohere, and it was as if Derrick watched dust or pollen swirled away by the gusting wind. Dust. Pollen. Pixels. One of those artistic effects, so beloved by critics, because you had to have paid attention to have caught it. Some unintelligible conversation continued, maybe just the buzz of mosquitoes, as the credits began to roll.

The credits rolled, and the camera hung liked a hanged man in the air, no longer dipping and diving but focused on the porch. Ana had exited the scene. No party guests remained in view. A minute passed. Another. Derrick might have thought the house an image frozen in time, but for the shadows of the unseen clouds that drifted across the darkening sky. A minute passed and another, and Derrick's attention shifted to the credits themselves. Amateurish and without sufficient contrast to distinguish the text from the image of the porch behind, but perhaps that was the intent.

The Lansing chamber of commerce was thanked for location shooting. That, at least, he could make out. But the year of the film's release? He couldn't decipher the Roman numerals even though he froze the screen. His old housemates, of those he had recognized in that final scene before they were extinguished, they looked exactly as he remembered them, ageless.

This all seemed to prove something. But maybe the movie was trying too hard to be meaningful. Artifice layered over artifice, the tired idea that our world is a nested set of Russian dolls, all of these, large or small, but a crude facsimile of humanity. Derrick thought of the tabby cat and its hideous face, how it of all his housemates now seemed the most real.

Ana reentered the scene. Skeletal fingers slid along Derrick's backbone. Derrick didn't remember having started the film up again. Ana ascended the steps to the porch. She avoided the protruding nail with a delicious side-step. She was the only one remaining from the cast party. Almost, because now the ugly cat wound its way into camera's eye just as the picture began to fade, yellows becoming ghostly until, even as the cat wrapped itself around Ana's ankles and she reached for the doorknob, the screen flared to white.

Derrick had always hated that cat. Maybe it was because he saw too much of himself in it. They were both deformed, one visibly, the other psychologically, but now he saw that, regardless of the hand they had been dealt in life, they had both survived. His former housemates were all gone, the house desolate but for the cat. The cat had survived and so had Derrick. That had to count for something.

He thought of the house, how it had slipped into ruin. More ruinous than when he had lived there all those years ago, the houses in the neighborhood now retailing for a dime a dozen. He had saved up some money, could possibly afford to purchase the house. Even if he couldn't live there, he could be its caretaker. Maybe the cat would be there. He could still remember how, in the old days, he would awaken to and inhale the tabby's hot corpse-scented breath. Derrick could almost laugh about that now. Hindsight and all that. Maybe the cat would still be there. Maybe something more.

III.

Future Tense

Automata

"Here." Ramona tapped her bared forearm with a dessert fork. "Stab me here."

This by way of making a point.

Something about definitions: the living, and the dead, and the dead that approximate the living.

Richard's recollections were sketchy on some of the specifics because Ramona and he had drunk a fair quantity of red wine with dinner. He didn't remember the name of the wine or even the exact variety, a merlot or perhaps a cabernet sauvignon. The label suggested, if only because of its lack of decoration, a certain importance to the vintage, the sort of self-satisfied smugness that assumes familiarity. He had in fact bought the bottle precisely because the label projected these qualities. Ramona and he were not intimidated, however, and polished the bottle off with sufficient alacrity to make him wish that he had brought two bottles instead of the one. Luckily, Ramona was prepared for such a possibility and sacrificed a bottle of her own, one whose label displayed a goat wreathed in grape vines.

Dinner, to fill in the details, was a spinach salad topped with shrimp and sea scallops, squash soup, and fresh crusty bread from Ramona's electronic breadmaker. It was a light meal, high on protein and low on carbohydrates, just the food to inspire conversation rather than sleep. More importantly, it was the breadmaker that inspired their conversation on automata. Unless this subject was already waiting in the back of Ramona's mind, the breadmaker simply an impetus, a launchpad for a rocket she had previously armed.

Richard was sure, in retrospect, that Ramona had invited him to dinner because of her thesis. Ramona, dear sweet unattainable Ramona, was working on her graduate degree in English literature at Columbia and writing her thesis on *Automata in Western Literature as Symbol and Subject.* Or something like that. She knew of Richard's background in engineering and of his occasional forays into science fiction. He liked to think some of his stories might work their way into her thesis, although he was not egotistical enough to assume this would be the case. But at the time she simply said they should get together because she now lived in New York City. She said she always remembered his visits to her family in Connecticut with fondness, that in some ways she saw him as an uncle.

How could anyone resist such an invitation?

And so dinner, his hostess a woman young enough to be his daughter, but who was not his daughter. Ramona's hair shadowed one eye with the broad sweep of a raven's wing. She smiled enigmatically as a sphinx. "Could you have even imagined an electronic breadmaker thirty, forty years ago?"

She spoke plainly, but when Richard thought about what she said it seemed a riddle of a depth he could not fathom. "I just wrote about robots," he said. "About as simple as it got was the vacuum cleaner robot in the Jetsons. Not that I wrote the Jetsons."

"You can't get much simpler than making bread."

After dinner, Ramona cleared away the plates over Richard's protestations that, because she had prepared the meal, he should now clear and wash. She busied herself in the kitchen and returned with two wedges of chocolate cheesecake topped with raspberries and mint leaves.

At some point she mentioned her thesis.

At some point they debated definitions for the term automata.

Did Richard say "The dead that approximate the living?" He was sure he said something like that during his conversation with Ramona. But he was equally sure he corrected himself, no doubt in response to a raised eyebrow that communicated derision more expressively than words. Let him correct himself now as he did then. Death has nothing to do with it. Automata are non-biological, and thus neither dead nor alive, but assume aspects that we associate with the living.

Another raised eyebrow. A further refinement. There needs of course to be a maker with intent: a creator. Furthermore, the automata besides having the appearance of life, such as would be found with a doll, must also be capable of movement. And so: the non-biological fashioned to assume aspects of the living, with appearance and movement both being necessary aspects.

"Does this definition seem reasonable?" he asked.

Ramona nodded. "For the sake of argument, provisionally, yes."

Argument did naturally ensue, sporadically over the next couple of hours between mouthfuls of dessert, and sips of wine or coffee, the greatest heat being reserved for what might seem the most minor details. But it was at this point, before they began to cut and splice wires as it were to create a more perfect monster, a Rube Goldberg-like definition that would run on for pages of text, that Richard remembered an episode from his childhood. Truth be told, although he had used the conventions of science fiction in his stories, he had not given them much thought, employing robots and spaceships as one might the words and grammar of one's native language. Now, he saw connections he had never seen before.

He remembered lying in bed as a boy, the covers pulled up around his neck, the top sheet folded over so the blue woolen blanket would not scratch his face. He remembered his mother sitting beside the bed, with the lights out, telling him the stories she knew by heart, stories passed down to her from her mother, and so on back who knew how many generations. Some of the stories he later discovered in books when he began to read to himself, others he never found and these may have existed only in the oral tradition of his family.

"Do you mind," he asked Ramona, "if I tell you a story I learned from my mother?"

"Of course not," she said, shaving off a thin forkful of cheesecake.

So he told her the tale of the boy Levi, who lived in Egypt during the time of Moses, and who created a Golem of blue clay. He told her of the adventures these two friends shared, how once they sealed the temple cats in earthen jugs so their shrieks drowned out the priests' incantations, how another time they floated a burning man of reeds down the river so the fishermen fled to shore crying that the spirits of the underworld were loosed, and how yet another time they paraded an old blind crocodile among the market stalls and took donations in the name of Sobek, the long-jawed god of the Pharaohs.

Ramona clapped her hands. "Why that's wonderful," she said. "You say it was your mother who told you this story? But tell me what happened to the Golem. In all the stories I know, they are destroyed."

Richard nodded, impressed that she had seen where the story was headed. He had considered leaving off the ending, which touched on troubling aspects of Levi's character, but now felt compelled to continue. He told Ramona how Levi fled with Moses and the Israelites from the Pharaoh's army, but surrendered to fear and attempted to swim the Red Sea. The Golem, ever at Levi's side, bore him on the waters when the boy's strength failed. But the Golem was only as strong as the materials from which it was made...

Richard paused, letting the implications of clay and water sink in.

Ramona closed her eyes and took a deep breath, inhaling as if the story carried a scent, a combination of smoky desert fires, spice-impregnated clothing, brackish water, and acrid fear. "So it ends."

"No!" He had been afraid she might think so. "Levi lived. When Moses led the Israelites between the parted waters of the Red Sea, he discovered Levi kneeling in the silt among the stranded fish and aquatic monsters. The boy was weeping, scooping up handfuls of mud and attempting to mold it as if dough, but it would not hold shape and trickled between his fingers. Moses lifted the boy onto his shoulders and told him to dry his eyes, he said the day was not one for tears but for rejoicing because on this day Levi was free."

Ramona nodded. Richard's words appeared to confirm, even strengthen her previous assessment of the story. "But Moses was right," Richard said. "There was cause for celebration. Levi crossed the Red Sea carried first by the Golem and then by Moses. My mother said Levi survived to father many children and, in later years, told them that during the Exodus he crossed the Red Sea in just two steps, only once touching the bottom of the sea. When his children asked how this was possible, he then told them this same tale."

Ramona and Richard did not argue further, if in fact they had been arguing, about the relative measures of pleasure and sorrow to be found in Levi's story. Instead they turned their attentions again to the definition of automata, elaborating and refining it in terms of the materials for their construction. The conversation became heated and, in his excitement, Richard forgot himself. He reached across the table to seize Ramona's hand, confusing the passions of intellectual discourse with those of desire.

Ramona stiffened. She sprang from the table, her chair squealing across the floor and her fork clattering on her dessert plate, calling attention to the fact that, as yet, she had barely nibbled at her cheesecake. "Hold on a second. I've got something you might like." She opened the door to what Richard assumed was her bedroom, although his brief glimpse inside revealed just the corner of a roll-top desk overburdened with books and papers and, on the wall above, the framed cover of a pulp magazine that depicted a woman, her blouse hanging in rags from her bosom, shrinking in terror from a towering robot.

Ramona returned waving a tattered green hardcover, the pages liberally marked with torn scraps of paper. "The seventeenth volume of Burton's *The Thousand Nights and One Night*, originally published as one of the unexpurgated supplements in 1888. This is a reprint of course."

Ah, Richard thought, remembering the story of a flying horse, fabricated by a magician, that the rider controlled by manipulating pins on its neck. But Ramona surprised him and read a tale with which he had no familiarity. "King Saleh of ancient times valued his daughter Farasche more than any treasure in his kingdom," she began, and then told of how the king's daughter took a giant Blackamoor as her lover. The king, upon discovering Farasche naked in her lover's arms, beheaded the man, chopping his body into pieces small enough to pass through the ring of his pinky finger.

Ramona did not read the story straight through but skipped from section to section, picking out the "good parts" as she called them, which Richard took to be those most relevant to her thesis. It soon became apparent that this was a tale of revenge, for the Blackamoor's father was a king in his own right and loved his son with an intensity equal to that born by King Saleh for his own daughter. The agent of the Moorish king's revenge was a golden falcon, so realistic that it might have hatched from a golden egg, delivered to King Saleh as a gift. But concealed behind the breast feathers of the falcon were twelve tiny golden men and, each night, these marched forth into the darkness of King Saleh's treasure room then returned to their safe haven, arms loaded with stolen gemstones. And each day, when the golden falcon was released into mechanical flight, it delivered the stolen gems to the Moorish king who now lurked by the castle gates in the disguise of a beggar.

This thievery went on for months, King Saleh all the time becoming more distraught at his inability to discover the culprit. Eventually, to protect his prized golden falcon, he brought it into his own bedroom. Richard knew from the way Ramona's voice rose that they were reaching the climax to the tale. "Hardly had the king's eyelids closed," she read, her own eyes widening, her cheeks glowing, "but the falcon's metal breast feathers parted and the troop of tiny golden men departed their barracks. The tiny men did not search for treasure this time. They each took up stations next to the sleeping king and, with one uniform motion, drew forth twelve tiny swords and raised them high. Then, as if they were not twelve men but one with but one thought in mind, they let fall their blades. In a single instant, King Saleh lost an eye, both ears, his nose, two fingers from his left hand, three from his right, two toes, and his organ for procreation."

Richard found this last part discomforting, as would any male, and crossed his legs and covered his lap with his hands. As a result, he almost missed hearing how the falcon hopped down from its perch and with one strike punctured the king's ribcage and retreated with his bloody heart in its beak.

Richard felt his own heart pound and, more disturbingly, a vague sense of embarrassment. He wondered if the story was intended for his benefit, a pointed reminder of his own earlier indiscretion.

Ramona looked at him expectantly, unaware of his discomfort.

"Revenge is a dish best served cold," he said, thinking it appropriate to the circumstances of the tale, and added that this was a Klingon proverb he had learned from an episode of *Star Trek*.

Ramona corrected him, pointing out that the correct attribution for the proverb was to the French novel, *Les Liasons Dangereuses*. She then said that although the Moorish king of the tale had taken his revenge, still he had lost his son and now he had nothing, not even his revenge, to keep him going. He was, in effect, as dead to life as the enemy whose life he had stolen. He had become an automaton.

Richard decided that he had been utterly mistaken as to Ramona's intent. If anything, she intended him to understand that passion is what makes us human. He chastised himself for his cowardliness and reached again across the table to where Ramona's hand rested upon her placemat.

But before his action was half completed, as if Ramona anticipated just such an expression on his part, she pushed herself to her feet and excused herself from the table. Richard made to rise as well, but she held out her hand. "Relax. I just remembered another story that you must hear. Back in a moment."

Richard wondered, while staring at her still unfinished wedge of cheesecake, how often she shared the results of her studies with her parents, how sympathetic they were to her research. He then downed the remainder of his wine and refilled the glass, topping off Ramona's glass as well. The goat on the bottle's label seemed to regard him with a lecherous eye and he turned the bottle ninety degrees to the left.

Ramona returned with a sheaf of papers, a draft of her actual thesis. "It's in here somewhere," she said, shuffling the sheets like an unwieldy deck of cards. By this point in the evening Richard's mind was swimming with so many ideas, not to mention wine, that he could scarcely follow the tale once she began. Her tale ebbed and flowed like the sea, following the changing fortunes of a watchmaker who achieved fame from the innovative dioramas he built for the clock towers of his alpine home, but who then accepted a commission from an unnamed benefactor. Richard understood Ramona's interests better now and was not surprised when the commission was revealed to be for a mechanical Venus, a woman automaton perfect down to the smallest detail, from the arch of her backbone to the downy hairs on her arms. Such an enterprise was doomed, Richard knew, to spectacular failure.

It may have been during this tale, or another of remarkable similarity, that Richard remembered a scrap of story from his mother's measureless horde. He interrupted Ramona, perhaps rudely, but for once his enthusiasm matched hers. He told her of a Christmas gift, a masterpiece of the Nuremberg toy-makers art that, to his mind, seemed a strange reflection of their own evening meal. The toy featured a well-to-do family of mechanical dolls—a father, mother, and boy in short pants—assembled beside an outdoor picnic table. When the mechanism was wound, the already seated grandmother waved her hand, calling the rest of the family to sit down and say grace. The little family was then served lunch by a bandy-legged chimpanzee dressed in the uniform of a butler. Meanwhile, high above the feast, shadowy forms swung among the leaves of a great spreading plane tree. These spies were first glimpsed as a pair of eyes here, a waving arm there, until being revealed as a mischievous band of wild chimps, which then disrupted the picnic by throwing bananas down upon the diners.

But if Richard had been impolite for interrupting Ramona, she now fully repaid the favor, exclaiming, "Why I know this story! 'The Darkling Feast', right?"

He stared at her, knowing nothing of its provenance outside of his mother's voice.

"The boy who receives the gift at first finds great pleasure in it," Ramona said. "But then abruptly refuses to play with it any further. His parents do not understand this change in his affections. The automaton is, after all, an expensive present. A doctor, an old family friend, is brought in to examine the child but finds no defect in his body or mind. But the boy implores the doctor to stay the night and this he agrees to do."

Ramona raised her small chin and rested it in the cup of her hand. "Is this the same story you remember?" she asked, "There are, as you say, interesting similarities to our own evening. A doctor and his young charge, alone together."

Richard nodded, although he felt uncomfortable agreeing, as she now seemed to read more into the story than he intended.

"Together that night," Ramona continued, "the boy in his bed and the doctor seated beside him, with no illumination but moonlight reflected off the snow, together they watch the automaton while the clocks of the city slowly tick off the hours. The chimes of midnight pass. One o'clock, two o'clock, three o'clock, four. They fall asleep, but then start into wakefulness at a small scraping sound that emanates from the automaton. It is the chimp, the one dressed as the family's butler. The chimp is in motion although the automaton has not been wound. He removes his jacket, his vest, his ruffled shirt, and then, hopping first on one leg and then the other, he strips off his breeches and drops these to the ground. Now naked but for his natural suit of hair, he climbs up into the tree to rejoin his cousins, who greet him and pull him into the darkened interior of the foliage."

"And the boy. Let's not forget the boy," Richard said. "He takes the doctor's hand and says 'In the dark, he is free.'"

"In the dark, we are all free," Ramona said, smiling that same enigmatic and infuriating smile. "Speaking of which, don't you think candlelight would be more appropriate for this time of night?" She winked and then, without waiting for an answer, retreated again to the kitchen. She returned with a candlestick holder and two white candles. The candlestick holder was thickly coated with wax drippings but it took only a little imagination for Richard to discern the shapes of two twined bodies joined in either passion or anger.

"A gift," Ramona said, as if this explained everything. She screwed the candles into the waiting arms of the recipients. "Would you do the honors?" She passed a matchbook to Richard.

Richard succeeded after only three matches and one burnt finger. In spite of the romantic shadows flickering about the ceiling and on Ramona's face, he was still a little miffed. Not only had he discovering his family story was written by a stranger, but it had somehow been hijacked that evening by Ramona. And Ramona, dear sweet Ramona, who he had known since before she could read, did nothing but communicate in riddles. "What exactly is your thesis about?" he asked. His smile could not mask his petulant tone.

"Power."

"Power? Surely that's not all."

"Power comes in many forms." Ramona's voice changed into the parody of some foreign accent and she added "political, economical, and sexual." She emphasized each word by thumping her fork on her placemat.

Richard asked why she spoke in the funny voice, and she laughed. "Sorry, I didn't notice," she said. "There's a radio show that comes on in the evening. I think the DJ is from the Caribbean, maybe Jamaica, and he repeated that phrase three or four times during a single broadcast. It's become part of the common vernacular among my circle of friends. I'm most interested in the sexual dimensions of power, as you might guess, although they all become intertwined."

She then began a dry discourse on power structures of which all Richard would later remember is her saying how automata can either represent the current power structure, thereby reinforcing it, or they can stand in opposition to it, in that case being an example of wish-fulfillment by the dispossessed. Richard breathed deeply to avoid yawning, then raised a hand to hide a yawn that could not be prevented. He tried to focus on her eyes, her lips, the way her tongue flickered outside the cage of her teeth. He nodded at what he thought were appropriate times.

Perhaps Richard's gaze inadvertently drifted toward Ramona's breasts, or maybe what she next said had nothing to do with any particular action of his, but was the natural progression of a line of argument that he had missed.

"Have you ever thought about your power?" she said, the sudden intensity of her voice shocking him into alertness. "Your power here tonight. You a man. I a woman. A woman who invited you, an old friend, into her apartment. A woman with whom you shared dinner and wine. How much wine have we had? One bottle, two bottles? Now let's say something happened, something you wanted but I did not. What would you call that?"

He knew the word she was looking for, although he was uncomfortable saying it aloud. Nevertheless, he answered her, framing the word with his lips although he did not truly speak it, merely mouthed it. "Rape," he said.

"Yes. Of course. It would be rape." She did not have any trouble speaking, pausing only long enough to give her subject an additional emphasis. "But, given the situation, given your power in the situation, you would not be found guilty by a jury of your peers. Let us not forget that your peers would be men. Your peers would excuse you. They would point to the invitation. They would point to the wine."

Richard did not know how the conversation had so quickly changed from something light and fanciful to its antithesis. Perhaps, he wondered, he had been mistaken about the conversation all along. "What exactly do you mean?"

"Let me show you," she said. She lifted her fork and licked it to remove the last few crumbs from the tines. "A simple fork. Hardly in the same category as a knife. But an instrument nevertheless capable of inflicting damage."

Ramona wore a long-sleeved purple dress that buttoned at the wrists. The dress was vaguely Japanese in its severity and contrasted so sharply with the cut-off shorts and pink T-shirts she wore as a child that Richard could scarcely believe this was the same person. She now shifted the fork from right hand to left and, without releasing it, unbuttoned the two buttons that cinched her right cuff and rolled the sleeve up to expose her naked forearm. She rested her arm upon the table, elbow braced against the wood, pale interior upturned and glowing orange in the candlelight.

"What I want you to do," she said, so matter-of-factly that she might have asked Richard to pass the salt, "is to stab me with this fork. Stab me here." She tapped her bared forearm with the desert fork.

Richard laughed. A little nervously, but laughter nevertheless. The request was too ludicrous to entertain.

Ramona smiled, and her smile was cold as winter dawn. "Of course, you laugh," she said. "Of course, you refuse, even though you are a man and have the power in the situation. You see me as the weaker sex. To attack me offends your sense of self." She put down the fork and settled back into her chair. She fingered the coral necklace at her throat. "You do not want to see my blood."

Richard nodded, knowing that some response was called for but feeling, deep down, that he had been put into a position where he affirmed more than he believed.

Ramona sensed this. "Oh, but I've confused you," she said. "Worried you. Really, I was just trying to make a point. We were talking about power and what it means to be human." She reached across the distance that separated them, taking his hand in her own and running her thumb back and forth across its veined back. She used the same arm she had so recently asked Richard to mutilate, and this gesture, this choice of which arm to use, he found strangely erotic. His breath quickened and his skin pimpled with gooseflesh. Without releasing his hand, Ramona said, "Look closely at my arm. What do you see?"

"It's very pretty," he said.

"Look more closely." She squeezed his hand.

He shrugged, smiled a little. "Like the arm of a goddess," he said, trying to be poetic.

Her grip became almost painful.

"You must work out," he said, making light of his discomfort. He pulled back, testing her grip, but her fingers did not budge.

"You just don't get it, do you?" Ramona suddenly released him so he flopped backward into the wooden arms of his chair. "Can't you see? There are no freckles. No scars. No hair." She thrust her arm out again for his inspection. "It's not real."

She was right of course. In spite of the fact that her arm had the feel of flesh and her palm was marked with the creases and lines so beloved by fortunetellers, her skin was unblemished. Richard flexed his bruised fingers. "That explains a lot," he said. He was tempted to disbelieve her but, now that he knew what to look for, he could detect a hair-thin line that ran from the bunched-up cloth of her sleeve down to her wrist, which it circled like a scribed meridian.

Ramona caught the movement of his eyes. "That's better," she said. She slid the fingernails of her left hand into this thin crevice and rolled back her skin to expose the plastic and metal armature beneath. In some places the plastic was the pink of a naked Barbie doll, in others the black of old licorice. The metal supports shone with the pure silver-white of aluminum. The skin flap was supported by a flexible black mesh.

Her arm no longer looked in the least bit human.

Richard must have gasped, because Ramona immediately said, "It's just my arm. My forearm. The rest is still me." She raised her left arm: "This is me." She placed her palm between her breasts in the vicinity of her heart: "This." She tapped her forehead: "And this."

"How did it happen? No one told me." He flushed. It had been years, many years, since he had sent her family a Christmas card.

"It's not exactly the sort of thing you advertise. Do you really want to hear the gruesome details?"

Her sarcasm set him more at ease. "Sure."

"This was about seven years ago, back while I was in high school. I didn't go to many parties then. I had friends but they weren't in the right groups, if you know what I mean. We might get together to study, to talk about this and that, for dinner or a sleepover, but nothing too wild. Parties seemed an excuse for drinking and letting pimply-faced boys grope under your sweater." Ramona lifted a coffee mug and took a sip. At some point, Richard realized, although he was not sure when, Ramona had removed the emptied wine glasses and brought coffee to the table. "I'm sure I gave off an aura that said I had better things to do."

He tasted his own coffee, glad for the warmth, glad to have something to do with his hands.

"Anyway, during my senior year" Ramona said, "I became friends with a girl who moved in the circles that had parties and I ended up going to a party with her that winter. There were more familiar faces than I had expected, familiar as in comfortable, people that I could relax and be myself with. I even ended up talking with people that I didn't talk with much at school. I enjoyed myself more than I would have guessed."

Something about the look on Richard's face must have given away his thoughts. "It's not one of those stories," Ramona said. "Not where a bunch of snobs pretend to be friends only to play a trick on the odd-girl-out. There were cliques, sure, and I am sure that they followed various socio-economic patterns. Political, economical, sexual." Ramona smiled again at her joke, and Richard now smiled also, recognizing it as such. "But there wasn't a concerted attempt to reinforce these structures. Such structures tend to reinforce themselves anyway. Although, that said, I am sure that I was uncomfortable interacting in a novel situation with people that were not part of my group, even if I did not consciously recognize the fact at the time.

"When I left the party, a bit on the early side, but I was certainly not the first to leave, I found my car had a flat tire. My parents' car, I should say, that I had borrowed to drive to the party.

"I had never had a flat tire before.

"I stared at it. I pressed the toe of my shoe against the bulging rubber. I tried to see if there was something stuck in the tire, but this was difficult at night with only the porch and garage lights and strange shadows everywhere.

"I reached what seemed the only conclusion possible and stormed back into the party. 'Who let the air out of my tire?' I cried. 'My tire's flat. Did someone let the air out?'

"In memory, I see everyone within earshot looking at me as if I had gone off my rocker. Of course, no one had let the air out. Sometimes a flat tire is just a flat tire.

"Two of the boys came out with me, set their beers down in a snow bank, and changed the tire. They used the spare from the trunk and showed such proficiency with the jack that I was astonished. Their breath puffed like smoke in the cold. The spinning tire iron flickered like a strobe. When they were done, they clanked beer bottles together. One said, 'How about a kiss?' I said, 'Okay,' and gave them each a kiss. I walked with them back into the party, found the friend who I had come with and told her everything was all right, and then left.

"I got into my car and tried to turn it around in the driveway, but there were too many other parked cars. I didn't want to embarrass myself by going back into the party again to ask people to move their cars, so I backed down the driveway.

"It was night. It was winter. The driveway was steep and slick with ice. I hadn't had my driver's license very long. Maybe I had drunk too much alcohol, but I don't think so. I am sure that my mind was a whirl what with my stupid accusation at the party and because I had just kissed two boys.

"To make a long story short, I got stuck in a snowbank part way down the driveway. I tried to go forward, then switched into reverse. My wheels spun but the car did not move. I pressed down harder on the accelerator. Then suddenly I was loose and speeding backward down the driveway. Then, instead of hitting the brake as I intended, I stomped down on the accelerator again.

"The car shot down the driveway, crossed the road, plowed through a snowbank, and slid down the hillside. Backward. I hit a tree. Next thing I knew, I was lying on my back in the snow. People were helping me up. Trying to get me out of the snow. I tried to move my arm but I couldn't. I couldn't feel it. I'm lucky that someone tied a tourniquet around it. Otherwise I might have bled to death. My forearm was nearly severed at the elbow."

Ramona raised her arm, the motion smooth and unhurried, so that the loose coil of rubbery skin barely shifted. She held her palm out vertically and bent each finger in turn first downward to touch her palm then back up to its original position. She then separated the second from the third fingers in the time-honored "Live long and prosper" Vulcan greeting of *Star Trek*. "Pretty good really," she said.

Like a well-oiled machine, Richard could not avoid thinking.

"I've also got scars all over the top of my head but those don't show." Ramona shook her dark hair so it slithered across her shoulders.

"I'm sorry," Richard said. He was fascinated by the arm's mechanism from an engineering perspective and wished he could examine it in more detail. But to voice these thoughts seemed an invasion of her privacy.

Ramona picked up her fork again and held it out to Richard. "Here," she said, placing her hand over his and prying apart his fingers with her own. "Take it." Richard had no choice. To not respond would have been to let the fork fall.

Richard's stomach lurched. He had thought the fork episode over but here it was happening again.

"Knowing what you now know, could you stab me?" She pulled aside the skin flap so the plastic and metal underneath were clearly visible. "I would not feel it. Nor could you hurt or damage the arm. So what is there to stop you?" She raised her voice. "Stab me now." No longer a question, but an order.

Richard stared at his fist and the protruding fork. There were hairs on the back of his hand and on the areas between his knuckles. His skin was dry and crinkled, crowned with the gray remnant of scab from a week-old scrape. His hand trembled. The fork, jutting from his fist at the same awkward angle he used as a kid to spear green beans off his plate, also trembled.

He looked at Ramona, hoping her face, her eyes, might give away her thoughts. She stared back at him. Her lower lip protruded and her breath came in short angry bursts through her nose.

"Stab me. It's very simple."

Richard grimaced. He shook his head. "You know I can't do that. It's too much a part of you."

He thought he had made the correct decision. He thought perhaps this was another test and maybe she now approved of his answer. But then she grabbed the fork from him, as if he might fight her for its possession, and jabbed it hard against her forearm. The fork glanced off. She stabbed at her arm again. And again. Three times in all, each time brutally direct, without the hesitation one might expect in an attack on one's own body. She then laid the fork with its bent tines very carefully beside her plate. She extended her artificial arm for Richard's inspection, rotating it back and forth at the elbow. "See, you cannot hurt it."

Richard nodded. He said nothing about the pockmarks he now noticed in the plastic, the shiny scratches in the metal. There were many more than she could have made just then. "I'm sorry," Richard said. He didn't know what else to say.

"Sorry?" Ramona snorted. "Sorry? This was the best thing that ever happened to me. It's the new improved me. The stain-free, accept-no-substitutes, every-day's-like-Sunday, bionic super me. And, do you want to know what?" She didn't give him a chance to answer. "If I had my choice, if I had the money—the economical power—every bit of me would be like this. This would be me." She swiveled the fingers and thumb of her false hand and formed a fist.

Dinner might as well have ended at that point, but it went on for another half hour.

Ramona got up to clear the table and, while her back was turned, Richard stole the mangled fork from her placemat and slipped it into his pants pocket. She must have noticed but, thankfully, she said nothing. She just carried the stacked saucers, the rattling coffee cups, and the plate with its crumbled wedge of cheesecake into the kitchen.

When she returned, the right sleeve of her dress was once again buttoned at her wrist. She and Richard sat on opposite sides of the empty table and conversed like wary strangers. Richard asked Ramona about her parents and her sister, about any bit of personal information he could dredge from memory. But he did not hear her answers. Instead he watched her arm, the gestures she made, trying to detect the movements by which he might differentiate the real from the fake. Each time she actually moved her right arm, he shrank into his chair. He was convinced that at any moment, in spite of his preventative measures, she would again strip back her sleeve and force him to participate in a violent demonstration.

After a suitable length of time had passed, so that his leaving could not be ascribed to aversion, Richard stretched, yawned, and said it was well past the hour he usually turned in. Ramona saw him to the door of her apartment. She hugged him goodbye after a fashion, circling him with her arms although her body did not press against his, and gave him a peck on the cheek. Out of politeness, he said how much he had enjoyed the evening. She suggested they get together again. He said that would be nice.

Richard didn't take a cab, preferring the bustle of late-night pedestrians along Broadway, the sense of connectedness to the human horde. He walked, hands thrust into his pockets, fabric tight against his knuckles, and thought about how, somewhere along the path between childhood and adulthood, he had lost Ramona. Or maybe she had lost herself. The little girl who sat in his lap at Christmas and tied ribbons in his hair was long gone, replaced by... maybe he should have asked her more about her arm, about why she would, if given a choice, replace herself with a manufactured creature of plastic and metal. But he knew what Ramona would have said in response. The same thing she always said: something about power, about the relations between men and women, about matters political, economical, and sexual.

"Political, economical, and sexual." Richard spoke these words aloud, unconsciously aping the accent Ramona had employed, and elicited a puzzled glance from a passing co-ed.

But Richard found it hard to believe Ramona would reject her own body all because of politics, because of a misplaced idea about oppression. He told himself that she was just young. Foolishly idealistic. He considered calling her parents. He considered searching on-line to see if this was the manifestation of some crazed urban subculture. He wondered what he would do if, in spite of their rather ambivalent parting, she should phone.

He turned the ideas, the possibilities over in his mind in much the same way he fingered the bent fork in his pocket as he walked along. He explored the fork's blade-like handle with its faint decorative scrollwork, the smooth flare of metal at its working end, and the three misshapen tines. He pressed the sharp points against his finger pads. The sensation was not pleasurable, but it assured him that he was alive.

Monkey Shines

I. King Kong vs. Mecha Kong

King Kong was all of six feet tall on a good day. He had a barrel chest and a belly tight and round as a beach ball, the kind of physique you earn from a combination of genetics, cabernet sauvignon, and long hours sitting in front of a computer. His fur was synthetic and his teeth bared in a permanent smile. Whether you thought his growl sounded more angry than sexual, or vice versa, depended only upon which side of the bed you awoke. "Goddamn it," King Kong said, "stop fooling around and get over here."

Mecha Kong was seven feet tall, but almost two feet of that was owed to her metal headdress. Maybe the headdress was intended as a radar antenna, what with its bifurcating wires and glittering saucers, but it looked about as functional as foil antlers. Mecha Kong's fur was tinsel and she had pointed silver breasts. When she moved metal whispered against metal and the scent of graphite filled the air. "You don't own me," she said in a voice like an amplified music box.

"I never said I did." King Kong lunged for her, but she jumped behind a brick-red couch, leaving strands of tinsel clinging to his outstretched paw. "Stop that," he said. "I don't want to fight."

"Then stop chasing me. Treat me like an adult. I'm not a child. I'm not one of your toys." While Mecha Kong talked, King Kong rocked on the balls of his feet, prepared for her to dash off in any direction. But she knew his tricks and had a few of her own. She grabbed an embroidered pillow and threw it at him. He knocked it aside, but she had already bolted for the stairway.

"Come back here." King Kong vaulted to the top of the couch and pounded his chest with wide swinging blows of his hairy fists. He howled. This was his domain and he wanted everyone to know it. But the world was not truly his to command. When he leaped to the floor, the rug slipped out from under him and he tumbled furry ass over elbows to end up on his back, legs kicking holes in the air.

Mecha Kong was already taking the stairs two at a time, but she stopped and turned when she heard the crash behind her. She leaned over the banister and laughed, reprising a tune stolen from "South Pacific." "Maybe I should spray your ass with Pledge, then you can dust the floor while you're down there."

"The only thing I'm going to dust the floor with is you." King Kong kicked the rug away and climbed to his feet.

"Oh dear me. Whatever shall I do?" She wrung her hands, then raked her metal fingernails, each shaped like a perfect almond slice, along the banister.

"Don't do that." King Kong spoke but, like a master ventriloquist, you never saw his lips move. He spoke with the voice of someone who was tired, sweaty, and covered in synthetic fur.

"What's the matter? You worried that I'm going to damage one of your precious things?"

"Have some respect for good craftsmanship."

"Maybe if you started to have some respect for simple human feelings."

"Simple human feelings? Don't make me laugh. You're a machine. And not a particularly well made one at that." He thought he had her there. Trapped in a logical conundrum of the sort that caused evil robots to blow up in old sci-fi flicks: if I am a machine then I can't have emotions, but if I have emotions then I can't be a machine. Circuits overheat. Smoke pours out. Then boom! She had to appreciate that. But she surprised him.

"More human than you can ever hope to be."

He had no response to that but a wounded roar and was soon chasing her pell-mell up the stairs and down the hallway, his feet slapping the maple floorboards, his rubbery knuckles swinging alongside his ankles. He caught up with her at the master bedroom. She tried to slam the door, but he had already shoved his shoulder through the entrance, and she didn't slam the door very hard anyway.

"I've got you now."

She backed up against the bed, one hand extended in front of her chest, the other steadying her headdress. Mecha Kong was really much better crafted than King Kong gave her credit for. She was made of lightweight and dent-proof plasticized aluminum, with rivets every inch, and a money-back

guarantee. It was all that tinsel floating around that made her look cheap.
The tinsel was always sloughing off, and she was always gluing more back on.
When the servants searched through the vacuum cleaner bags for valuable
trinkets, all they ever came up with were thick tangles of silver tinsel.

It was Sunday.

The servants had the day off.

King Kong tackled Mecha Kong, and she fell backward across the bed.
"Oh," she said. "Oh my." He pawed at her, grunting and pulling out tufts of
tinsel, gnawing at the lobes of her metal ears. His breath smelt of garlic and
chocolate. She guided his fumbling hands to the catches along her hips and
thighs and, released, slipped out of her metal leggings like a shucked oyster,
her skin smooth and glistening with sweat. A shove and the leggings clattered
to the floor. She bent forward and parted the fur between King Kong's legs.
She found and pulled the tab of the exposed zipper, then circled him with
her metal arms and dragged him down on top of her.

King Kong and Mecha Kong fell asleep after they made love. He was
naked, except for a pair of cotton briefs, and slept curled on his side, genitals
clutched in both hands as if afraid that burglars would steal them under cover
of the night. She wore a Hawaiian shirt decorated with martinis and palm
trees that she had bought on their last vacation together. She slept on her
back, one arm thrown across her face, as if she dreamed that she was still on
the beach at Honolulu and was protecting her eyes from the sun.

She woke well before dawn. The only sounds were those of the rain:
the spatter of drops against the slate shingles and the gurgle of water that
wormed its way through leaf-clogged gutters. The window was ajar and the
air smelt of grass and ferns and garden flowers, of mushrooms and mildew.
Of growing things.

She had felt a change come over her body, and it was that change which
had awakened her.

She was pregnant.

With a daughter.

She looked at the man sleeping beside her but she did not wake him. He
would not believe her, even though it was the same with her mother. "I knew,"
her mother said, "I knew the moment you were conceived."

Across the room, two hulking silhouettes were outlined against a pearly
window. The body suits, both now discarded husks, sat on stuffed chairs
and eyed each other across the small table where breakfast was sometimes
served. They seemed at peace, engaged in idle chatter over coffee. But that

was a deceit. The only time they were truly alive was when they were fighting, or making love.

She giggled.

Her husband woke and looked up at her with puffy eyes, his mouth already set in a grimace. "What is it?"

Mecha Kong shook her head. She had been granted a vision of what lay in store for her, for the man with whom she has chosen to share her life, and for the unborn daughter that she now carried. She foresaw the day when their daughter was three or four years old. Blond and blue-eyed. Old enough for Halloween. Old enough to go trick-or-treating. Old enough to be the center of an argument over whether she should wear the costume of a Furry or a Mech. It was a vision of the future that was ludicrous but, even should it never come to pass, still somehow true.

"Nothing," Mecha Kong said to King Kong. "Nothing with which you need concern yourself." She said no more but, as she lay beside her husband waiting for sleep to return, she ran through possible baby names in her mind. She eventually eliminated all names but one, her mother's middle name Samantha.

II. The Plastic Jungle

Who knew when it started? There were always houseplants. Clay pots of purple, white, and pink violets. Geraniums on the kitchen table. A spiderplant hanging in the bathroom window. But one day Sal realized that there were plants he could not identify. "What's that?" He pointed at a scaly brown bulb the size of a coconut crowned with long green spikes. Its leaves were the expected green but had the texture of wood.

"A cycad," Sarah said. "They're ancient, from the time of the dinosaurs."

"What about the plant upstairs?"

Sarah looked puzzled.

"You know. The one with all the arms, like a family of octopuses that got caught in a whirlpool."

"Do you mean the night-blooming cereus?"

"It has flowers?"

"Not yet. But it will. The flowers open and die off in a single night."

"Seems a waste."

"They're pollinated by bats who find the flowers by smell. Just wait. They say you can smell a single flower from a mile away."

Sal assumed she was exaggerating and so he was surprised when he came home from work one evening, opened the front door, and smelled a perfume that he did not recognize, pervasive but subtle as a siren's song. He should have guessed its origin but he had already forgotten his conversation with Sarah. He tracked the scent to the upstairs guest room, where he found Sarah seated among the greenery, their daughter Samantha swaddled in a pile blanket and asleep in her lap. Even then he did not understand until Sarah placed a finger to her lips and whispered, "The night-blooming cereus is blooming." He spent the next hour in the room listening to Sarah read a book of poetry aloud that neither Samantha, he, nor the cereus understood.

In the months that followed, Sarah's plant menagerie continued to expand until it reached the limits dictated by available light and suitable living space. That should have been the end of it, but Sal came home from a business trip to find that contractors had ripped a hole in the outer wall of the living room and erected the metal skeleton for a two-story greenhouse. Naturally, Sal and Sarah had an argument. Naturally, they ended up in bed together, and, as he drifted off to sleep breathing in the briny scent of her skin, Sal agreed to her project.

They had a private celebration when the greenhouse was finished. They wandered, footsteps cushioned by springy moss, beneath the canopy of interlaced leaves made by the palms, bananas, pomegranates, and aromatic hardwoods. Sal tugged at a bearded lichen, ran a finger along the lacey edge of an orchid's bloom, and bent back the tender young frond of a fiddlehead fern, its tip curled as tightly as a baby's fist. They sat on a Victorian bench imported from England and toasted each other with glasses of Vive Cliquot. "It's like an exotic Olympic Peninsula," Sal said, genuinely astonished at Sarah's creation.

Then the animals arrived. Frogs, who hid during the daylight hours, but sent up a chorus of competing voices as soon as the sun set. Silvery fish that darted among the papyrus and lily stems in a circular pond. Guinea fowl. Finches. And, finally, the monkey. The monkey was a filthy thing, a scrawny shadow that hid among the leaves, trailing Sal from above, then suddenly screamed and unleashed a barrage of twigs, half-eaten fruit, and dung. Sal was not sure if this was simply the way of all monkeys or if this one was defective. Maybe, he thought, the monkey would behave more like a proper pet if it didn't have a jungle in which to play.

Their daughter Samantha was the only person for whom the monkey seemed to truly care. Maybe it was her small size, so similar to his own that he considered her a relation. Or perhaps it was the unadulterated joy that

Samantha found in playing the simplest games: passing a stick from hand to hand, balancing pebbles one atop the other, splashing water at the fish in the tiny pond. Samantha was the one who named the monkey Bobo. "Why Bobo?" Sal asked. "All monkeys are named Bobo," Samantha said with the implacable logic of a four-year old. She and Bobo would play together for hours, and when she left for meals or a nap, Bobo would mope, only rousing himself to vent his frustrations upon intruders in the greenhouse.

Sarah said that everything was perfect, even the tempestuous monkey. But if everything was perfect, then why did she leave Sal one autumn day? Why did she pack two suitcases with clothing, jewelry, and her favorite Hiroshige print, the one showing pedestrians crossing a bridge in the slanting rain, and drive off with Samantha in the red convertible, leaving Sal behind with everything they had built together?

In his youth, Sal had been perceived as selfish by even his family and closest friends, a behavior that he had excused with a smile and the phrase: "Nothing personal, it's just business." But if marriage had changed him, divorce changed him still more. He fired the servants, took to wearing a nylon running suit, and only left his bedroom to buy groceries. He bought Campbell's tomato soup, Nabisco saltines, and Hungry Man TV dinners, the same foods that had been his favorites when he was a kid.

Then the monkey died.

Sal had neglected the greenhouse like everything else, treating it like a foreign country that he dimly remembered once visiting. But the scent of death was unmistakable and led him to a maggoty corpse surrounded by buzzing flies. The dead monkey lay on a bed of yellowed leaves and dried moss. The small pond was also dry and the fish that once swam in it were gone, probably victims of the monkey's hunger. Sal poked at the monkey with a stick. In death, the monkey seemed much smaller than in life.

The next day, Sal called a contractor and had all the vegetation removed from the greenhouse. Maybe the contractor sold some of the plants. Maybe he had them all burned at the dump. Sal didn't care. The jungle as he had known it was gone. In its place, over the next six months, he assembled a plastic reproduction that was as close to the original as time and his memory allowed.

On the day of its completion, he walked his familiar route beneath the shiny green leaves and hanging fruit. The moss compressed beneath his shoes, but sprang back to its original height as soon as he passed. Cinnamon and clove wafted through the air from hidden vents. The orchids, the lichens, and even the fiddlehead ferns were all as he remembered. Better than he remembered because the orchid did not show a bruise, not a single blemish, when he pinched its petals.

He sat on a cast-iron bench and stared at his reflection in the central pond. Plastic lilies, each in bloom, floated on the pond's hard mirrored surface. If a coin were tossed it would glance off the pond without a ripple. A frog's chirp sounded from a speaker hidden among the lily pads, the trill of a finch from another speaker wired to a tree branch.

The leaves rustled nearby, a tentative sound easily confused with the effect of a breeze, but no breeze was blowing. Sal did not look up. Palm fronds rasped against each other, then stilled. Sal glanced at his wristwatch. He did not look up, even when the rustling began again from directly overhead. The leaves rustled but did not fall.

Seconds flickered by on Sal's wristwatch and, at exactly three o'clock, a monkey dropped from the tree above Sal. The monkey landed in a crouch by the pool but immediately righted himself to stand on his bandy legs. The monkey had large dark eyes set in a wise face. His fur was so well groomed and of such a russet hue that he appeared to be wearing a tailored jacket. If not for his tail, he might have been confused with an elderly gentleman come to discuss financial matters with Sal.

The monkey had landed facing the bench to the right of where Sal sat. The monkey now cocked his head first to one side and then the other, appearing to evaluate the empty spot on the bench. Sal slid over so as to be directly in front of monkey. The monkey nodded his head in apparent satisfaction, then extended his hand toward where Sal sat on the bench. In the monkey's hand was a bright red fruit, brighter and redder than any apple or pomegranate Sal had ever seen.

Sal looked at the fruit but did not take it.

After exactly one minute, during which he held his pose immobile as a statue, the monkey withdrew his offering. The monkey then walked twice around the bench, on the second circuit stepping precisely where he had on the first, and came to a stop in front of Sal once again. The monkey held out the fruit in exactly the same manner as before, but Sal refused to do anything but look at it. After one minute, the monkey withdrew his offering, but this time walked over to and shinnied up a palm tree, glancing back once before he disappeared among the fronds, which rustled and then were still.

After the monkey left, Sal rose from the bench to leave. The monkey was a miracle of rare device, he thought, a descriptive phrase that he had once heard, although he no longer remembered where. He planned to return tomorrow at the same time to watch the same scenario play itself out again. He would return and he knew that he could count on the monkey to return as well. There was a consistency to life in the plastic jungle that he liked. A consistency to which he already looked forward. But one day, not tomorrow, or even the day after tomorrow, he would take the offered fruit and eat it.

III. Rise and Shine

The young woman had hitchhiked all summer up and down the west coast. She had no set destination but, if you believed her, she let the wind carry her along in whatever direction it was blowing. It's easier to walk with the wind than against it she said and, should you catch a ride, it still saves on gas.

Her friends called her Sam. So did everyone else for that matter.

Her blond hair was cut short and stuffed inside a Greek fisherman's cap, a few stray strands on her forehead, tufts beside her temples that could pass for sideburns. She carried a tent strapped to an oversized backpack, but the tent leaked in the rain and she had become adept at finding free shelter. This skill had become more important ever since she made her way up to Washington state.

She had slept the previous night on an old logging road. It had been a gorgeous afternoon when she set up her tent, but the clouds had closed in during the night and when she awoke the next morning it was to a steady drizzle and the pungent aroma of damp pine needles. She ate a breakfast of granola, dried apricots, and instant coffee. She wrapped a garbage bag around her backpack, shouldered it, and then pulled an orange plastic poncho over both herself and her backpack. She looked like a day-glo hunchback as she stomped along the mist-shrouded track back to the highway, a south wind tugging at the skirt of her poncho.

The van that slowed to pick her up, once she reached the main road, sent a spray of muddy water across her boots. The driver, a young man in his mid-twenties with a scraggly beard and a chipped front tooth, cracked the passenger door ajar. "Hey, climb on up man. Where you headed?"

"Which way are you going?"

"Tacoma, then on to Seattle. I've got half a dozen deliveries to make. You help me unload, and I'll buy you lunch and drop you wherever you want."

The van was hauling glazed hams. The driver told Sam that the best part of his job was when he used a blowtorch to melt the brown sugar on the hams back at the factory. It was a good story but apparently his only story and, each time he told it, he sprayed spittle through the hole in his tooth when making the sound effect of a torch. But he was as good as his word and, after cheeseburgers and strawberry milkshakes, dropped Sam at the address she told him.

The house was a Victorian monstrosity at the end of a dead-end street, barely contained behind an iron fence, with peeling white paint and mossy shingles. There were four brick chimneystacks but no smoke, and the windows were covered with plywood.

"You sure this is it? Doesn't look like anybody's home."

"I have a key." Which was true, in a manner of speaking.

Sam ignored the front door and splashed across the soggy lawn, circling around the back of the house. She glanced at but did not linger by the twisted and blackened remnants of the greenhouse, globs of melted plastic hanging like alien fruit from the broken glass and girders. Her father, his body burnt almost beyond recognition, had been found in the greenhouse by the firemen who responded to the emergency call. Sam's mother had felt it best that neither she nor Sam attend the funeral. What could be gained by opening up old wounds? But soon thereafter Sam ran away from home, and she made a regular habit of running away until she turned eighteen. Past the age of eighteen, you couldn't really call it running away from home. It was just life on the road.

Sam pressed her thumb against a plastic box mounted by the rear door. There was a click, and the door swung open. Sam looked at her thumb. The last time she was here, she had needed a stool to reach the sensor panel. But even after all these years, the house still recognized her.

She dumped her backpack just inside the doorway, found a flashlight in one of the zippered outer pockets, and began to explore the shuttered house. Everything was new and old at the same time, familiar but dislocated with the intervening years. She maneuvered around the living room furniture, fingered yellow curtains that were now faded to ivory, and listened to the creak of floorboards beneath her adult weight. Most striking was the filth. Tin cans and the foil trays from TV dinners were everywhere; they spilled out of garbage bags, cluttered the kitchen counters, and were piled high on the couches, tables, and bookshelves. Didn't her father ever clean up after himself? The bedroom was the worst. She opened the door, but shut it again almost immediately, having picked out with her flashlight the erratic reflections of crumpled metal that extended from floor to ceiling.

Her father's study provided a retreat. There was the large cherry desk, an antique office chair upholstered in leather, and built-in bookshelves on every wall. The study was also still remarkably clean. She sat in the chair, one foot drawn up and tucked beneath her hip, the other touching the floor so that, by exerting just a little pressure, she could swivel the chair from side to side. She had crawled up onto this chair when she was a toddler, sometimes to sit in her father's lap while he typed at the computer, sometimes to play by herself, pushing off from the desk so that the chair would roll across the floor or spin like a merry-go-round.

Her father had collected toys but these were placed on the upper shelves where she could not reach them as a child. Now, yielding to a long repressed temptation, she began to pick through her father's collection. Her father's taste in toys extended from old-fashioned pull toys to mementos of the space age, tidily arranged but with no apparent organization. She found a wooden rabbit on wheels next to a sparking ray gun, a plastic Donald Duck ring next to a handheld pinball game. Training her flashlight on the top shelf, she started at the sight of eyes glistening in the darkened corner where the bookshelves met the ceiling. Then recognizing it as a doll of some sort, she pulled the office chair over so as to climb up and investigate.

It was a monkey. A toy monkey. He sat bent nearly double, his back against the ceiling, head thrust forward, and hands clasped in his lap. He had large black eyes, unblinking but animated by the beam from her flashlight. "Bobo," she said, whispering the name of her childhood pet but knowing even as she spoke that it was not he. Bobo was dead and gone for who knew how many years. She turned away, unable to look at the grin that stretched across the monkey's felt muzzle.

She rolled the chair back to its proper location and began an inspection of the desk's contents, unsure for what she was looking, but nevertheless confident that whatever artifacts it contained would reveal something of its former owner. But the desk had been cleaned out. The top drawer contained only paperclips, rubber bands, and some wintergreen lifesavers lying loose among the silver, green, and white confetti of their torn wrapper. There was also some Canadian change that her father had dumped into the drawer so it wouldn't contaminate the American money he kept in his pockets. Sam was stacking the coins in preparation for counting when, at a little before three o'clock, she heard a noise.

She dropped the coins and looked around, the light from her flashlight skittering across the bookshelves.

Nothing.

She took a deep breath and sat perfectly still. She cupped the head of the flashlight with her left palm, holding the flashlight below the level of the desk so that its glow would not give her away.

Something loose and wooden banged in the wind, and rain thrummed against the study window.

Her chair suddenly settled beneath her with a protracted groan.

Then she heard it again. A sound more rhythmic than anything perpetrated by the weather: feet being set down one after the other, but muted as if by socks. Then a jingle jangle from directly overhead.

She swung the flashlight upward. A reddish brown blur disengaged itself from the chain of the lamp hanging above her.

Sam ducked, throwing an arm up for protection.

It was exactly three o'clock.

The monkey landed on the floor facing her. He straightened and cocked his head from side to side, a mimicry of intelligence that suggested he was considering the identity of the woman who sat before him. Apparently satisfied, he extended a cupped but empty hand toward her. The monkey held this pose without a blink or a twitch.

Sam drew both her legs up onto the chair and hugged her knees. Her lips quivered. "Go away."

The monkey did nothing.

"You're not real. You're not Bobo."

The monkey did not move, but held his arm extended as if he had all the time in the world. Spotlighted by the flashlight, the monkey's shadow was huge upon the wall.

"You're nothing. Just some stupid toy of my Dad's."

The monkey seemed oblivious to her words but then, ten seconds later, abruptly turned as if finished and walked away, body swaying as he lifted and placed each foot in turn.

Sam exhaled in relief.

But upon reaching the edge of the desk, the monkey pivoted so that his path traced the desk's circumference. He took four steps then turned again as if he planned to circle back around the desk to reach the chair on which Sam sat.

Sam tumbled out of her chair and scrambled for the office door, cursing under her breath when she realized too late that the clattering she heard was from the flashlight she had dropped.

But she knew the house well enough even in the dark to find the rear door. She crossed the living room at a trot, her right arm waving back and forth in front of her like a metronome. She kicked an end table, bumped into and rolled around the couch, then, groping for the expected wall, stumbled forward until she found it. She ran alongside the wall, fingertips brushing its surface. A right turn to cut along the edge of the dining room. Another right turn. The first door was a bathroom, the next were the double doors to the coat closet, and after that was the one she wanted. She found the handle and opened the rear door, letting in the greenish-gray light of the drizzly afternoon. Her backpack was still there beside the door, braced against the wall, and she shouldered it with the ease of long familiarity.

She could have left then. But she hesitated just long enough to look back into the darkened interior of the house. All was silence. Standing there in a muddle of her own bootprints, her damp backpack hanging from her shoulders, Sam had a vision of the future, the same sort of damned thing her mother was always going on about. Sam saw the house slip further and further into decay as the lawyers fought over it. She saw the roof leak and the plaster ceilings crack, sag, and break loose from their pins. She saw the woodwork rot and bloom with mildew, the paint flake, the wallpaper peel, the pipes break, the events of years passing by in seconds as in a time-lapse movie. But, while the house disappeared around him, she saw the monkey repeat his simple journey every day, crawling down from his shelf to make his short perambulation around her father's office, then clambering back up the bookcase to his seat in the corner by the ceiling. His timing was as regular as clockwork but there was no one left to bear him witness.

Sam took a deep breath, turned, and headed back into the depths of the house.

When she emerged again, her backpack was noticeably larger because of the bulging and awkwardly shaped garbage bag strapped to its frame with bungee cords. She pulled her hat down over her forehead, cinched the straps on her pack, and stepped outside into the rain. She wasn't sure where she was going but that had never slowed her down before. She slogged across the lawn, her boots making sucking noises with each step.

When she reached the sidewalk, a van flashed its headlights at her. On the side of the van was the image of a glazed ham stuck with cloves and arranged on a bed of pineapple slices.

"Were you waiting for me?" she asked the driver after swinging herself up into the cab. The cab was toasty, and the old tune "I Walk the Line" played on the stereo. She wasn't fond of country music, but Johnny Cash was all right.

"No. I came back." Stuffed between the front seats was a rolled up magazine, something to do with cars, that the driver had been reading. "I couldn't picture you spending the night in that place."

"Thanks. You didn't have to do that. I just had to pick up some stuff."

"So I see. What's with your friend there?" With his thumb the driver indicated the backpack that Sam had set on the rubber floor mat between her legs. A furry arm had worked its way loose from the attached garbage bag. The raised arm trembled from the engine vibrations such that it had an air of expectancy, like a confident student hoping to be called upon in class.

"That's my monkey, Bobo."

"Bobo? Why's he called Bobo?"

Sam gave the driver the same answer that she gave her father many years before: "All monkeys are named Bobo."

Christmas in the Altai

A blue angel. On December 18, a week before Christmas, Jake explored the remnants of a dream as he shuffled across the ice. In the dream, he had joined Peter, Ganbaatar, Chuka, and the family of sheepherders from down-valley in the largest of the two gers. They toasted each other with shots of vodka and exchanged gifts. Jake had bars of Hershey chocolate for everyone and, because he felt guilty about the sweets, toothbrushes and toothpaste for the sheepherder's children. These were in fact the gifts Jake had stored in preparation for Christmas. What was unique to the dream was the card passed to him by the herdsman, something he could not as yet know. The blue angel on the card was crudely printed and the ink had bled. A thumbprint obscured the angel's faded blue halo, snowflakes glittered dully, and a dove flew skyward from an evergreen tree surrounded by local fauna. Everything was wrongly sized: the tree too small and the animals too large. The Mongolians grinned and laughed, pleased with themselves for their understanding of western culture. Jake felt only embarrassment and mumbled his thank-you's.

Jake grimaced and adjusted the hay bale on his back. The makeshift rope harness cut into his shoulders. This was his job: to trudge up and down the valley twice a day, a roundtrip of four miles each morning and evening, slippery and cold, all to feed one damned goat in a live trap. He'd hoped to try out some of Peter's movie cameras but, although Peter had grudgingly allowed him to test-drive an older model, and although Jake had followed Peter's example of sleeping with the batteries in his down-fill bag so as to keep them warm, there had been no opportunity, no *charismatic megafauna* yet to capture.

Jake scanned the valley and the sky. The light in the valley was gray, the sky a distant sliver of indigo, sparkling with a hint of snow. A lammergeier circled, and its eight-foot wingspan dipped to cut the blue ceiling like a knife. Then just as easily, just as dangerously, Jake's foot slipped on the ice. "Christ!" A slip but not a fall. There were white bubbles trapped in the treacherous ice and, in revenge, he crushed these with his sneakers—duct-taped replacements for the new boots that had aggravated his Achilles tendon—and luxuriated in the wicked crunch.

He focused on the icy trail. He might slip again. Rocks frozen in place might trip him up. It was a small miracle that he paused on reaching a stretch of open valley, looked around, and saw what Peter and Ganbaatar, who had made the same trek two hours earlier, admittedly in dim light, had missed. A yak knelt in the scrub a few hundred feet away. The yak was brown and calm as the earth, so alike to the earth that it might as well have been birthed from it. The yak's coat was a tawny tangle but it contained a bright streak, a red so intense it was fluorescent. Jake at first thought it paint, perhaps an identifying mark by a herdsman. Then, his heart thudding a rhythmic reminder, Jake realized the fluorescent trickle could be nothing but blood. Frozen blood.

Jake stared at the yak from the cavern of his parka hood. A sharp wind tugged tears from his eyes. The yak stared back at Jake with calm acceptance. The yak's innocent brown eyes said that it had always suspected that something like this would happen and, now that it had, the yak was not in the least surprised. After all, didn't the yak and the snow leopard live in the same locale? Their catastrophic meeting was pre-ordained.

The yak exhaled and its breath condensed into fog. Moisture dribbled from its nose. Its right leg was clotted with blood, up high where the leg joined the shaggy undercoat. There was also a gash in the yak's back, thickly frosted, the steam having frozen into ice on the brown hair, the intense white emphasizing a line of equally intense red, the fluorescent signature that had caught Jake's eye.

Jake dropped the hay bale and pulled loose a handful of straw. The yak extended a hairy upper lip, seized upon the straw, and chewed slowly, almost contentedly, without rising from its kneeling position.

There was more than just calm acceptance in the yak's eyes. There was also faith. A faith in the ability of Jake to set things right. The yak had traveled all the way from the desolate high peaks, many kilometers down from the mountain scrub. It had left behind the other yaks, its comrades, its blood relations to reach the dusty floor of the Altai valley. It had traveled all this lonely way with a wound shining brightly in its side, and it had done all this because it knew that rescue awaited in the valley, that humans lived in the valley. Humans were the closest thing to god that an animal domesticated millennia ago could ever know and, when it found a human, a human like Jake, everything would be made right.

"What took you so long?" Peter Beamish, wildlife film-maker extraordinaire, laughed his caustic laugh. He didn't wear a facemask and his curly red beard was thick with ice. It had taken Jake three weeks to learn that Peter only laughed when he wasn't joking.

Jake was too exhausted to reply. The cold raked his throat.

"Did you forget the hay?" Peter laughed again and slapped the wooden frame of the live trap for emphasis. The young goat, nubs for horns, bleated. Two years ago, back when Jake had accompanied his father Leonard Morgan to the Altai Mountains, they and the sheepherders had constructed three gargantuan live traps in the valley, each divided into two sections: one open and inviting, the other closed and containing a live goat as bait. Jake had fed the goats and checked the traps twice a day because neither he nor his father knew how a snow leopard would behave if trapped. It might batter itself bruised and bloody. It might sleep. It had been too much to ask that all three traps remain intact for Peter's subsequent film-making expedition, not with firewood in short supply for the sheepherders. They were lucky to still have the one.

"You forgot the hay." Peter spoke slowly as if forced to deal with a child.

Ganbaatar, stationed at one of Peter's cameras, the tripod legs braced with rocks, pressed finger to lips. He pointed along the line of the telephoto lens.

Jake heard the distant sound of hooves. He didn't see the sheep but they were up there on the mountainside, retreating.

Peter frowned.

"There's a yak, back near our camp," Jake said. "I think it was attacked by a snow leopard."

Ganbaatar did the hard work. He hiked down valley, past the research encampment, to the sheepherders' gers and returned with one of the herdsmen. The herdsman wore a bristling fur hat and a long, felt coat cinched at the waist with an orange sash. He had the deep wrinkles and leathery skin that came from daily exposure to sun and cold. He ran his fingers along the yak's neck and uncovered frost-edged bite marks. Then, miming fangs with his curled fingers, his own teeth bared, he confirmed the leopard attack. He left, smiling and shaking hands.

"What's going on," Jake asked Ganbaatar. "Doesn't he care about the yak?"

Ganbaatar shrugged. "Dirty," he said. "Dirty from the snow leopard."

"Sick?"

"Not sick. Dirty."

"Dirty?"

"What is the word for it?"

"Contaminated?"

"Yes, contaminated from the bite."

"Can we save it?"

Ganbaatar shrugged again.

Jake remembered something his father had once said, about the danger of infection from cat bites. But didn't that relate to lions and the Maasai? Or was it tigers in India? "It can't be infected. Not in this short a time."

Peter patted Jake's shoulder in his most patronizing fashion. "Don't mess with the locals. Or their traditions." He then traipsed after the herdsman. He carried his handheld camera with him and was maybe hoping to score an interview, some local color, translated after the fact since the herdsman spoke no English.

Jake and Ganbaatar grabbed the yak by her horns and pulled her to her feet. The yak wobbled but did not kneel. She could walk. Ganbaatar steered her across the ice by positioning himself behind her and slapping her rear. They steered the yak to a small stone corral intended for sheep and goats. The corral walls would provide protection from the wind and cold during the night.

Dinner that evening was the usual: ribs of stringy sheep meat and cubes of fat bobbing in a broth flavored with potato and onion, the aluminum pot so large it might as well have been a cauldron. Jake squeezed into a space between Ganbaatar and their driver, Chuka, as far as possible from Peter. The stove fire had been burning throughout the day and the interior of the ger was tropical. The forehead of the camp cook, Khangal, glistened with sweat.

Ganbaatar slipped his arms out of his insulated coveralls, a relic from a Russian Antarctic expedition, and let them sag around his waist. Chuka wore a white t-shirt and smelled of sweat and machine oil. The Mongolians weren't fond of spice and, when handed his bowl, Jake added pepper and salt from the Ziploc bags he kept in his coat pocket. He gnawed on the ribs and wiped his hands clean on his khaki pants. The thighs of his pants were gray, almost translucent, with grease. Ganbaatar told a story about how much he had missed the sweetness of Mongolian sheep fat when he had once visited New York City. "Your fat has no flavor," he said.

After dinner, while walking from the main ger back to the one he shared with Peter, Jake saw a shooting star. It burned so brightly it might have been a lit match waved overhead, inches out of reach.

He made a wish.

The generator ran until 9 PM each night. Jake used the remaining hour of light to write a letter to his girlfriend, Samantha. He didn't write to her every day. Sometimes he just read himself to sleep, but he had lent his Hemingway collection to Ganbaatar, who wanted to read the stories in their original English. Jake's letters were similar to his journal entries, personalized by an "I miss you," although he had no way of knowing how much Sammy missed him; and with "Wish you were here," although he knew Sammy would hate the cold, the dirt, and the greasy flavorless food. Still, he really did wish she were there with him, an antidote to his loneliness and isolation. Jake's letters were written with the understanding that they would not be mailed for another month and that he might still beat them home if, in fact, the letters ever made it back to his home city of Madison, in the state of Wisconsin, in the very distant USA. That sense of futility was integral to his letters.

Jake had just written the word, "contaminated," when Peter returned from the main ger, swinging wide the insulated door and inviting in a frigid blast of the January cold. Fifteen minutes of electric light remained. Peter stripped down to his underwear and slid into his sleeping bag. "What you got there?" he asked, gesturing at Jake's pile of script.

"Nothing."

"That's a whole lot of nothing."

Jake wore three layers on his upper torso: a silk undershirt, a long-sleeved shirt, and a Kashmir sweater purchased at a Beijing market stall. His sleeping bag added a fourth layer. Even so, the chill that transited from nose and cheeks, to fingers, to his stockinged feet, incriminated him as a lesser mortal in comparison to Peter. "It's a letter to my girlfriend."

"Your true love?"

Jake liked that term. It harkened back to a simpler time, a pledge that stood steadfast against the illicit fingers of desire. "I guess."

Peter laughed. "There's no such thing as true love. The best you can hope for is a bottle of soda that fizzes over when you pop its cap." Peter snapped his fingers, a percussive blast beyond anything that Jake could have managed. "There's surprise, confusion, and, yes, lustful anticipation. That's what you call love. But that soda goes flat before you know it and, more often than not, it's some sugar-free substitute. Aspartame."

"Is that what you believe?"

"You know my history." Peter was the sort of minor celebrity who assumed everyone knew his history. He had been married and divorced twice. "I lost more than I ever gained by love. You've much less to lose in pursuit of the fairer sex." He was referring to money, of course. The generator kicked off and the interior of the ger inhaled darkness. Jake weighted the papers beside his sleeping bag down with his pen. The battery pack he kept warm in his sleeping bag shifted uncomfortably. Jake wondered if Peter had noted its protruding bulk, if he secretly acknowledged Jake's preparedness to participate in the filmmaking aspect of the expedition.

"Go ahead, write your little letter," Peter said in the darkness. "Just don't expect it to provide any comfort when your relationship goes tits-up on the road to Hell."

In spite of Jake's wish on the shooting star, he found the yak dead the next morning. Frozen bile clung to her lips and beard. She might have died of shock or, because she was lying on her side, suffocation, her rumen shoved against her diaphragm so she couldn't breathe. A small goat tethered in the corral cuddled against the yak's dead body, sucking in the little warmth that remained.

Two years ago, Jake and his dad had determined that one in ten yak deaths were owed to the predation of snow leopards. Yaks, unlike goats who were corralled each night, wandered freely to graze in the mountains, free to encounter death in all its forms. Jake was sure *this* yak, his yak, would have survived if the herdsman had been willing to care for her, if he had not written her off as contaminated.

Contaminated.

Snow leopard prey.

Peter, however, was elated. He saw cheap profit to be made from the dead yak, an unexpected boon for the stalled expedition. Accompanied by

Ganbaatar as cameraman and translator, and Jake as a witness, Peter made a deal with the herdsman. The monetary exchange involved more than just ownership of the yak's corpse. The herdsman looped a rope around the yak's frozen forelegs and dragged her by horse a half-mile to a side valley. This was in all likelihood the same valley the yak had followed down from the upper fields, from where it had been attacked by the snow leopard but not killed, surviving long enough to return to its home only to be discovered by Jake, by its owners, and to then be abandoned to its preordained fate, death.

Peter, of course, insisted on spending the first night in the icy tent they erected near the kill. He returned home the next morning tired and angry. He was even angrier when he learned a snow leopard had circled the live trap at the far end of the valley. There was a dusting of snow and the leopard's fresh prints were everywhere. That's where Peter would now spend every night up until Christmas. "You stay with the yak," he told Jake. "You found her. You find her killer."

Peter loaned Jake the necessary equipment. *Loaned* was the operative word. Jake had the responsibility and would bear the cost of any misadventure that befell the movie camera, the battery packs, and the night vision goggles. Jake, fully clothed, shivered in his sleeping bag. The cumbersome movie camera would be useless for much of the night, the hope being that the snow leopard would reveal itself during the dimly lit hours of evening or morning. Nevertheless, Jake set his alarm on vibrate-mode to wake him each hour on the hour.

Nothing happened on the first night of Jake's watch, and he arose the next morning bone tired but still obligated to hike a hay bale up-valley to the live trap. Peter was in an even worse mood. Nothing had happened at his end either. The goat in the live trap frisked about as if every day was the first day of creation and hay an unexpected bonus.

The second night, at 5 AM, alarm a bumble bee in his pocket, Jake shook sleep from his head and then, remembering where he was, opened up the tent. The yak was in motion. Her foreleg scraped the air. Her ribcage heaved. She stilled and for several long minutes Jake thought it was all nocturnal conjuring, but then the beast hiccupped, not a human hiccup, more like a bark. *My camera.* Peter's camera, Jake corrected himself. He rolled over and, dragging the tripod along, was just in time to see, although he was too late to capture it on film, a shadow disengage itself from the yak's stomach and disappear into the rocks.

A fox as it turned out, based on the tracks Jake discovered beside the dead yak. He rolled the frozen yak over to protect the hole gnawed into its stomach. The third night, that's the charm, Jake promised himself. He was due for a reward, for some magic to enter into his life. In truth, there was a beautiful sunset the next night. The sky caught fire, flickered as if the dying light was captured and reflected back from thousands, millions of snowflakes. But it was only the fox that returned. It spent the long dark hours scraping at the frozen ground alongside the frozen yak, a vain burrow that never broached the entrance it had laboriously gnawed through the thick skin the night before. The fox's flawed effort was amplified in Jake's dreams like nails screeched across a chalkboard.

Khangal, the camp cook, wrapped a rag around the handle of a large metal teapot the next morning and, tilting it over a cup, disgorged a milky brew swimming with tea leaves. Jake gladly accepted the cup. Peter was still up-valley, triangulating the presumptive reappearance of the snow leopard based on temperature, day length, and the lure of fresh goat meat, a feat of divination with as much likelihood for success as conjuring the carnivore out of wood smoke. Ganbaatar slurped his tea. "Why did Hemingway write about the dead leopard?" he asked. It took Jake a few seconds to connect the question to Hemingway's story, "The Snows of Kilimanjaro," one of the tales in the collection Jake had lent him. "What is it doing near the summit?"

"Maybe it has something to do with why people climb mountains, why they seek danger," Jake said. The question seemed strangely personal. "Why they do stupid things that make no sense."

"No sense?"

"Why they do stupid things that get them killed."

Ganbaatar nodded as if he understood, although Jake was already second-guessing his own answer. "Hemingway writes about a dead leopard on a mountain in Africa," Ganbaatar said. "He never visited Mongolia. He never met our snow leopard."

"What do you mean?"

"Our snow leopard is not that easy to find. It does not die for our..."

"Convenience?"

"Yes. It is not convenient. You will not find a snow leopard waiting for you in the Altai. Not dead. Not alive. You think you will catch a leopard because you have expensive equipment. These are expensive toys. You cannot catch it."

"I won't see the leopard?"

"I followed snow leopard tracks when I was a boy. I climbed high. I followed the leopard's tracks in the snow." Ganbaatar raised his hand until it was extended above his head and then snapped his fingers. "The tracks ended. There was no snow leopard. A snow leopard will vanish. A snow leopard will leave you alone with nothing."

Khangal, perhaps sensing Jake's consternation, pointed upward. He said something to Ganbaatar in Mongolian.

"What did he say?" Jake asked.

"He said, 'The moon will be full tonight. Maybe you will be lucky.'"

That night, the air sparkled silver. The hairs of the dead yak also sparkled. Jake's phone alarm vibrated each hour on the hour. He awoke due to something else. It was 2:34 in the morning. Jake pushed himself up onto his elbows in the soft glow of the tent's interior and listened. His bones were stiff with cold. His breath hung in ragged crystals from the tent ceiling. It was so silent he might as well have been on the moon. A pebble scraped, just a hint of sound. Maybe it was the fox. Maybe it had gnawed its way back into the yak's belly.

Jake unzipped and rolled back the tent door. He did the same with the tent fly, wincing at the incriminating *tch tch tch* of the zipper's teeth. Cold clawed his cheeks and raked his throat. He pushed his woolen hat back from where it had settled across his eyebrows. The frosted crust on the yak glinted in the moonlight.

Movement! The yak's chest rose, subtle as a prayer. Jake searched for the fox, for its slinking shadow, for a dark rip in the yak's belly. No fox, no shadow, no bodily excavation. But then, subtlety be damned, the yak lurched to its hooves. Its frozen guts spilled and crashed to earth. Laboriously, the yak turned its head toward its home valley in the mountains. Laboriously, the yak began the long hike up the valley, stony entrails dragged along the frozen ground, questing for the higher elevations, to where its brethren gathered and gnawed at the meager grass.

Jake, heart pounding, wrapped his sleeping bag around his shoulders and stumbled from the tent. The decrepit yak's wounds glowed in the moonlight. Its hooves snagged on the rocks. The yak seemed to have been raised by the moon's distant gravity, as if Jake's secret prayers had been heard and had rekindled in the yak a desire for rejuvenation.

The ground and air were astir. Silvery motes peppered Jake's eyes. It was too late for Jake to return to his tent and collect his camera and batteries, his clothing, to prepare for a nighttime expedition. He slapped at the stinging crystals. He would have to continue on alone with what he carried and, as ever, hope it was sufficient.

The dead yak passed beyond a bend in the stony valley. The silhouetted face of the projecting rock glowered at Jake. Jake threw aside his sleeping bag. There had been no time to put on his shoes, but he still wore woolen socks and polypropylene liners. He ran. He slapped at his pants pocket: his phone with its camera was missing. He thought he had brought it along but, just his luck, it was still back in the tent buzzing each hour on the hour.

Jake, hacking on billowing snow, rounded the rock outcropping and discovered the yak crumpled in its tracks. The yak was meat, dead and contaminated meat. It was hair, tangled and bloody hair, hair encrusted with frost and bright as metal. Its eyes were closed, the silvery lids pasted across the dead orbs. Jake wiped his brow—with a naked hand, he had forgotten his mittens—and dislodged cold trickles of sweat.

Cold burrowed its way up from the stony ground to pierce his stockinged feet. His moonlit shadow. Another shadow, drifting, rippled across the frozen ground and joined his own. His breath caught in his throat. He looked up. Maybe he should never have given in to that impulse. His future might have been so simple. He might never have felt the need to hide what he had seen, almost embarrassed as if the holy, the immaculate, the miraculous was on the same level as masturbation.

What he saw in the night sky, silhouetted against the Milky Way, splayed, arms and legs spread-eagled, puffy tail extended, fur protruding like effervescent needles: a snow leopard.

A snow leopard. *Charismatic megafauna.* A great cat taken captive and now flying up into the sky. A scared cat will howl. A scared cat will scream. This snow leopard never howled, never screamed. It rose into the starry night without a sound. The stars whirled and coalesced around the cat. The color of the leopard's fur had evolved over countless eons to meld into the snowy peaks, and now it melded into the scintillant sky, and then...

Bones crackling like ruptured ice, the dead yak, cradled in snow crystals, elevated to follow. Jake could have reached out and grabbed onto its scruff if he had responded quickly enough. If he were foolish enough to seize onto the unknown. It was in that moment Jake understood just how inconsequential he was. Here he was witness to a miracle, a snow leopard taken captive, swirled

ERIC SCHALLER

away in a crystalline storm, and because an animal needs food, its prey, the dead yak, also raised by the same process, it now rising above Jake, disgorging scraps of gnawed and frozen intestine to patter down on Jake's upturned face and shoulders. Jake was irrelevant, an observer. Whatever had stolen the snow leopard and its prey did not care that he was witness.

Jake watched for long minutes after the snow leopard and the yak disappeared into the verticality of the night sky. He did not know the constellations of the southern hemisphere. There were stars overhead and they were brilliant. There was the Milky Way and it was as thick as clotted cream. Somewhere to the left of the Milky Way, one of the faint stars shifted in place, as if preparing for a complicated dance step, and streaked toward the horizon.

A star that wasn't a star.

Jake did not bother making a wish.

They had Mongolian barbeque for Christmas dinner. Khangal heated stones red hot in the stove then placed these in a metal can and layered them with sliced mutton. He added water. He forced a lid onto the can against the pressure of the steam and set the can back onto the flaring coals. The lid popped loose, and the ger filled with smoke and steam. They replaced the lid, and Chuka leaned on it with a stick. The lid popped loose again. Peter arrived back at the ger, having spent the day and evening waiting in vain for the snow leopard, and smoke poured out of the opened door.

Everyone laughed, including Peter.

The meat was tender and good.

The herdsman, along with two of his children, came over after dinner, just in time for vodka. There were offerings to the local spirits, done by dipping a finger in the vodka and flicking it toward the sky, the ground, and touching one's forehead, and the glasses then drained at a swallow. A full belly, alcohol swirling in his brain, Jake dragged his belt pack up from the floor, settled it in his lap, and pulled out the dozen bars of Hershey chocolate he had reserved as holiday gifts. He distributed these, even pressing one on Peter who tried to wave it aside, claiming he abhorred empty calories. Then, because Jake felt guilty about the sweets and the likelihood of cavities, he handed out toothbrushes and small tubes of toothpaste to the sheepherder's children. They smiled and thanked him with the exact same expression that had greeted the chocolate bars.

Jake had just returned to his seat, was glancing around to determine where the bottle of vodka had migrated, when the herdsman tugged at his sleeve.

"He has a gift for you," Ganbaatar said.

It was then that Jake saw the envelope. The herdsman grinned and waited until Jake had taken the envelope before resuming his seat. He raised a toast. Jake's glass was still empty.

"Open it," Ganbaatar said.

Jake felt the adrenalin rush of déjà vu. He hadn't yet seen what was in the envelope, but he knew what he would find based on his week-old dream. He ripped open the spit-sealed flap. "Thank you," he said, before he even looked at the card. It was as if the image on the card held a secret validation, or disproval, of the rules he had always assumed governed existence.

The card was the same as that in his dream, bluish and printed on cheap paper, probably purchased on a recent trip to Ulaanbaatar but already smudged. The angel he remembered from his dream was in fact a Mongolian girl in a fur-trimmed coat, her arms upraised like wings, her dark hair haloed by a white cloud that dissipated into snowflakes. She stood taller than a nearby evergreen tree laden with snow. A white goat with nubbin horns, much like the one he fed each morning, a rabbit, and a hedgehog danced on their hind legs around the tree. The tree was too small and the animals too large. Doves erupted skyward to herald all that was good in the world.

All this happened some years ago. Jake returned home, and his girlfriend presented him with a bundle of letters she had written in his absence and which he, after reading, folded and stored in the back of his Mongolia journal. Jake never told her or anyone else about the ascension of the snow leopard. Jake has learned from experience which stories of his winter in Mongolia play best to a dinner-party audience. He talks about the cubes of sheep fat bobbing in the dinner cauldron and how he carried Ziploc bags of salt and pepper in his coat pocket. He talks about how, as an occasional gustatory relief, they enjoyed sheep intestines stuffed with fat and blood and crisped on the coals. Strangers always want to know if Jake ever saw a snow leopard. "On the first trip with my dad," Jake says, "and even then it was at a distance and hard to distinguish from the rocks." They ask what the snow leopard was doing. Jake laughs. "Sleeping," he says. "Big or small, that's all cats ever do." Then he shrugs and changes the subject, as if there is little more to tell.

Get a few more glasses of wine into Jake and he'll expound on his theory of precognition. "It's my conviction that we all have the ability to foresee the future," he says. "The problem is there are many possible futures and, in the chaos of our modern world, these futures are limitless. As a result, most people never see their future."

Nod your head, go along with it. Jake's on a roll.

"The only way to see the future is to get far away from all these crazy distractions. In my case, this was on a trip to the Altai Mountains of Mongolia. In the middle of winter. I did the same thing every day, day in and day out. The day-to-day predictability to all of our lives was significant."

Jake leans toward you and gesticulates with his wine glass. "I had a dream," he says. "A week before Christmas, I dreamed about what would happen in the future. I didn't know I was dreaming about the future, but then it happened the same way I dreamed it." He tells you about the herdsman and the Christmas card.

"That's amazing," you say.

"Not really," he says. "But I've learned three things from that experience." He holds up three fingers and, in doing so, sloshes Pinot Noir onto the couch, so tipsy he doesn't notice, only licking a bloody trickle from off his glass's rim. "First, as you have probably already figured out, even if granted a vision of the future, you won't know it for what it is until later, when it happens."

You nod. "Second?"

"Second, you won't know what it feels like until you have lived it."

"What do you mean?"

Even drunk, Jake is suspicious, as if you are a journalist or maybe his former employer, Peter Beamish, inquiring as to how the dead yak could have possibly disappeared, vanished as if into thin air. Jake shrugs. "You can know the future, but when it happens to you it will *feel* completely different."

Jake remembers how, when he received the Christmas card, he ducked his head and wiped his eyes on his coat sleeve, so touched that the Mongolians had included him, a stranger, in their celebration. He hugged the herdsman and his children, then each member of the film team, even Peter who stiffly relented to his embrace. Khangal poured another round of vodka, and they drained each glass at a swallow before slamming it down. Jake went to bed drunk and happy. He imagined a world where everyone shared the Christmas spirit, a spirit he now entertained as universal and independent of religion.

Jake smiles, reliving that bountiful moment. But his smile doesn't last, not when you ask him, "And the third?"

"The third?"

"The third thing you learned about precognition?"

Jake stumbles over his words. "Just those two things, I guess. That's what I learned." His wine glass is empty. "I could use some water," he says. "Rule of three. No more than three drinks in an evening, and a glass of water between each if you want to stay sober." He winks as he stumbles away. "Now where's the kitchen?"

The refrigerator is equipped with an ice dispenser. Jake presses his glass against the lever and, as the cubes tinkle and crash, he thinks back to that bitter cold night in the Altai Mountains. "It doesn't matter," he says, to no one in particular. "None of it matters."

There are things Jake talks about from his two trips to Mongolia. Likewise, there are things he never talks about, no matter how many glasses of wine you might ply him with. It's not much really, that third thing, probably the sort of thing that matters more to the speaker than to his audience. Only this, that no matter the optimum conditions for precognition, the most significant event in your life might be excluded. There will be no dream vision of a snow leopard rising spread-eagled into the air, nested within a haze of silvery confetti, each sparkling like a winter snowflake falling in reverse, falling into the night sky, into a future in which you have no part.

How the Future Got Better

The FoTax process. "Your taxes fo' nothing," is how Uncle Walt defined it. He stole that joke from a late-night talk show. But even though he didn't bother to read the brochure, he had caught at least one TV special and knew that *Fo* stood for *photon* and *Tax* for *tachyon*. "Now pass me another roll," he said, "a warm one from the bottom of the bucket."

Mom always insisted that everyone sit down as a family for dinner, but had consented to eating a half-hour earlier than usual so we could watch when FoTax went live. Five-thirty in the pee-em, would you believe it? "Might as well be eating lunch twice," is how Uncle Walt phrased it, but he said it softly so that Mom couldn't hear, and out of the corner of his mouth just in case she could lip read. "Hey! What about that roll? A man could die from hunger at his own table." Little sister Susie, Suz to the family, passed him the bucket and let him dig for his own roll. He probably fingered every one, muttering the whole time: "Cold and hard as a goddamn rock. Probably break a tooth and wouldn't that be just my luck. There's a sucker born every minute and, by God, this time that sucker is me." Took him so long to find his roll and butter it that, by the time he got around to taking a bite, we were already talking about ice cream. "Hold your cotton-picking horses," Uncle Walt said. "What's the future got that we ain't got now?" But he powered through his chicken, coleslaw, and dessert and long-legged it to the living room before anyone grabbed his favorite lounger.

Mom played with the settings on the new Sony receiver by the TV set, squinting at a pamphlet in her hand labeled READ THIS FIRST. "Set it five minutes ahead," big sister Elizabeth called from her seat on the couch between Dad and Gramps. Elizabeth insisted upon being called by all four syllables of her given name but, to her credit, had memorized the instruction manual as soon as it was out of its plastic wrapper. Probably memorized the Spanish edition too, just in case. "Setting the time closer to now reduces the chance of gray spaces and ghosting," she said. "Don't forget to tune to channel one-hundred-and-thirty-one."

She might have said more but was interrupted by a frantic knocking at our apartment door. It was the Willard family, Pa Willard in the lead, Ma at his elbow, and all the little Willards, indistinguishable from each other with their chocolate-smeared mouths and cherubic curls, peering through the bars of their parents' legs. "Can we join you?" Pa Willard asked. "Our receiver didn't arrive." Ma Willard shot him a dirty look. "You forgot to sign up," she said. Before the argument could escalate, and the Willards were always arguing, Mom said, "Come on in. Everyone's in the living room. Suz, would you grab some more chairs for the Willards?"

Which is why, when FoTax went live, there were fourteen of us crammed together in one small room. Our TV was seven feet on the diagonal, and the Willards might have come over even if Pa Willard had remembered to order their receiver. Last anyone knew they still had their old 42-inch model. As you might guess with both families together, and even granting that Grammy started to nod off as soon as she settled into her chair, it was kind of noisy. But everyone went quiet and stared at the TV screen when the little green numbers on the receiver flickered to six o'clock.

But nothing happened.

Nothing changed.

All you could see was the blue of an empty channel.

"What a con," said Uncle Walt. "You made me rush dessert for this?"

"Maybe it's not set to the right channel," said Elizabeth. "One-hundred-and-thirty-one is what the manual said."

Mom reacted like she had just been called stupid, but got up and checked the setting again anyway. "One-three-one," she said, "See, it says one-three-one."

Then without preamble or warning, while Mom tapped her finger on the illuminated part of the screen that, to her credit, did display the proper channel designation, an image abruptly replaced the blue background.

An image of us.

Or most of us anyway. The vantage point looked to be above and a little behind from where we were sitting. But you could see Uncle Walt's balding head protruding above his lounger, the shoulders and hair of Dad and Elizabeth and Gramps on the couch, and, beside them, Mom sitting rigidly in one of the wooden chairs brought in from the dining table. Two of the golden-haired Willard kids shared another wooden chair beside her. In the image, they, or rather we were all watching the TV. You could see just about one-third of the TV screen, and on that image of the TV there were tinier versions of us clustered around a still tinier version of the TV. And on that miniature TV... well, you get the picture.

Suz, surprisingly, was the first to notice the difference between the image on TV and the positioning of those of us clustered around it. "Hey Mom," she said, "you're sitting down in the TV picture. On a chair." Which of course was true. But just as true was the fact that here, in the real world, Mom was still standing beside the TV where she had been checking the channel.

"That's because it's the future. And in the future Mom's already sat down again." Elizabeth said this using her most infuriating know-it-all voice, as if she had also seen the same thing but hadn't bothered to say a word because it was all so self-evident.

"What if I chose not to sit down?" said Mom, suddenly inspired as she looked at the seated image of herself on the screen. "What if I continued to stand here by the TV?" Even as she said this, before she had finished speaking, her image on the TV started to turn gray and fade away like smoke.

"Hey, you're ghosting," said Elizabeth, genuinely excited. "I read about that. Maybe you'll disappear altogether."

"Oh, I don't like that," said Mom. She sat down in the nearest empty chair, and the image of her on TV came back clear and sharp.

"I want to ghost too," said one of the Willard kids, already making a move like he was going to jump out of his chair and dance around the room.

"No you don't," said Ma Willard, and shot him a look that could freeze, and did.

Uncle Walt was the next one to make a discovery. "You know what?"

"What?" Mom said. She didn't look at him but kept her eyes fixed on her seated TV image.

"I was wrong."

"You wrong? Now that I find hard to believe." Uncle Walt was Mom's younger brother and, according to her, had been so spoiled while growing up it was a wonder he didn't stink all the way to China. "Not that I find it hard to believe you were wrong, mind you," Mom said. "But that you would admit it. That I find hard to believe. Please tell, and I hope to God someone is recording this."

"I was wrong about the future. It does look better."

"Better than what?"

"Better than now."

"How's that?"

"In the future, I got a beer." Uncle Walt gave a little nod like he had just scored a major debating point, but was too polite to rub it in. He was right. The TV version of Uncle Walt was reclined in his lounger, an extra pillow behind his head, just like the real version here in the living room. But on the TV, in the cup holder of his lounger, was a silver can of Coors Light.

Uncle Walt got up, went to the kitchen, and returned brandishing his Coors Light like it was the Holy Grail. He triumphantly popped its top and settled back into his lounger. Now there was absolutely no difference between the version of Uncle Walt on TV and the one in our living room.

We watched then in silence, waiting to see if we could pick out anything else, waiting to see what we would do next, even trying to make out what was being shown on those screens within screens within screens that should, by rights, show us the future in five-minute increments. In some ways it was like a What's Wrong With This Picture game where you study two seemingly identical pictures and try to discover the differences. Only here they didn't tell you how many differences there were.

And that wasn't really fair.

Pretty soon Mom started talking about the obits with Ma Willard. Dad told Pa Willard about the funny noise our refrigerator made, sometimes squealing like there was a mouse trapped inside it, and Pa Willard responded with the obvious, "Well maybe there is a mouse trapped inside it." Elizabeth told the Willard kids a ghost story, with Suz adding atmospheric wailings at the appropriate moments. Gramps asked Gramma if she wanted a bedtime martini, then laughed when all he got in response was a colossal snore.

Uncle Walt wasn't the sort to say he was getting bored with a program, at least when he was one of the stars. But after about fifteen minutes, he leaned over to me and asked, "Isn't there a new episode of *Nut Jobs* on?"

I tried to remember what day of the week *Nut Jobs* ran, and if they were maybe already into repeats. I was just about to check the listings when I saw it. I spotted a difference. Me. Not Suz. Not Uncle Walt. And certainly not all four syllables of Elizabeth.

"No," I told him. "*Nut Jobs* isn't on. But there's something just as good."

"How do you know?"

I pointed at the TV.

Five minutes into the future we were already watching it.

Red Hood

There was a young girl whose grandma loved her fiercely, and so made for her a suit of skin. Her grandma brined the skin, scraped it free of fat and flesh, and soaked it in a brainy mash until it was soft and milky as a baby's breath. She crafted an opening in the suit with leather cords to tie the flaps. "Promise me," said the girl's grandma, while she adjusted the fit, "that you'll always wear this when you go outside."

The girl shook her arm and the skin waggled. "It's still loose."

"That way you won't outgrow it. Now promise me... "

"I promise," said the girl.

Her grandma then showed the girl how to smear the blood and offal of the Risen over the skin for camouflage, including onto the hairy scalp of its cowl. The girl kept to her promise. She never left home without the blood-smeared suit, and so everyone called her Red Hood.

One day her mother gave Red Hood two tins of soup and a bottle of cough syrup. "Go, my darling, and see how your grandma is doing. She is sick and could use our help." Red Hood loaded the supplies into her knapsack and put on her skin suit. Her mother applied blood from a pot they kept by their apartment door and handed her a sheathed knife, its wooden handle split and repaired with duct tape. "With luck, you won't need this."

"It's broken," Red Hood said.

"The worth of a knife is in its blade, not its handle," her mother said. She then gave Red Hood a few last words of advice. "Don't follow the road because your shadow will show in the sunlight, and don't talk to anyone until you get to your grandma's apartment."

Red Hood descended the stairs until she reached the sub-basement of their apartment building, and then followed the dusty trail of footprints her mother called the Lost Highway. The trail twisted and turned in the darkness, leading from one building to the next. Red Hood maneuvered past hulking furnaces, octopus-armed duct systems, and grimy cars abandoned in parking garages. Sometimes her flashlight picked out the decapitated bodies of the Risen. Sometimes the dust tickled her nose. She pressed a finger hard above her lip—a trick she had learned from grandma—so that she did not sneeze.

She did not encounter anyone animated until she had completed half her journey. Tinny and wan, like the mating cry of an insect, music was the first indication that she was not alone. She swung her flashlight around. A stranger leaned against a desolate sports car. He wore a squirrel-fur hat and had kindly eyes. He held a tiny machine in his hands and cranked its handle with the tips of his thumb and forefinger. "What's that?" Red Hood asked. Then remembering her mother's admonition against strangers, she added, "Who are you?"

"A friend." The music stopped and was replaced by a silence that felt like loneliness.

Red Hood looked longingly at the tiny machine.

"It's called a music box. A genie lives inside and he sings when I poke his ribs." He cranked the handle, and Red Hood heard the startled genie's tune. This time the stranger sang along with it. His voice was rough, but the words were pretty:

Away upon a rainbow way on high
There's a land that I learned of once from a butterfly
Away upon a rainbow bluebirds sing
Of warmth and food and all the love that you can dream.

Red Hood had never heard anything so wonderful. She clapped her hands. "Please play it again." She said *please* and so the kindly stranger obliged.

"Would you like my music box for your own?" the stranger asked.

"Oh yes," said Red Hood.

"I can't give it to you, but you can earn it."

"How?"

The stranger's forehead wrinkled. He stroked his naked chin. Then his eyebrows shot up. "I have it. We'll have a race to the next apartment building. First one to tag the EXIT sign wins."

Red Hood had visited her grandma many times and knew the Lost Highway well. She knew its dangers and obstructions: the cave-ins, the flooded levels, and, most importantly, where a Risen might lurk at a dark intersection.

She gained two full steps on the stranger before he even knew the race had begun, but her skin suit slapped and dragged at her ankles. She slowed and the stranger passed her like she was a rooted in the concrete. He wasn't even panting by the time she caught up with him at the EXIT sign.

"My suit tangled in my legs," Red Hood said. "Otherwise I could have beaten you."

The stranger looked so sorrowful it was surprising his eyes were dry. He placed the music box on the floor and ground it beneath his heel until it squealed. Nothing was left of it but a mess of crushed metal and plastic. "See what you made me do," he said. "That's the music box and the genie also." There was a spot of rust on the floor that might have been genie blood.

"I'm sorry," Red Hood said.

"Will you pay the forfeit?"

"Forfeit?" He had said nothing of this before.

"I'm not asking for anything of value. Just a kiss."

Red Hood had kissed family members, even a few boys. This kiss was different, hungry, and just when she thought it over, the stranger bit her lip. She gasped, tasted blood.

"Now," said the stranger. "I have something that your mother would like." He rummaged through his pack and exhumed a plastic comb, pink and with a floral design. "Will you race me for it?"

"To the next apartment building?"

"Yes."

Why dwell on the details of this race? All happened as before. Red Hood took a head start but the skin tangled in her legs and she slowed. She would have cried over her failure but for the sympathy of the stranger. "See what you made me do," he said. He cracked the comb across his knee and threw the splintered pieces away as if to hide these from their sight.

"Is there another forfeit to pay?" Red Hood asked.

He nodded.

"The same as before?"

He nodded again.

In truth, this kiss was nothing like the first. The stranger's tongue pummeled her lips and teeth and, when she relented, pursued her own tongue like a hungry salamander. He only withdrew after he had wrestled her tongue into bruised submission.

The stranger wiped spittle from his lips and smoothed his eyebrows. He removed a crystalline flask from his pack. "If you can beat me to the next building," he said, "I'll give you this medicine for your grandma." He uncorked the bottle, swirled the amber liquid inside, and let her smell its honeyed aroma.

"I can't win," Red Hood said. She fought back tears.

"Of course you can. You just have to set aside your suit. Without it, you'd be as swift as the North Wind." This was the best comparison the stranger could make, for the North Wind is the liveliest and cruelest of the four cardinal winds. "Hang your suit on this nail where it will be safe."

Red Hood stripped off her suit and hung it on the basement wall. She felt naked without it, but won the race easily. The kindly stranger had been morose in victory but accepted loss like a champion. "You do not need a suit if you are quick," he said. He rummaged once more through his pack and found a flask that looked much like the one he had shown her. "Take this to your grandma. It will assist her health."

"Thank you," Red Hood said. The medicine was murkier than she remembered. She wondered about the forfeit she had missed. Would it have been like a rat, or a salamander, or another animal altogether? She started to retrace her steps.

"Where are you going?"

"To get my suit."

"But you are almost at your grandma's."

Red Hood was tired from the races, but knew she shouldn't leave her suit behind. Luckily, the stranger was as wise as he was kind, and proposed a solution. "I'll watch over your suit and keep it safe. We mustn't keep your grandma waiting."

"But *you* might have to wait a long time."

"I won't be lonely." The stranger squeezed his pack and it rattled merrily. Perhaps it contained miracles more entertaining than anything he had yet shared.

Red Hood glanced back once after they parted, just long enough to see the kindly stranger tip his squirrel-fur hat. If she had followed him, she would have seen him give a little skip as if he had just won a lottery. If she had followed him still further, she would have seen him take her skin suit down from its nail and try it on for size. And lastly—although of course she did not, for she continued on to her grandma's apartment—she would have seen that the suit fitted the stranger so perfectly that he, not she, might just as well be called Red Hood.

*

Red Hood found her grandma shivering in bed, although her apartment was roasting hot. A fire crackled in the wood stove. Red Hood sat beside her grandma and, using the hem of her undershirt, daubed at the chill sweat on her forehead. "Where is your suit?" her grandma asked.

Red Hood flushed. "There was a tear in its sleeve and I had to leave it behind."

"Couldn't your mother repair it?"

"She's doing that now." Red Hood's excuse felt too much like a lie and she evaded her grandma's eyes by fumbling inside her knapsack. "I brought you soup and cough syrup." She set these on the bedside table. "And something better." She added the crystalline flask of medicine. It sparkled with light stolen from the fire.

Grandma reached toward the flask as if it were a source of warmth. "That's beautiful. What is it?"

"Medicine." Red Hood thought back on the kindly stranger and how he had given her the flask so freely. "From a friend."

"A rare gift."

Red Hood used her knife to break the seal of sticky stuff that adhered to the cork. "Smell this," she said. "Doesn't it smell just like a summer's day?"

Grandma sniffed the opened flask and jerked away as if slapped. "My mother used to tell me the best medicine tasted foul. But sometimes evil cannot hide its fangs. Dump that down the sink."

Red Hood did as commanded. The medicine bubbled and fumed and its stench hung in the air. Red Hood opened a can of soup and heated it on the wood stove. It was tomato soup and it smelled wonderful. Her grandma stirred the soup, inhaled its aroma, and thanked Red Hood for her kindness. But she only sipped at her spoon, and the soup cooled in its dish.

"Will you be better soon?" Red Hood asked.

"I will never be better." Grandma pulled her nightgown down to reveal a wound that was wet and red and shaped like a mouth. It pained Red Hood to look at the wound, but she did not turn aside. Her grandma reassembled her clothing and sank back into her pillows. "You brought me three gifts from home and so I will tell you a story of three's. While I am talking, you will know that I'm alive. When I stop, you will know that I am dead. When that happens, you must take your knife and stab me through the temple."

Red Hood nodded. This was one reason her mother had given her the knife. She fetched it from her knapsack and set it on the table close at hand.

"I'm cold. Please add a log to the fire."

Red Hood fed the stove even though the room was stifling.

"There was once a young woman who lived in a small town. She knew everyone in the town and everyone knew her. One day, a handsome stranger arrived. He told comical tales of outwitting the Risen, played a scuffed guitar, and sang songs to her. The best songs were those in which he compared her eyes to pools of starlight or oceans of violets. The stranger was canny enough to also charm her parents and, with their blessings, he took the young woman away to his distant home.

"They spent the cold seasons beneath a down comforter and the following summer she gave birth to a baby boy. The baby entertained her even when her man did not. Another year passed, and the young woman gave birth to a second baby more handsome than the first. She missed her family and friends, but her man discouraged her from visiting them, sometimes with words and sometimes with blows. The young woman gave birth to a third baby boy, the prettiest of them all, and, while her man was out scavenging, she escaped with her children and began the long journey back to her hometown.

"One of the Risen caught her scent, and then another, and soon it was a fearsome pack that trailed her, howling and crashing through the underbrush. She reached a river and tried to hide with her children among the rushes. The youngest began to cry and could not be quieted. The young woman knew they would soon be discovered and so she wove a basket of reeds and set her youngest in it. She kissed her baby one last time, pinched his cheek, and shoved the basket out into the current. The baby's cries attracted the Risen and the young woman escaped with her two remaining boys.

"The meal was small and the pack was many, and soon the Risen took up the chase again. This time they caught up with the young woman in the forest. The Risen gathered around the tree in which she hid and howled for the sweetness of her flesh and the richness of her blood. The young woman crawled to the end of a branch. She knit a nest of leaves and set her next youngest in it. She kissed her baby one last time, pinched his cheek... "

The room was hot, and the voice of her grandma dwindled until it seemed the rustle of leaves itself. Red Hood had promised to stay awake but she could not keep her promise. When she awoke, her grandma's story was long completed and the fire almost out. She fed a log into the stove and stirred the embers into flame.

Grandma's eyes sparkled.

"Oh grandma, what big eyes you have."

Grandma pulled at her blankets.

"Oh grandma, what big hands you have."

Grandma yawned.

"Oh grandma, what a horribly big mouth you have!"

Grandma stretched her stiff limbs. She was newly dead and still slow. Yet, even dead, grandma had already cast aside her blankets. She tried to speak, but the words caught in her throat, and all that emerged was a painful moan.

Red Hood stumbled backward. She spotted her knife but in her haste knocked it off the table. It skittered across the floor.

The Risen never laugh, not even at another's misfortune, and that distinguishes them from true men and women. Grandma stood and sniffed the air. Her nightgown slipped down to expose the dreadful wound in her side, and she tore at the fabric as if it had attacked her.

Red Hood's horror was like a boulder in her belly. She still loved her grandma, even though she was now on level with a beast. Who knows what would have happened if there had not been a knock at the door? This knock was followed by two more, each louder than the last. Grandma hugged the tattered nightgown against her bony chest and hunched to the door. She pressed her eye against the spy hole and howled in delight. She undid the deadbolt and opened the door.

The kindly stranger stood outside. One of his hands was extended in greeting, the other hidden behind his back. He wore Red Hood's skin suit.

"Red Hood," grandma cried. The suit fooled her. Her words sounded almost human, but were not human enough to fool the stranger. The stranger swung his arm out from behind his back. He wielded a machete. The blade flashed and grandma dropped to her knees. The blade flashed again, and grandma's head bounced across the floor. "Go to the bathroom," the stranger said to Red Hood. "You should not see what I now must do."

Red Hood heard thumpings and rattlings and dragging noises, and sometimes a joyful whistling. Finally, after thirty minutes that carried the weight of hours, she heard the stranger's footsteps approach. He knocked politely and then opened the bathroom door. He no longer wore the skin suit and once again looked as kindly and as handsome as when she had first met him on the Lost Highway. "I need your help," the stranger said.

"What must I do?" Red Hood asked. She wanted to sound brave, but her voice squeaked. The body of her grandma was nowhere to be seen.

"Help me barricade the door." The apartment door was thick, but not so thick that it could shut out the howlings of the Risen. Even more disturbing was how they scraped at the wood, as if they might peel the door apart sliver by sliver.

"Help me with this couch," the stranger said. Red Hood and the stranger wrestled the couch into position by the door. They then flipped a table upside down onto its cushions and searched the apartment for heavy objects—pots and pans and plates from the kitchen, drawers from a bureau, rolled-up rugs, anything and everything—to add to the pile.

"That's enough." The kindly stranger wiped sweat from his eyes. "Bring me the kitchen knives."

"Why?" Red Hood's arms ached.

"This is no time for questions."

Red Hood was too tired to debate and did as commanded. The stranger dumped the knives into his pack and cinched it shut. He then smoothed the sheets of her grandma's bed, straightened the blankets, and fluffed its pillows. "We're safe now. Sit beside me and share the warmth of the fire." He patted the mattress.

Red Hood took a seat near the footboard.

"Do you still have the bottle of medicine I gave you?"

"That's finished," she said.

"No matter. I have more." The stranger pulled a crystalline bottle from his pack. Uncorked, its honeyed aroma was just as she remembered. "Drink this," the stranger said. "It will restore your strength."

Red Hood took a sip and felt fire burn across her tongue and run down her throat. She coughed. "Have another taste," the stranger said. "Each sip is easier than the last."

The stranger, as always, spoke the truth. "Do you know why I came back for you?" he asked. He had moved so close to Red Hood that she could smell the medicine on his breath and feel the heat of his body.

Red Hood took another sip from the bottle. She felt warm and a little too comfortable. "Why?" she said.

The stranger smiled. "Because you still owe me one last kiss."

Red Hood was confused. She licked her lips clean. Kisses, she had learned, were unpredictable. "Will it be like the others?"

"It will be nothing like those." If a smile can be said to smile, the stranger's smile wore itself out with trying. The stranger loosened the cord that cinched his pack shut. The leather puckered around the cord like withered lips and, once parted, the entrance gaped like a mouth.

Red Hood leaned forward. She could see nothing inside the pack. "For this kiss," the stranger said, "you must climb into my pack." The pack bulged with its hidden freight and anyway was too small to hold a person, even someone as young and small as Red Hood. Red Hood wasn't sure if the stranger was making a joke, but she laughed just the same.

The stranger dug at his teeth with a fingernail and flicked a pinkish morsel aside. The gristle hissed on the warm bricks by the stove. "Just a little kiss. You promised."

Red Hood could not have said why she thought of her grandma at that moment. Maybe it was only because memories, like ghosts, know no barriers and enter unbidden. Whatever the reason, Red Hood remembered the story her grandma had told her earlier. Red Hood had not stayed awake to hear the story's end, but she had heard its beginning and its middle and that was enough. No matter how small the pack appeared, she knew that it could swallow her and then the stranger would take her away. "If I give you this kiss, will you carry me with you to your home?"

"I live far away but, yes, I will take you with me. We will live together and you will share in all that I own." The stranger hefted his pack and it rattled merrily, suggested the wealth contained within. There was a murmuring also, like distant voices.

"What is that?"

"Those are the voices of my hometown," the stranger said. "Before I left on my travels, I stopped by the market and I listened to the laughter and chatter of the crowd and the haggling of the merchants. I gathered just a little of what I heard into my pack so I might feel less lonely on the road."

"If I give you this kiss and join you in your travels," Red Hood said, "you will never feel lonely again."

"*When* you give me this kiss."

"*If* I give you this kiss." Red Hood bounded from the bed. She grabbed the pack's strap and dragged it past the stranger's legs. She shook the pack. The first time she shook it, the voices inside came tumbling out and echoed all around her. "Run," they cried. "Run for your life." The second time she shook the pack, spoons clattered forth and scattered across the floor. Spoons, not the knives she had hoped for. "Run," they cried with their blunt metallic tongues. The third time she shook the pack, bones tumbled forth. There were leg bones, rib bones, finger bones, knucklebones, vertebrae, and broken pieces of skull. Most of the bones were white but some were pink. "Run," the jawbones cried. Red Hood now knew where her grandma's body had disappeared. She also knew why the stranger walked the earth alone but with a full pack.

The stranger laughed. He had not moved from his seat on the bed. He smiled at her indulgently, as if she were a child easily tamed.

Red Hood looked about for a means of escape. The door was barricaded, the window three levels above the street. She had lost the kitchen knives to the stranger and his pack. But there was still the knife she had brought with her from home. She had set it on the table and then knocked it to the floor when her grandma woke from the dead. Where had it gone?

The stranger caught her eye. He reached into his boot and brought out her knife. Its blade flickered in concert with the fire. "Is this what you are looking for?" He inserted the blade's point between his teeth and picked loose another sliver of flesh. He licked the flesh from the metal. He then opened the door to the stove and tossed her knife into the fire.

"You still owe me a kiss." The stranger reclaimed his pack from the floor and shook it open. The mouth of the pack gaped. Its sides caved like a stomach accustomed to richness but which has gone hungry for too long. "Now climb into my pack."

The fire crackled behind its mica window, perhaps in laughter, perhaps in simple enjoyment of the knife's wooden handle. The remains of Red Hood's knife glowed within the heart of the fire. She remembered her mother's words: *The worth of a knife is in its blade not its handle.*

She dropped to her knees before the stove and swung its door open. Sparks cascaded forth. Her knife's handle had burned to ashes, but the blade remained. She plunged her hand into the coals. The knife seared her flesh and the heel of its blade sliced into the meat of her thumb. The stink of burnt flesh filled the room. Her skin blistered but she did not drop the knife. Tears blinded her but she gripped the knife all the more tightly. She screamed and she struck.

Red Hood's first strike cut loose a hank of the stranger's hair. He laughed and caught her by the arm, spinning her around as if he were a prince and she his princess engaged in a dance. "You owe me a kiss," he whispered, his breath tickling her ear. He twisted her arm behind her back. She cried out in pain, but this was not the arm that held the knife.

Her second strike slashed the stranger across his bicep, slicing through his sleeve and drawing a trickle of blood. He cried out in surprise and released her. "You cut me," he said. He shook his head in disbelief. "All over a kiss."

Her third strike pierced the stranger through the eye. He stumbled back. The knife protruded from his eye socket, and he crumpled dead to the floor.

Afterward, Red Hood bandaged her hand and tidied the apartment. She gathered up her belongings, not forgetting her knife, the remaining can of soup, and the cough syrup, and slipped into her suit of skin. She freshened the suit with the kindly stranger's blood and then shoved his body out the window.

She watched it tumble through the air and smack against the pavement, and continued to watch as the Risen shambled from the shadows and shredded his flesh. On her way home, she passed one of the Risen gnawing on a bone. The creature growled when she approached, and followed her. Red Hood had nothing to fear. She wore her suit of skin and the creature fawned about her bloody heels like a dog loyal to its master.

Story Notes

The Five Cigars of Abu Ali

After reading the Oxford edition of the *Arabian Nights' Entertainments*, I was inspired to write some stories that involved the narrative structures I found so entrancing. This was the first such story I wrote, featuring tales nested within tales. Ellen Datlow accepted "The Five Cigars of Abu Ali" for publication at *SCI FICTION*, Ellen having earlier selected my story "The Assistant to Dr. Jacob," originally published in *Nemonymous*, for her annual year's best anthology. I used the unexpected windfall to purchase an etching by Peter Milton, "Hidden Cities II: Embarkation for Cythera," a print that reminded me of the summer I had spent in New York City living with my uncle and aunt in an apartment bordering Riverside Park on the Hudson. More about my uncle and aunt later in these notes.

"The Five Cigars of Abu Ali" is based in part on the time I lived in Pakistan, and in particular a trip I took with my father, brother, and a Pakistani conservationist up along the Karakoram highway during a time when it was briefly opened for non-military travel. I was in seventh grade, my brother in sixth grade, and we both wore our hair long and bleached to a greenish blonde from swimming in the chlorinated pool near our apartment. Seeing our long hair, my father's colleague congratulated him on his two beautiful daughters. This was a wondrous trip. We gorged on apricots and cherries freshly picked from the village orchards. My father, a wildlife biologist, met with local officials and inspected the horns of antelope strung along rooflines for their provenance and age. I learned to use birch bark for my pen and ink sketches of the looming mountains. Something that does not appear in the story, but which had some significance many decades later, is that we spent a night early in our trip at Abbottabad, the same city where Osama bin Laden took refuge and was eventually killed in a U.S. raid. The only significant event worthy of mention about Abbottabad in my journal of our trip is that I bought a Spider-Man comic there.

The Watchmaker

This story springs (pun intended) from my long-term love for automata. Two such stories appeared in my previous short-story collection *Meet Me in the Middle of the Air*, and several more are included in this collection. I'm not sure what about automata captivates me so, at a minimum it has to do with how such mechanical creations, going through the same motions again and again, embody some essential aspect of our meaty human nature, a preservation as if in amber of who we are but are not always sure we want to be.

North of Lake Winnipesaukee

This story is directly inspired by Angela Carter's wolfish stories, some of which appeared in her collection *The Bloody Chamber*, and which were later basis for the film *The Company of Wolves*. As a historical work I wanted to set the story in my home state of New Hampshire, rather than directly emulate Angela Carter and the influence of her British homeland, although the early paragraphs in my story serve as an intentional reminder of the umbilical cord that links the New World settlements to Mother Europe.

Lake Winnipesaukee is famous in New Hampshire for its bass fishing. It's in the Lakes Region of the state that also provided fertile ground for the Academy Award-winning movie *On Golden Pond* and is suggestive of the bucolic ideal of a New Hampshire retreat from the hustle and bustle of big city living. The lake itself plays no major part in this story, set as it is long ago, and not on Lake Winnipesaukee, but in the barely settled northerly region. The lake is a landmark, not a destination.

A Study in Abnormal Physiology

This is a Holmesian tale, I'll make no bones about that inspiration. I knew this before I started writing. Like many of us, I've read and reread Sir Arthur Conan Doyle's tales ever since a child. These mystery adventures stand the test of time and deservedly so. But for me, in my career as a scientist, as a biologist, Darwin is always adjacent and inspirational. I've written other works that feature Darwin, most notably in a contribution to *The Field Guide to Surreal Botany*[1], edited by Janet Chui and Jason Lundberg, an anthology that was reviewed and recommended as a holiday gift by the premier scientific journal *Science*. The parallelism of Sherlock and Watson to Darwin and Huxley almost insisted itself upon me.

A historical tale, a scientific tale, is an open invitation to reading and research. In this case, I am greatly indebted to Janet Browne's two-volume biography of Darwin, its pages now dog-eared across the whole trajectory of Darwin's life, although my story captures but a tiny fraction of that history. Although only mentioned tangentially, the realization that Darwin and Huxley participated in the X Club, something like a Victorian legion of science heroes, only confirmed the appropriateness of the direction I was taking with Darwin's life. More integral to the emotional core of the story was the discovery that both Darwin and Huxley had lost children in infancy, all too common back their day but, even if common, something no parent could ever be reconciled to.

The conclusion to the tale came to me essentially as a gift from the aether and because it seems a gift, it still warms me like fire on a blustery winter's night. Although not necessarily obvious, this section, if only because of how it structurally relates to earlier aspects of the story, exists only because of the glorious fiction of Gene Wolfe. Gene Wolfe passed away a few years ago, but in this and so many other stories and influences, his legacy lives on.

Smoke, Ash, and Whatever Comes After

This story was inspired by a dream, one in which I was reading a short story by Simon Strantzas. I knew of Simon's work but had not read his stories at the time. After having had the dream, I picked up two of his collections—any of his collections is well worth your while—and, of course, discovered that my dream story had little to do with his actual work. That gave me license to write the story.

In this case that presented problems. Dream logic often does. I ended up using the initial premise of the dream—the problematic bureau—as a jumping off point. Later, when revising the story for publication, I also eliminated much of the initial section, that portion of the story most closely related to the dream, and focused on the where the premise had led me. In case you are wondering, the part that I couldn't handle—Simon undoubtedly could—was a black hole leading to some other dimension within the bureau.

Three Urban Folk Tales

This is one of those stories that took many, many years to become a true story. I wrote the first section after reading and being inspired by Italo Calvino's collection of Italian folk tales. There was a spareness, a simplicity to his versions that got to the heart of each one. A folk tale, as opposed to a fairy tale, without the inclusion of magic reminded me that such tales could involve and be a commentary on their own time rather than rooted in the past. I wrote the first of my three urban folk tales remembering a garbage strike in New York City from my summer after high school, where I had lived in the City with my aunt and uncle while working at Memorial Sloan Kettering. That first tale, alone, is a simple sketch without sufficient complexity or depth to be a story. Years later, I returned to that initial sketch and, inspired by the story's rats[2], the following two interconnected tales revealed themselves to me, probably in large part because I no longer felt as beholden to the initial inspiration for the tale.

Wildflowers

I teach biochemistry and, not surprisingly given my interest in the fantastic, I am fascinated by the scientific basis for monsters such as vampires, werewolves, giants, and so on. The genesis for this story, as described by the story's veterinarian, is the relationship of a cholesterol-like molecule from plants to cyclopia in animals. When I introduce this topic in my biochemistry course, I start off with a brief clip from the movie *The 7th Voyage of Sinbad*. It's the marvelous stop-motion animation sequence by Ray Harryhausen in which the giant horned cyclops fights a dragon while Sinbad and the princess sneak away.

All We Inherit

This story owes some inspiration to the marvelous short story "Blood" by my friend Matt Cheney, to the story "A Tropical Horror" by William Hope Hodgson in which the bulk of the story is a murderous fight, and to "Country Death Song" by the Violent Femmes, all well worth seeking out. There's also a cousin of mine, since passed, who toward the end of his days and living alone in a house in Wisconsin sent us a list of the secret compartments he had constructed throughout his home to fool thieves.

What I really want to write about here is something small, the story's title. I have always loved how James Tiptree, Jr. found the perfect line from a poem for their stories, and so, often as not, I perform Google searches in hopes of finding something better than my working title for a story. My working title for this story was the moribund "Fathers and Sons." Then I found the e e cummings poem, "my father moved through dooms of love." At first, I went with the obvious title "Dooms of Love." That phrase alone with a bit too vague, but then there was this one verse:

though dull were all we taste as bright,
bitter all utterly things sweet,
maggoty minus and dumb death
all we inherit, all bequeath

I had forgotten where my story title originated until, by chance, when recently reading Susan Cheever's biography of her father John Cheever, *Home Before Dark*, I found these lines were the ones she had read to eulogize her father on his death. John Cheever is one of my all-time favorite short-story writers, and so this title seems even more appropriate.

A long tangential aside now but, if anything, this aside reveals more about my writing process and what I consider significant in that regard, than anything else in these notes. John Cheever is not only one of my favorite writers, but he lived in Ossining NY, a stone's throw up the Hudson River from where my uncle and aunt live. My uncle once took me for a ride beneath the imposing walls of Sing Sing Prison, where Cheever taught writing and which was the inspiration for his novel *Falconer*, and, because we paused too long and too close to the wall, a guard yelled at us from his high tower to move along.

Just down the road from my uncle and aunt's house is the small Scarborough Park on the banks of the Hudson, where we went to watch sunsets, to spar with the geese who called this stretch of greenery home, and where, one rapturous midnight, we drove to watch the fireworks from across the river announce a new year freshly born. The Scarborough train station is there as well, and it was here that my wife and I would take a commuter train into the City, leaving our car parked on my uncle and aunt's front lawn, whenever we wanted to experience the magical joys of the new Atlantis that is New York City.

Cheever wrote exquisitely about the life of residents in Westchester County, about the adulteries, monotony, and ecstasies of the commuters, and, what's more, at one time, he rented a space on the second story of the rail station at Scarborough for his writings. It seems, and maybe is a fact, that I breathe the same molecules of air that Cheever did whenever I return to Scarborough Park and the Rail Station. I like to consider this some form of inheritance that exists beyond strict bloodlines.

Hell and a Day

In the film *A Nightmare on Elm Street*, Freddy Krueger can enter and kill his victims in their dreams. The soft spaces in my dreams, where others gain entrance, are more prosaic. I sometimes read mythical works by other authors, as if my dreams are attuned to the literature of a Borgesian alternative world. I wrote earlier how "Smoke, Ash, and Whatever Comes After," was inspired by a dream. In this case, in the dream, I was reading a story and watching a film based on the work of the writer Matthew Bartlett. Again, the dream really had nothing to do with the fine writing of Matthew and so I, again, felt it my prerogative to write the story contained in the dream. Unlike "Smoke, Ash, and Whatever Comes After," in which the dream served as a jumping off point for the story, I was able to include virtually everything from my dream in *"Hell and a Day."* I suspect that I might be accused of plagiarism should I ever acquire the ability to travel the multiverse.

Automata

This is the other significant piece, besides "The Five Cigars of Abu Ali, that I wrote inspired by the *Arabian Nights' Entertainments*. Here I chose a different strategy for encapsulating the sub-stories within the broader narrative, preserving the idea of taletelling, but now having the stand-ins for the king and Scheherazade trade tales with each other. At one point I considered writing complete short stories for each of the tales but soon realized that strategy slowed down the main story line. However, I did expand and complete one of the sub-stories: "The Watchmaker," which appears earlier in this collection. I shared a draft of "Automata" with the fine historian and short-story writer Minsoo Kang—author of the nonfiction book *Sublime Dreams of Living Machines: The Automaton in the European Imagination*—and was moved by the positive remarks he made and how aspects of the story meshed with his own interests.

Monkey Shines

This story has a lot to do with the emotional connections we build to the toys of our childhood, particularly dolls and stuffed animals, so much so that many adults hang onto and continue to collect these throughout their lives. My strongest such attachment was to a stuffed toy gorilla. He was about a foot in height, had a kindly but not sentimentalized smile, and wore a small white t-shirt I dressed him in. His arms and legs were positioned as if always reaching out for a hug. Wear and tear resulted in his armpit seams ripping, and my mom would repair these wounds with a curved sewing needle and thick thread.

Christmas in the Altai

This story, like "The Five Cigars of Abu Ali," owes itself to a trip I took with my father, this time as an adult. I joined my father for a zoological study in the Altai Mountains of Mongolia, working with local conservationists to gather data on the snow leopards and their range. As usual when traveling, I kept a journal and many key elements in this story come from that journal. However, this story isn't the story of that trip itself, but imagines a subsequent trip to the same location.

What can I add that is not in the story but is still documented in my journal? How about this lesson learned? On the way to Mongolia, and then again on my return, I flew through Beijing. On my way in, I explored the Beijing Friendship store, a gigantic, many-storied building with goods from throughout China and the world. I was shopping in spirit, mentally cataloguing what I would purchase for my girlfriend, later my wife, Paulette, as well as for other friends back in the States. Most wonderful were the sumi ink brushes and the solid sticks of sumi ink. Many of the ink sticks had designs printed on them in gold and silver and one caught my eye: it depicted a turtle dancing upright upon the waves lit by a yin-yang moon. Magical. But I didn't buy it, knowing I would have a chance to do so when I returned to Beijing on my way home. Of course, when I did so, although there were still plenty of brushes and ink sticks available, the one design I coveted was gone. Somewhere that turtle dances, but not in my home.

How the Future Got Better

Scott Nicolay, notable not only for his short stories but also for his translations of Jean Ray, once posted on Facebook that he would like to see someone write a story based on Bob Dylan's song "Clothes Line Saga." I responded that I had previously done so, although I did not reveal that the song served as this story's inspiration. I think what Scott and I respond to in the song is its deadpan delivery and focus on how laundry and neighbors can be of greater importance to a family than the momentous news of the world. This story was reprinted in the anthology *The Time Traveler's Almanac* (Ann and Jeff VanderMeer, editors), and one reviewer referred to my story as "the *Seinfeld* of short stories," a description I love.

Red Hood

I've always loved fairy tales and folk tales, but it was only with the passing of Richard Adams that I wondered how much his novel *Watership Down* influenced me as a storyteller. I first read this novel in high school, but I've reread it many times since then, including right after his death. I was struck by how Adams integrated folk tales into the novel's narrative. Most significantly, these were *rabbit* folk tales, told by them and expressing their point of view. If you read these alone, you still understand a lot about the rabbit culture, their hopes, fears, and value system. That's an approach I've taken with several of my stories: telling a folk tale but not explicitly describing the narrator to the reader. In "Three Urban Folk Tales," found earlier in this collection, and "The Three Familiars," found in my collection *Meet Me in the Middle of the Air*, I created new tales that were primarily derived from our urban culture, the later story being told from a witch's perspective and morality.

"Red Hood" is the first time that I took an established folk tale and reworked it, evolving it to reflect the priorities of a dark future. A key element in the gestation of "Red Hood" was a 2013 article by Jamshid J. Tehrani, published in the science journal *PLoS ONE*, titled "The Phylogeny of Little Red Riding Hood." Tehrani analyzed 58 different versions of the tale and used 72 plot variables to create an evolutionary tree that related all these different versions to each other. This article was revelatory as it made it suddenly clear that the same story template I knew so well from Perrault and the Brothers Grimm also has Asian and African analogues, and that the villain is not necessarily a wolf but might be a tiger, an ogre, or a crow. As a scientist, I also got a kick out of the idea that you can use evolutionary theory and computational approaches to characterize the relationships between all these alternative versions of the same tale which extend back for over 1500 years. Evolving the tale into some future version gave me the freedom to retell it from a new perspective.

[1]Bonus Track:
Darwin's Orchid

Common name: Queen Victoria's Bloomers
Systematic name: *Caligulus homocopulus.* (class: Liliopsida, order: Asparagales, family: Orchidaceae, genus: Caligulus, species: homocopulus)
Appearance: The first recorded description of C. homocopulus comes from Charles Darwin who, in 1862, published the book On the Various Contrivances by which British and Foreign Orchids are Fertilized by Insects. Unfortunately, due to the mores of the time, this was an expurgated text and some of the Darwin's most interesting observations were confined to an appendix available only by subscription to men over the age of 30. It is here that we find the following description:

"Although dried, pressed, and sectioned into various folios at the Royal Herbarium and thus lacking the intense color and unrivaled immediacy of the bloom *in situ,* I do not hesitate in declaring this orchid the King or rather the Queen of flora. I have measured the dimensions of the reassembled bloom and find it to be three-feet nine-inches in width and fully five-feet four-inches in height! In color it is of a deep reddish purple, the two outer petals edged with a fringe such as one might find on a curtain. But it is not the size or the color of the flower that must most excite the admiration of travelers in Madagascar, it is rather the perfect mimicry exhibited by the orchid labellum to the lower torso of a human female. Discretion forbids my dwelling overmuch on this aspect of the flower, but the reader can be assured that this mimicry is exact down to the smallest detail. The appearance of this bloom, and possibly the excitement attendant upon discovering it in the jungle, calls to my mind what a young man experiences on his wedding night as he draws near his bride in her canopied bed."

Ecology and geographic location: Historically, the natural habitat of *C. homocopulus* is the tropical broadleaf forests along the eastern coastal strip of Madagascar, and extends to an elevation of 1000 meters in the subhumid highland forests. Deforestation has severely impacted its habitat, however, and greater numbers of the species are now found in collections than in the rain forest.

Life cycle: C. *homocopulus* is a perennial, flowering once a year, with the flower persisting until pollinated after which it rapidly senesces. Darwin hypothesized that the "pseudomimicry" exhibited by the flower played an important role in the life cycle of the plant, luring animal pollinators to the orchid by sexual deception. Darwin predicted that the pollinator was a large lemur and declared that "naturalists who visit Madagascar should search for this primate with as much confidence as astronomers search for the planet Neptune, and I venture they will be equally successful."

It was not until 1886 that Darwin's prediction of the pollinator was put to the test by Alfred Russel Wallace, the father of biogeography. It was from his personal journals that the following account is taken:

"That evening, I stationed myself behind a rosewood tree, gaining a good vantage on the orchid but exposing little of myself to the pollinator regardless of the direction from which it might approach. The flower was swollen within its bud but, although I waited hour after hour through the long night, it was not until the stars disappeared from the sky in the gray light of dawn, that the flower finally opened. In truth, I had fallen asleep and was awakened by a musky smell that reminded me of youthful indiscretions that I need not dwell on here [see journals 8, 11, and 12]. The mimicry exhibited by the opened blossom was greater than I would have believed possible. The two petals curved downward to hide all but the pseudolegs of the labellum, but these crossed and uncrossed in the slightest breeze such that it seemed a real woman waited impatiently for her lover. Indeed, hardly had this thought entered my mind, but I detected a disturbance in the underbrush and beheld the approach of a wild hairy creature, which flung itself upon the flower with great ardor. Not fifteen minutes had passed, however, but the creature withdrew from its amorous embrace and proceeded on to another bloom, and from there on to yet another, flitting from blossom to blossom like a large disheveled moth, and moving all the time further away from my observation post. Leaving my station, I slipped from tree to tree so as to gain a closer look at the pollinator, whose identity was obscured in the dim light. Imagine my surprise then, following its withdrawal from a flower not fifteen feet from me, when I beheld that it was my old mentor Charles Darwin. Truly my surprise cannot be accurately measured for the good man I now saw had been buried four years previous at Westminster Abbey. But the truth of his identity was proved when he with equal incredulity cried, "Alfred," then hastily pulled up his trousers. He subsequently revealed that his coffin had contained a straw dummy with a melon for its head, and that this had served as a distraction so that he might embark on a new set of travels. Neither of us, however, desired to linger in conversation because of the discomfort attendant upon the circumstances, and Charles soon bid me good-bye. 'Please don't tell Emma,' he said, from which I understood that he had not taken his wife into confidence. As he turned to leave, I noticed a dusting of golden pollen now decorated the shoulders of his jacket, and I could not help but think that although his solution to the riddle of the pollinator had been a near miss, he had probably known the correct answer all along."

Accompanying notes on specimen and how others may find it: Those in the field of paleobotany are all too familiar with how any learned discussion at scientific meetings on the evolutionary history of *C. homocopulus* invariably results in a shouting match. On the one side are the neo-Darwinists with their insistent chants of "Darwin was right." They claim that even if lemurs no longer pollinate the orchid, that the pseudomimicry originally arose to take advantage of the indigenous population of giant lemurs, and only upon their extinction did the orchid morphology adapt to the increasing human population. On the other side are the Wallaconians with their cries of "Darwin sucks sap." They insist that hominids have always been the pollinators and that *C. homocopulus* represents a remarkable case of co-evolution between flower and pollinator that extends back to prehistoric man.

What is clear is just how rapidly the *C. homocopulus* flower has changed in the last few hundred years, resulting in a plethora of subspecies that mimic women of every form and nationality. It has been suggested that this is due to selective breeding initiated in the 1700's by local entrepreneurs catering to the pirate colonies that sprang up at Fort Dauphin and St. Mary's Island. Indeed, modern-day visitors to Madagascar interested in viewing a living example of C. homocopulus need not bushwack through the jungles but can instead visit any one of a dozen "hot houses" still in existence. Upon payment of a modest fee, the visitor will be escorted to a private room wherein he or she may view the specimen for up to 30 minutes. Unfortunately, neither photography or videotaping is allowed, but good reproductions in a variety of formats may be purchased at the front desk.

The Ballad of the Ugly-Nest Rat

Where have they gone these inhabitants of upended baskets, hollow trees, and musty catacombs? Theirs was an unquiet stillness. So easy to recognize with their noses a-twitch for the slightest scent of danger, both real and imagined, their hands fluttering as if trapped between anticipation and fear, and their smiles... yes their smiles—if any creature can be said to smile, they smiled—but their smiles were haunted by an immaculate sorrow.

I refer, of course, to the ugly-nest rat.

At one time their visibility was such that they earned a place in Aristotle's epic treatise, "The History of the Animals." In the section on habitations, following descriptions of the dwellings founded by moles, mice, ants, and bees, Aristotle calls attention to a bastard creature from the Far East. The natives from the subcontinent of India, Aristotle notes, "lock a female rat and a hound together in a basket: if the dog is in an amorous mood he will pair with her; if not he will devour her, and this casualty is of frequent occurrence. But if progeny is produced, the new breed walks on its two hind-legs; its front legs small and its hind legs long. These rats are desirous of a greatness like that of man, but lacking a rational soul, the temples they build are dung-heaps of squalor and wash away with the rain."

Aristotle's description can refer to none other than the ugly-nest rat.

But it is not just Aristotle. Others too have contributed to the recorded history of this sad creature, links in a chain that extends across time and space, starting millennia ago with the words of Aristotle and ending, perhaps, within the pages of this Bestiary. For example, from his journals and written in his distinctive mirrored script, we find this fable by Leonardo da Vinci:

A rat called the woodland animals over to show off his new house, its construction revealing his amateur hand. Most of the rat's guests were polite and, because they also enjoyed the food and drink he provided, complemented him on his craftsmanship. But the weasel did not like nuts, grain, or fermented berries. He laughed and flashed his smile of a thousand teeth. "Your house is a heap of rubbish. Why there are so many holes in it that you cannot escape the wind, much less me." And with that he gave chase. But no sooner did the weasel bump against a wall but the house collapsed, killing the weasel instantly. However the rat escaped and rejoined his guests outside to finish the feast. The woodland creatures congratulated the rat on his good luck but he was silent and left the celebration early. Not all victories are to be savored.

The domestic atmosphere of da Vinci's tale suggests that the ugly-nest rat was a common enough feature of the Italian woods to be familiar to his audience, supporting the theory that in the millennium since Aristotle's description, the species had migrated from Asia to the European continent. But, if so, the ugly-nest rats were destroyed or moved away within the next few centuries. No physical relics of the ugly-nest rat have been recovered in Europe, and the skull fragment on display at the Ashmolean Museum in Oxford was in fact acquired by Henry Stanley during one of his famed expeditions to the Congo.

Yes, Stanley. That Stanley. The Welsh explorer who exemplifies the best and the worst of Victorian Britain. The Stanley who retroactively coined the phrase, "Doctor Livingston, I presume," the Stanley who decorated his trail across the African continent with the diseased and bullet-ridden dead, and the Stanley who, while in a nameless village a dozen days' travel north of Nyangwe, rediscovered this enigmatic creature. The chief of the village offered Stanley and his men the best food his impoverished people could provide. But this was not enough. "Have you nothing more?" Stanley asked. "My men are hungry and, when they are hungry, I cannot be held responsible for their actions." The chief proffered his empty hands, a gesture that needed no translation. "What about there?" Stanley asked, pointing with his rifle's barrel toward what he took to be an animal shed on the village outskirts. The chief frowned and, through Stanley's translator, communicated that this crude imitation of a hut had been built by a colony of "ugly-nest rats," the name by which these creatures have been known ever since. These creatures were not to be disturbed, the chief said, voicing a superstition born from the belief that their sterile imagination was contagious. Stanley, of course, was not deterred and had his men butcher and roast the entire colony, later describing the meat as "gamey but not unpleasant."

From India to Italy to the Congo: over the course of two millennia, the ugly-nest rats made their slow, halting way across three continents. Always they existed in our shadow, at the edge of our awareness, sometimes hunted, sometime persecuted, often simply ignored. But they persisted. They survived. And when not welcome in one area they moved on, wandering the world in search of a home.

But everything ends. Even the wanderings of the ugly-nest rat.

The last reported sighting of an ugly-nest rat occurred in 1959 at a ranch outside of Dar es Salaam, Tanganyika. James Sinclair, Jr., the only child of British diplomats, was left alone one endless afternoon and chose to entertain his small cadre of inanimate friends—toy versions of Noddy, Big Ears, Tubby Bear, and a Golliwog—by building a bonfire. Unfortunately, he situated the bonfire under his bed. First the sheets, then the drapes, and then the entire house went up in flames. Coughing, hacking, tears streaming down his cheeks, James Junior still had the presence of mind, when asked by his rescuers as to the cause of the conflagration, to lead them to a termite mound beneath a spreading acacia tree. The mound had been abandoned long ago by its original builders but, appropriated by a family of ugly-nest rats, had been modified into the crude approximation of a castle. The rescuers smashed the mirrored glass and beads studding the walls, tore down the flags of discarded women's underwear flying from the turrets, and broke into the mound with shovels and axes. The ugly-nest rats were then either killed or driven away. James Junior himself did not live much longer, catching a fever during the Laughter Epidemic of 1962, but revealed to his doctors the truth behind the fire before his untimely passing.

The end?

Not quite.

In 2006, 47 years after the last sighting of an ugly-nest rat, 44 years after the death of James Junior, his body was disinterred to resolve an issue of paternity and inheritance. Inside the diminutive coffin was found a skeleton stripped clean of flesh and stuffed with the decayed remnants of a nest. What's more, the skeleton had been gnawed by sharp incisors so that the bones were more like lace, sea froth, or some baroque architecture than anything designed to carry the weight of a man. "Weird," the lawyers said, "yet beautiful." But that's not all. Modern computational methods of cryptography suggest that what was always taken for architecture is in fact something more: a written language, idiographic in content but far more malleable than cuneiform.

What is written into the bones of James Junior? The calcified arabesques resolve into four simple lines if the translation of Whitfield Ellis (Distinguished Fellow of the Marconi Society) is to be believed:

To descend
To sail upon the earthen waves
The flaming sun at my back
The black star beneath my feet

Four lines, that's all.

But that's enough to give me hope.

I like to believe the strange noises reported by miners are not the tectonic groans of the earth's crust, but rather signs of viviparous life. In caverns deep below the earth's surface, protected from bad weather and the caustic comments of men, the ugly-nest rats invent new architectures and build cathedrals of their own devising. There in the sheltering darkness, they feast on pale wheels of cheese and on loaves milled from their own fields of etiolated wheat. There they raise families of countless young. There they lift voices in laughter and in song. There they smile and these smiles hold not a trace of fear or sorrow or shame. There... but no, I'll write no more for otherwise you might think that I evoke a Paradise when all I really describe is the seeking and finding of a home, the ugly-nest rat coming home at last.

Original Publication Information

"**The Five Cigars of Abu Ali,**" *SciFiction*, Jan. 2005

"**The Watchmaker,**" *A cappella Zoo #4*, Spring 2010
    *reprinted in *Bestiary: The Best of A cappella Zoo*, 2013

"**North of Lake Winnipesaukee,**" previously unpublished, and also to appear in *The Dark Heart of the Wood* (Duane Pesice, ed.)

"**A Study in Abnormal Physiology,**" *Dim Shores Presents Vol 1* (Sam Cowan, ed.) Dim Shores, Summer 2020

"**Smoke, Ash, and Whatever Comes After,**" *Black Static #56*, Jan/Feb 2017
    *reprinted in *The Dark*, Jan 2018

"**Three Urban Folk Tales,**" *Lady Churchill's Rosebud Wristlet #16*, July 2005
    *reprinted in *Fantasy: The Best of the Year 2006* (ed. Rich Horton), 2006
    *reprinted in *Best of the Rest #4* (ed. Brian Youmans), 2006
    *reprinted in *Lightspeed*, issue 118, March 2020

"**Wildflowers,**" previously unpublished

"**All We Inherit,**" *Black Static #67*, Jan/Feb 2019

"***Hell and a Day,***" *Black Static #77*, Nov/Dec 2020

"**Automata,**" *A cappella Zoo #12*, Spring 2014

"**Monkey Shines,**" *Text:UR, The New Book of Masks* (ed. Forrest Aguirre), Raw Dog Screaming Press, 2007

"**Christmas in the Altai,**" previously unpublished

"**How the Future Got Better,**" *Sybil's Garage #7*, 2010
    *reprinted in *The Time Traveler's Almanac* (eds. Ann and Jeff VanderMeer), Tor UK 2013, Tor US 2014

"**Red Hood,**" *Nightmare*, April 2017, issue 55
    *reprinted in *Year's Best Weird Fiction Volume 5* (Robert Shearman and Michael Kelly, eds.) 2018

"**Darwin's Orchid,**" *A Field Guide to Surreal Botany* (Janet Chui and Jason Lundberg, eds.), Two Cranes Press, 2008

"**The Ballad of the Ugly-Nest Rat,**" *The Bestiary* (Ann VanderMeer, ed.), Centipede Press 2016

Acknowledgments

This collection is dedicated to my Uncle Bill and Aunt Ani for the joy they bring to my life, literary and otherwise. First, last, and everywhere in between, I thank Steve Berman and Lethe Press for shepherding this story collection into your hands: you put the verse into diverse. I also thank the wonderful editors who published and championed these stories over the years, including Andy Cox, Ann and Jeff VanderMeer, Ellen Datlow, John Joseph Adams, Gavin Grant, Kelly Link, Sam Cowan, Rich Horton, Colin Meldrum, Brian Youmans, Forrest Aguirre, Mathew Kressel, Robert Shearman, Michael Kelly, Janet Chui, Jason Lundberg, Sean Wallace, and Duane Pesice. A special shout-out to Andy Cox because three of my stories made their initial appearance in Black Static. Finally and always, I thank Paulette Werger for her love and support.

About the Author

Eric Schaller is the author of the short story collection *Meet Me in the Middle of the Air* (Undertow). His fiction has appeared in *The Year's Best Fantasy and Horror, Fantasy: Best of the Year, Wilde Stories 2017, The Year's Best Weird Fiction, The Time Traveler's Almanac*, and many magazines and journals. Schaller's stories are influenced in part by his studies in the biological sciences, their inspiration, and the unease that originates in a world populated by billions of species—including humans—dependent on but also working at cross-purposes to each other. An active member of the Horror Writers Association, Schaller lives in a peach-colored house with his wife, Paulette, amid several mountain ranges of books.

CPSIA information can be obtained
at www.ICGtesting.com
Printed in the USA
BVHW031946130423
662292BV00006B/251